Beholden

C000157387

Twenty-eight-year-old Clare Littleford left Nottingham City Council where she used to work in the housing department, in order to take an MA in creative writing at Nottingham Trent University. *Beholden* is her first novel.

visit www.clarelittleford.net

Beholden

Clare Littleford

POCKET
BOOKS

LONDON · SYDNEY · NEW YORK · TOKYO · SINGAPORE · TORONTO

First published in Great Britain by Simon & Schuster UK
Ltd, 2003
This edition published by Pocket Books, 2003
An imprint of Simon & Schuster UK Ltd
A Viacom company

1 3 5 7 9 10 8 6 4 2

Simon & Schuster UK Ltd
Africa House
64–78 Kingsway
London WC2B 6AH

www.simonsays.co.uk

Simon & Schuster Australia
Sydney

A CIP catalogue record for this book is available
from the British Library

ISBN 0–7434–4105–2

Typeset by Palimpsest Book Production Limited,
Polmont, Stirlingshire
Printed and bound in Great Britain by
Cox & Wyman Ltd, Reading, Berkshire

To John Forbes

Acknowledgements

I would like to thank:

East Midlands Arts; Luigi Bonomi; Graham Joyce, Mahendra Solanki, Ellen De Vries, Julia Gaze, Hilary Heason, Helen Jayne Price, Victoria Waddell, and everyone else at Trent; Brian Snell, Katharine Clarke, Pat Lowe; and my family.

Peter

Chapter One

We caught the same bus from the same stop five mornings a week, and had never so much as smiled at one another. It didn't strike me as odd until the day she disappeared.

She lived in a flat above the hairdressers' on Vernon Road itself, almost directly across the road from the bus stop. I saw her in the window once, lifting up the curtains with one hand while she pulled her other arm into her coat, looking up the road for the bus. The entrance to her flat must have been at the back of the building, because sometimes when she was running late I would see her hurrying up the narrow passage at the side of the shop, and I would ask the bus driver to wait for her.

The first time I took any real notice of her was shortly after Christmas, a particularly cold day, drizzling rain that sneaked in through the fibres of my anorak to gnaw at my bones. Vernon Road is a straight road sentry-lined by red-brick terraces, and the wind fairly tears along in the winter. She was bundled up in an army-surplus coat with the hood up, a few strands of her long dark hair straying out to collect globules of rain. She had her knees slightly bent and her hands shoved deep into her pockets, and was moving from side to side in an attempt to keep warm. She was ten years younger than me, in her early twenties, and her skin was pale and clear, and there was a sharpness, an awareness in the way she moved. I waited for her to turn towards me so that I could catch her eye and speak, but I was cold with the rain that ran down my neck and under my shirt, and the moment passed me by.

She was running late on that last day. I saw her rushing up the passage, and the driver waited, and I was upstairs and in my seat too quickly to allow her to thank me. It wasn't that I didn't want to speak to her – in many ways it would have been nice to pass the slow crawl into the city centre in conversation with another passenger. Another man probably would have struck up conversation, about the weather, or the traffic, or the benefits of the proposed tram system.

The people I work with don't understand why I'm so excited by the tram scheme. I find that strange; the scheme is being run out of the office next to ours, and impinges on all the work we do. They seem to be obsessed with the big city centre schemes – the plans for the Broadmarsh shopping centre, the new international-standard ice stadium, the redevelopment of the canalside area into new offices and trendy wine bars and loft apartments. Me, give me something like transport, something that will change the way we move around the city. That's what gets me going.

Of course, the guys at work think I'm mad for using public transport at all. They often ask me why I come into work by bus rather than by car. 'You're crazy, Peter,' they say. 'Buses are a nightmare.' They're unreliable, slow, dirty. I could shave an hour off my daily commute if I only drove in. I have a number of stock replies; that parking is terrible in the city centre, that there are too many cars on the road already, that Alison needs the car for her work, that I can read on the bus. Actually, that last one is a lie; I tried very hard, but reading on buses makes me feel sick.

But the real reason I like to travel on buses, the reason I would rather not get into conversation with my fellow travellers, is that from my regular seat, on the top deck, kerbside, about halfway back, I can see the people waiting at the bus stops, and watch the ones who come upstairs.

People who travel regularly on buses tend to stick to certain zones. The pensioners and mothers with babies sit downstairs, for obvious reasons, joined by those only travelling a few stops and those who don't use buses regularly. Young children play driver upstairs at the front; teenagers and alienated youth lounge across the back with their feet up. The middle section upstairs is filled with novel-readers; slightly further back are the newspaper-readers and the watchers, who look at the houses and streets as we pass. It may be a gross oversimplification of the nuances of the zones, the crossovers and the time factors; but it is true, nevertheless.

I count the regulars on and off; it is satisfying to predict who will rise for each stop, and how many more or less there are than when I got on myself. In the mornings it is always more, in the evenings, less. A slow count up to a day at work, and a slow wind down at the end.

The girl – woman – who gets on at my stop sits near the front of the novel-readers, usually two rows in front of me and across the aisle, just behind the stairwell. She doesn't read, however – she writes. She has a thick hardback notebook and spends many journeys bent over with the book on her knee, writing and rewriting, thumbing back through the pages, looking up and frowning as the bus jolts her hand. There is something fascinating about watching her, seeing her movements, the physical evidence of the thoughts she is pursuing being marked down on the page. Watching her fills the moments between the bus stops much more satisfactorily than a conversation about the weather ever could. And she gets off the bus at the stop before the city centre, the last of my regulars before the mass changeover that occurs every morning in the Market Square.

Except, that last day, the day she disappeared, she didn't get off at her stop. I watched her, barely breathing, waiting for the daydreamer's sudden jerk awake, the lunge for the bell before the stop is missed. She didn't move.

I wanted to say to her, 'Quick!' I wanted to ring the

bell for her, to lean across two rows and the aisle to nudge her, but we didn't have that level of intimacy and I had to sit there and watch. She looked out of the window but made no effort to rise for her stop. Then it was too late, the bus did not even slow down, and she turned her head as if to see her stop from this new, going-on-past angle.

I wouldn't have thought too much of it, except that she was dressed for work – sensible shoes, thick black tights, black skirt that stopped just short of her knees, the red-and-white-striped shirt with the call centre's logo on the breast pocket, untucked at the back as usual, her denim jacket on the seat next to her. Her hair was scraped back into a low ponytail, a few wisps loose around her ears, as it usually was. She even had the swipecard for the security door clutched against the cover of the notebook in her hand.

We came into the city centre and pulled round towards the Market Square stop. She seemed to have made a decision, and put the swipecard between the notebook pages as a marker and shifted her open bag onto her shoulder. All of the other remaining regulars got up and moved towards the stairs. She put the notebook into the top of her bag and gathered up her jacket. I found myself hoping that she was doing some shopping or had an appointment somewhere in the city before work, but she didn't move. She seemed to be considering something, her shoulders hunched, looking down at her jacket scrunched up in her arms. Downstairs, the doors clattered open and people started to get off, but still she sat there.

The empty seats began to fill with the less familiar city centre passengers, and then we were pulling out of the square. She didn't get up at the Broadmarsh Centre, or even move as the bus stuttered up the hill towards the railway station. Half of those on the top deck got up and edged towards the stairs, but she stayed seated, looking up at those going past her. I watched her hesitate. The last in line began to move down the stairs, but still she hesitated. Then, just as I thought she had missed that stop too, she got up suddenly. As she swung herself down onto the first step her bag knocked against the rail – she pulled it onto her shoulder again, annoyed, and moved on down before the driver shut the doors.

Her actions surprised me. It was very rare for one of the regulars to get off at the wrong stop, but to dash to the railway station in clothes relating to four stops earlier was unprecedented. I looked around for support, but there were no regulars left to turn to. As I sat considering what this might mean, I realised that she had left something behind – her notebook, bookmarked with her swipecard. It must have fallen from her bag in her rush to get down the stairs, and now it lay on the floor in the aisle, half under a seat just in front of the stairwell.

Correct procedure would be to pick them up and hand them to the driver as I got off. The bus company would telephone her office and return them to her. But what if she didn't want that? I felt some sense of complicity, for having watched her get off at the wrong stop, for not having reminded her of her obligations. They wouldn't look kindly on her leaving that swipecard for just anybody to pick up. I looked around quickly and, before I could talk myself out of it, I gathered my things and moved up the bus, stooping to pick up the notebook, and quickly slid into the seat it had fallen under. One of the novel-readers glanced up, but went back to reading. I put my briefcase down on the seat next to me. Nobody appeared to be watching me, so I looked down at the notebook.

It was small, with a glossy black cover. The plastic coating on the cover had been scraped in a couple of places, the cardboard underneath rearing through, and the corners were dented and soft. I knew it was important to her, whatever state she kept it in – I had watched her often enough to realise the notebook's personal value. I could get off at the next stop, run back to the station and see if she was still there. I imagined myself on the platform, seeing her sitting on a bench, rummaging through her bag, close to panic as realisation unravelled. I saw myself running up to her, stopping slightly out of breath, handing her the notebook. She would take it and smile and say—

But going back would make me late for work myself, and I was on the Planning Hotline rota that morning. If I was going to get off at the next stop I should have gone down the stairs already – the driver had closed the doors and was preparing to pull away.

But, of course, I knew where she lived. She could cover the loss of the swipecard for one day – I would take the notebook round after work and return it to her then. I opened it up. She had written her name and address on the inside of the cover in blue biro. Sophie Taylor. Sophie. I sat back and watched as Trent Bridge and my stop approached. Yes, I would take the notebook round when I went to see Sophie later on.

Chapter Two

Malcolm was already in his office with the door open, talking loudly on the phone, and as I passed he raised his hand in greeting. I waved and went into the kitchenette to put my sandwiches in the fridge, then crossed the main office and switched on my computer. While I was waiting for Windows to load up, I turned off the Hotline answerphone and diverted the number to my extension. None of the others were in yet, and I sat for a moment savouring the calm of the empty office. I hadn't switched on the lights – I prefer to work in semi-gloom, despite the health and safety restrictions. The greyish light came in stripes through the open venetian blinds, settling like dust, washing out the colour. Each desk was piled high with folders and notepads and empty coffee mugs and coke cans, a stray cardigan on the back of a chair, scraps of fading paper pinned to the painted noticeboards that lined the walls, as if the occupants of the office had simply disappeared, the *Marie Celeste* of urban planning. I like a few moments in the empty office early in the morning; it

9

is a transition, a decompression chamber before the tumult descends – telephones ringing, the women chattering, the shuffle of paper, rhythms drummed out on the keyboards.

Malcolm had emerged from his office and now came over to my desk, jammed into a corner between the filing cabinets and the window. He jabbed the light switches as he passed them, and the lights flickered then kicked in, and I blinked at him through the fluorescence. He leaned against the nearest filing cabinet and handed me an orange envelope folder. He had written 'Peter Williams' in uneven black capitals across the flap, and I caught myself wondering how to re-use a folder with my name so prominently marked across it.

'The details of the Marston Street project,' he said. 'Thought you might like to read them on the train tomorrow.'

'Sure,' I said. It was a thick folder and when I opened the flap I could see architects' drawings and a bound proposal with a glossy cover. 'I'm driving over to Derby, but I'll have a look tonight anyway.'

Malcolm didn't turn to leave, but said instead, 'I'm sure you'll find the conference useful. There are a lot of projects coming on-stream with European funding.'

'I'm looking forward to it,' I said, wondering what was behind Malcolm's sudden friendliness.

Malcolm went to the window and looked out. I swivelled my chair to still be facing him. In the car park below Anthony was locking his BMW, the headlights flashing as he clicked the alarm on.

I said, 'The regeneration side is something I'm really interested in.'

He glanced at me. 'I know you are. The Marston Street project is a good place to start.'

I wanted to ask whether this would stand me in good stead for the next Senior Planning Officer's post, but I hesitated, not wanting to seem too pushy, not sure how to begin.

Malcolm said, 'Have they sent you the papers for tomorrow's conference?'

'Yes.' I located the envelope in my pending tray and passed it to him. Anthony had just entered the main office, and when he saw Malcolm at my desk he came over. Malcolm was looking at the conference agenda, and Anthony squinted at the front of the paperwork, setting his briefcase down between his feet.

'Ah, the urban planning thing,' he said. 'Are you going, Pete?'

I nodded, trying not to feel annoyed that Anthony always called me 'Pete', trying to remind myself that it wasn't Anthony's fault that he was promoted to SPO and I wasn't. That was down to Malcolm, now passing my conference papers to Anthony to scrutinise.

'Pete's going to look at the Marston Street stuff,' Malcolm said.

Anthony raised his eyes to meet mine. 'Good. I could use someone else's input.'

Yeah, I thought, I bet you could. But I said, 'No problem, it's an interesting project.'

Anthony ignored my words, handing me the conference papers and saying, 'Malcolm, I'd like you to cast your eye over something, if you've got a minute.'

'Sure, sure,' and Malcolm smiled a distracted smile at me before following Anthony towards the SPO's office. I took a deep breath and put the conference papers back into their envelope, trying not to think about Anthony getting that promotion. And the Marston Street stuff – that was SPO's work, but what could I say to object if I didn't want to jeopardise my chances of the next SPO post?

It was a quiet morning on the Hotline; a couple of enquiries about garage erections, someone living next to a pub who needed the difference between planning and licensing explained, and a handful of questions about the route of the proposed tram, which I redirected to the Tram Taskforce in the next office. By the time one of the girls took over from me, I was ready for a cheese and tomato sandwich at my desk before tackling the budget work piling up in my in-tray.

The afternoon passed fairly quickly, and I made a satisfying dent in my backlog before catching the bus for the tortuous crawl home through the traffic. Sophie wasn't on the bus home, but then she never was – her day must have finished earlier than mine, because in the winter I had often noticed the light on in her flat as the bus reached our stop. My earlier concerns about her trip to the railway station had subsided somewhat. There had to be a straight-forward explanation – picking up a ticket, perhaps. I was confident that when I returned the notebook to her I would see that there had been nothing to worry about. Alison always says that I concern myself too much with other people's problems.

I went slowly up the passage at the side of the hairdressers'. Now that the moment had come to actually speak to her, I wasn't sure what I was going to say. I imagined myself bumbling and stammering my way through a couple of sentences while she looked at me with pity, or amusement, or worse. The passage came out into a concrete yard, where an old brick outhouse sagged against a wooden fence trailing with ivy from the garden behind. There was an old sofa in the yard, the foam cushions rotting down into a carcass of springs and metal frame. Two doors led into the back of the building; one was a plain door peeling blue paint onto the concrete, the back entrance to the hairdressers', and the other was a varnished wood affair with 'Flat A' painted in white gloss above the brass letterbox. I rang the doorbell and stood waiting for feet to come down the stairs that must have lain on the other side of that door. Nothing. I rang again and waited, but she still didn't come. I considered putting a note through the door, but I had no paper apart from the pages of her own notebook, and I couldn't use that. So I told myself that I would come back later, and I went home.

Alison was still out at work, so I put my briefcase

in its corner under the coat hooks in the hall, checked the answerphone for messages and made myself a cup of tea before sitting down on the sofa to watch the news. I had Sophie's notebook in my hands. It was fairly tatty, as if she carried it around in the bottom of a bag. I ran my fingers over the soft cardboard on the corners and opened it to the first page. She wrote untidily, sloping looping handwriting that ran freely across the page.

I heard the car pull up outside the house and went into the hall to put the diary into my briefcase before slipping on my shoes and going outside. Alison was unloading shopping from the boot and I helped her bring the bags through into the kitchen. Once we'd put the bags down and had started to unpack, I said, 'How was your day?'

'Fine,' she said, wrist-deep in the grocery bags. Her light brown hair had fallen across her face like a curtain. 'Busy. Andrew's talking about office restructuring again. He knows I hate it when he makes decisions without consulting us advisors, but he still goes right ahead and does it.'

'Oh dear,' I said, taking out the pork chops that had been defrosting in the fridge since that morning. 'Do you want broccoli with this?'

'Yes, thanks,' she said, and rattled on about the reorganisation being a disaster for the customers, and the timing of it, and the threat to mutuality at the next AGM, and the City profiteers looking to loot the vaults. She was putting tins away in the cupboard as she spoke.

I scrubbed some potatoes at the sink and put them on to boil, then cut the fatty rind off the chops, nodding all the time at how important a principle it was that the advisors were listened to when decisions were made about the branches. Alison always looks tired when she comes in at the end of the day, but as she says, she has to work twice as hard because the graduate trainees get fast-tracked past her.

We ate dinner quickly, and I told her the details of the Derby conference, and we agreed to choose paint for the skirting boards at the weekend. I washed up and put everything away while Alison sat in front of *Coronation Street*. She always offers to help, but I usually send her away again, because she's always so tired, she's on her feet all day, and I know she would much rather be watching *Coronation Street*. By the time I had put everything away, Corrie had finished and she was into *EastEnders*. I took her a mug of coffee and sat down next to her on the sofa to lace up my shoes.

She stirred herself from the TV long enough to ask, 'Where are you going?'

'To post a letter,' I said, and gave her a quick kiss on the lips before standing up. 'Won't be long,' I said.

There were no lights on in Sophie's flat as I walked along Vernon Road. She could have been in a back room. It was dark in the passage at the side of the hairdressers', shadows that expanded as I stepped through, the dusk clinging in the air. I didn't see that someone was standing at Sophie's door until he had already seen me.

We looked at each other. He was a large shape, a bulk, his face sickly pale in the fading light, short dark dreadlocks casting shadows over his eyes.

'You after Sophie?' he asked.

'Isn't she in?'

He was wearing a hefty pair of paratroop boots, laced loosely over baggy army-surplus trousers, and he kicked the toe of one boot against the ground. He was looking directly at me, frowning or squinting, I couldn't tell.

'She's not answering. I was supposed to come round. She must've forgotten.'

I nodded, as if the same had happened to me. I wondered if I should explain my presence, but I thought he would offer to take the notebook from me if I did. He looked as if he was weighing me up, passing judgement on my shirt and tie, on the way my suit hung loose over my skinny body. The clothes Sophie would have seen – what would she have thought, seeing me on her doorstep in my office gear?

He said, 'You a friend of Sophie's, then?'

I didn't know what to say, so I said, 'Yes.'

I couldn't tell if he believed me. He looked up at the dark windows, as if she would suddenly appear. 'She never said she was going out, did she? I was supposed to come round.'

'Maybe she got held up at work,' I said.

'No.' He shook his head and his dreadlocks rattled

like tassels. 'I went to meet her. She never showed today. I thought she might be ill or something. Maybe she's ill and can't get help?'

He seemed strangely frightened by her absence, and I said, 'She seemed fine this morning.'

'This morning? Where was she going?'

'I don't know. She didn't say. I'll come back tomorrow,' I said, and turned to go. He followed me back down the passage, the boots thumping against the paving slabs behind me. I thought he was going to follow me along the street, but he stopped at the kerb, looking up the road as if he would see her coming towards him.

I left him where he was and hurried back home. Alison would wonder what had kept me so long, but she would quickly forget about that. The notebook pressed against me as I walked. I was curious now – I wanted to find out what was in the notebook, whether it was something that really did matter. Alison would be busy with the TV schedules for a while yet – I could run a bath, lie in the privacy of the water and start to read Sophie's words.

12 April

Never had a call like the one I had today. I can handle abuse, Mr Harris from Oakley Close yelling that we're robbing him blind, or that woman who threatened to come round and smash the computers until she started bawling, because her husband had cleaned out the joint bank account and her with three kids to feed. But the call today was different, weird. Maybe it was someone having a laugh, like the girls said, just a wind-up merchant, or Leanna might have been right – there's a lot of crackpots out there these days.

Because this caller never said a word. I went all the way through the corporate greeting, Trent-ElectricitySophieSpeaking, and they never said a thing. I'd have thought it was a dud connection except for the slightest sound of the person's breathing, picking up static on the line.

I said, 'Hello, hello, is anyone there?' but not a sound. I broke the connection, but then my extension lit up again, and I punched into the next call and it was the silence all over again. So I told them I'd have to hang up again if they didn't speak. Nothing. And the third time, the same silence, someone direct-dialling my extension, someone dialling to not talk to me.

I said, 'Leanna, is that you?' and turned in my seat to look across the office, but I could see Leanna's lips

18

moving, and her fingers tapping on her keyboard. I looked around the whole office, but I couldn't spot a joker looking for my reaction. So I asked if it was Jamie but got no reply.

I should have known better. I should have hung up again. Feel sorry for a weirdo and next thing they're harassing, waiting outside the office with flowers, like happened to Amy until she got the injunction. I wanted to get rid of the call and go onto the next one, a customer, get back into my rhythm, but I didn't want to break the connection again, I didn't want the caller back again.

Training never covered how to deal with this. After three years I've got my defusing tactics spot-on, and my certificate from the Dealing With Aggression training course, but this caller wasn't angry, and that gave me the chills. I'd have gone cold and efficient and talked about an account, the way Marion Barker likes us to, if there had been anything to go on. But it wasn't like the caller was having a go. I could tell that they weren't going to launch into some hate-the-company spiel, like the people who contest every penny on their bill because they're either miserly or broke. I can cope with that. Broke people are okay – they get emotional, but eventually they always say, 'Oh, it's not your fault, duck, you're all right.' Misers moaning about how hard they work for their money really piss me off, like work is a holiday for me, but let them say their piece and they soon run out of steam. But this caller wasn't saying a word, and that really freaked me out.

Marion Barker was coming up the aisle towards me,

and I knew I had to end the call because she wouldn't believe me if I told her I was listening to silence. So I said, 'I'm hanging up now,' and cut the connection again and, sure enough, my extension lit up straightaway, and what was I supposed to do, answer it?

Marion reached my desk, frowning sour lemons at me because I wasn't answering a call. Before she could start on one I told her about the caller, and asked if I should put the call in the Book. She got even sourer then, if that's possible, because I bet she wanted to say that I was skiving, she'd love to have the chance to say that. But she fed me the line about putting all threats in the Book, and when I said it wasn't threatening, not exactly, she just looked at me gone-out and walked off. She doesn't have much of a clue about how freaky stuff can start. They should take her off being Supervisor, let her cover the phones for just one day, or give her a personality transplant. If she wasn't ice cold she might have realised what I was trying to say to her.

Chapter Three

I never have liked driving. I don't like to be contained in a metal box, with all the other metal boxes hurtling past. It's not that I dislike sitting behind the wheel, following the routines of checking mirrors and blind spots, or changing through the gears, or balancing the clutch and the accelerator. It's other road users who make the experience so traumatic – anticipating traffic braking suddenly ahead, or pedestrians appearing from behind parked cars, or cyclists wobbling their way up a hill. The driver who jumps a red light, or pulls out of a side road without looking, or overtakes on a blind corner. When I am driving, everything about me locks and tenses up. I can imagine the moment of impact, the moment before impact when I cannot act to prevent it, the feel of hot metal and vinyl and glass crushing and piercing my body. I've had dreams about that. Alison says I just don't drive often enough to feel relaxed, I just don't trust other drivers to want to stay alive too, and I know she's right, I know that's what scares me, but it is a constant thought when I drive – what if someone else makes a stupid mistake?

Coming back from the Derby conference, the traffic snaking in towards the city added to the pressure I was feeling. Cars lined up, choking out exhaust fumes, and only one person in each car, an environmentalist's nightmare. Engines revving and horns sounding, and when I wound down the window to get some air in, warm sour fumes filled the car.

And the inside of the car just reeks of Alison. How could I feel confident when even the space I was seated in belonged to someone else? If I did crash, if I did die, the detritus of the car would be how I was seen by those who came after, the police and the fire crew and the paramedics, thinking of me and seeing Alison's belongings scattered across the tarmac. I know she's the one who uses the car every day, so it's bound to take on her imprint rather than mine, but it seems to be uncontrollably her. She left earlier than me in the morning, so after she had gone I spent ten minutes tidying up the car, because I knew that it would have irritated me too much while I was driving. It always amazes me that people can live their lives surrounded by rubbish. Alison drives around in that car every day with junk piling up in the footwells and spilling out over the seats, bits of paper that were once important reports folded over and footprinted on the floor, empty bottles of water and crisp packets thrown around, petrol receipts and old newspapers mixed in with stray jumpers and –

strangely, I always think – old pairs of tights. I would be embarrassed to leave the car out in broad daylight in that kind of state.

I think it's like a handbag. All the women I share my office with arrive carrying handbags that seem closer to survival kits. I've never understood the need to carry around a bag full of bits and pieces that don't need to be taken everywhere – make-up and tissues and aspirin and plasters and sewing kits and safety pins, just in case – but there it is, the need to be prepared for any domestic emergency. I see it all the time in my office – a button comes off someone's jacket or shirt, or someone complains of a migraine coming on, and instantly there are half a dozen women rummaging through their handbags. I think this is what Alison's car is – a huge moving handbag that she can dump everything into and then climb inside herself.

Whatever the reason for the car being in such a state, I couldn't leave it like that. When I got back from the Derby conference, I decided that I would gently suggest to Alison that she should clean the car out at the next available opportunity. A delicate matter to raise with somebody as stubbornly untidy as she. I was back later than I had intended to be, and to my relief she had already left for her college class by the time I parked up outside the house, and that meant that the job fell to me.

It was still light outside, so I fetched the car vac and a bin liner and got to work. There is something very satisfying about a big cleaning job. It took a good couple of hours to clean the inside properly, to pick up every bit of fluff and fibre from the boot and the upholstery, but when I had finished and stood back to admire my handiwork, I thought how pleased Alison would be at the transformation.

I deserved a break after that. Home cinema time, and with Alison out I could watch whatever I liked. So I settled down to watch the *Blade Runner Directors' Cut*, with the curtains drawn and the lights out so the steamy rain seemed to drift into the darkness of the room. I had barely finished Leon's interrogation scene before the phone rang.

It was Steve. 'I know Alison's out tonight,' he said, 'so there's no excuse for not coming to the pub with me.'

'I did have plans,' I said. I had paused the video, and Leon had stopped open-mouthed, half-way through saying, 'Let me tell you about my mother.'

Steve laughed down the phone. 'You can't be watching *Blade Runner* again. Come on, Pete, you've seen that film so often you must be wearing out the tape. Let's go for a drink. I'll even let you win at pool.'

'You must be desperate.'

'That's me. I'll see you there in half an hour.'

I didn't have any choice in the matter, so I rewound the video and put it back on the bookcase, then went upstairs and changed into jeans and a sweatshirt. I needed a shower really – my hair had done its usual trick of plastering itself down lankly against my head with a few random tufts sticking up at the back. I combed my hair through with water and hoped that that would do the trick.

By the time I got down to the Arms on Vernon Road, Steve was already there, racking up the pool table and having a stilted conversation about Forest with one of the old men who have been regulars since the start of history. He was halfway down his pint, so I ordered two pints of Kimberley Classic and carried them over.

Steve won the first game easily. As I racked up the second game he smiled and chalked his cue and said, 'Maybe I'll let you win this one.'

'Don't do me any favours,' I said. I sent the cue ball whistling down the table and in the resulting fracas a yellow rolled smoothly into the corner pocket. I lined up my next shot and pocketed another yellow.

'Hustler,' he said as I potted a third, but the luck ran out then, leaving him with an easy shot to the side pocket. He flashed me a grin as he potted the shot, then walked round the table to find his next shot.

'Do you fancy seeing that Cronenberg film?' I asked. 'It's on at the Broadway next week.'

He glanced towards me. 'Already seen it, mate.'

'Yeah?' I tried to sound casual. 'Any good?'

He screwed up his nose and then bent over to squint down the cue at the angle of the balls. 'It's okay, you know, typical weirdo Cronenberg.'

'Sure,' I said.

'Anyway,' he said, slamming the cue ball and a red against the far cushion. 'I'm tied up for most of next week. There's a whole load of us going to build a machine to enter Robot Wars.'

'Yeah?' I wanted to ask, to demand, when this had been decided, when they had got together, who was in this group. But I took all of the heat out of my tone before I asked, 'Who are you doing that with?'

He had put too much spin on the cue ball and the red had gone harmlessly clear of the pocket. He sucked air through his teeth then straightened up. 'Mate at work, his brother's in the engineering department at Trent Uni, so we're going to build it there.'

He had left me with an easy pot, and I wondered if he was being kind, but he drank from his pint glass without comment. I said, 'Have you got a name for it?'

'Sexorcet,' he said, without a hint of a smile.

'They'll never let you call it that,' I said. 'Not on the telly. There's kids who watch that show, you know.'

'It'll be fine,' he said, and then grinned. 'It'll be cool, you'll see. Going to use pram wheels so it can't get flipped, so it can run either way up, and have an axe for the weapon. Titanium alloy. We've got a wheelchair motor to drive it.'

'Nice,' I said, and missed the easy pot. He smiled again, still thinking about his robot. He was probably imagining annihilating the opposition against the spikes in the arena walls. He played a reasonable safety shot.

'Well,' he said. 'Time for another pint,' and drained his glass and headed to the bar.

I stood waiting for him to come back before playing my next shot. The pub was starting to fill up, as much as it did on a week night. It was badly in need of redecoration; the swirled artex on the walls had yellowed with age and nicotine, and the fabric on the seats was so worn it was hard to tell what the pattern had been like when new. The usual crowd of old men in stained shirts were grouped around the bar, and a gang of middle-aged women with voices shrill enough to peel paint sat in the booth nearest to the pool table. In the far corner, below the television, seated at a table piled with crisp packets and empty glasses, was a group of twenty-somethings, all laughing at a story being told by a chubby man with short dark dreadlocks.

I looked again, but it was definitely the man I'd seen outside Sophie's flat. His friends were all dressed in similar gear to him, a clan, and I looked carefully but Sophie wasn't there. I was just wondering what I would do if he saw me when he looked in my direction and raised his hand in recognition. I nodded and smiled back and went to turn back to the pool table, but he said something to the others and they all turned and looked towards me as he made his way out of the circle.

I pretended to be thinking about my next shot as

he crossed the bar to reach me. When he got to me, he said, 'Did you catch up with Sophie?'

'No,' I said, thinking suddenly of the notebook still in the pocket of my coat, now thrown across the bench behind us. What if the notebook was sticking out of the pocket? What if he could see it and demanded it back? I sneaked a look, but the pocket was folded under and nothing showed.

'Nobody's seen her,' he said. 'We're all worried. What did she say when you saw her?'

Steve had returned from the bar, but the man didn't even turn and look at him. I said, 'She didn't say anything.'

'Not even a hint?'

Steve was sipping his pint and pretending not to be interested. I said, 'Look, I didn't even speak to her. I just saw her on the bus that morning, that's all.'

'Where was she going?'

'I don't know,' I said. I wondered if I should say that I saw her get off at the railway station, but I could tell that Steve's ears were flapping, and it was going to be hard enough to explain as it was. 'I'm sorry, I can't help.'

'But you saw her on the bus. What time was that?'

'Eight o'clock,' I said.

'She must have been going to work. She never got there. I'm getting worried.'

'I'm sure she's fine,' I said.

Steve had opened his mouth to form a question, but the man said, 'If you see her, tell her to phone Jamie.'

'Sure,' I said.

He nodded, as if in thanks, and wandered back to the group. Steve handed me my pint and said, 'What was that all about?'

'Oh, nothing,' I said. 'He's looking for a girl who catches my bus to work, but I don't know where she is.'

'Why would you?'

'Exactly my point,' I said.

He looked back towards the group again, and I saw that Jamie was back in its midst. I lined up my cue and played a spectacularly bad shot that brought Steve's attention back to the game, but I couldn't resist the occasional glance across at Jamie as we played. I was thinking that the notebook might tell someone where Sophie had gone. I knew I should give it to Jamie – he was the one who knew her, he was the one who was worried – and I did think about it. But I couldn't see how I could do that – I couldn't imagine going over and handing it to him, and all his friends listening, and having to give reasons for not having explained the situation before, and what would I say if Jamie asked me if I'd read it? How did I even know if it would be useful? I could cause a lot of problems for myself for no good reason at all. It seemed to me that I had no choice but to keep reading the notebook myself, until it became apparent what I should do with it.

16 April

Female
Sister of Jonathan

Okay, the first few times it might have been a bit of a laugh, trying to guess who the caller was, and I can take a joke as well as the next person, but now I don't know what to do about the calls. Three times this week, and each time the same – silence, jamming up the switchboard and taking over my extension. I'm going to miss my call targets for the month and I need my bonus. I'm in danger of screaming down the phone the next time the caller rings, too, and that isn't allowed. I can feel the rage burning me up inside, and if Marion Barker thinks she can intimidate me into keeping on answering those calls, she's got another thing coming.

I phoned in sick this morning, put on a bad throat and a weakened voice and told them I hoped it was a twenty-four-hour thing and I'd be back tomorrow. I feel like never going back.

By the time I'd faked my way through Marion Barker's built-in lie-detector, I really did feel weak and ill, so I lay on the sofa for a while watching daytime TV and drinking Diet Coke from the bottle, but being on my own didn't do any good at all. I kept thinking that the person making the calls knew my extension, and that meant they knew something about me, and could that mean they knew where I lived as well? When Amy had that trouble that time, she had the bloke waiting outside her house all hours, and it was only her dad going for the bloke with a garden fork that stopped him coming around. That and the injunction, of course. And how did he find out where she lived? I always think that stuff's so private, but is it really? It wouldn't take much to find out my work number – it's hardly secret, they don't hide them from customers – and I'm in the phone book, right there with my address.

It freaks me out, thinking that the guy might be stood outside my flat, looking up at my windows, maybe even able to see me moving around when I've got the lights on. The flat always seemed so safe – burglar-proof, Mr Assif said when he showed me around. Just as well, seeing as I don't have any insurance.

But actually, someone could break in if they really wanted. Kick down the door – I don't suppose anyone would take any notice really, the hairdressers' dryers are going all hours, I can hear them humming all the time in the front room, and on a really busy day, if they're all going at once, sometimes the floor even vibrates.

I couldn't sit where I was, and I knew it was Mum's day off, so I wrapped myself up in my sick clothes (jogging bottoms and oversized woolly jumper) and walked down to Mum and Dad's. Mum wasn't at all surprised to see me. I swear she thinks that if it's her day off the rest of the world must be off as well. She was in the middle of hoovering the front room when I went in, so I put the kettle on and made a pot of tea, and she came and joined me at the kitchen table when she was done. She didn't ask why I'd come round, she never does. But it was one of her good days – she told me all about what the cousins were up to, and how her new shift pattern was working out, and how Dad would have to pay for Jonathan to fix the car because he needed some tool that his boss wouldn't lend him from the garage.

'Tight, that's what I say,' Mum said. 'It's not like he's going to break it, is it?'

I tried to imagine Jonathan having the guts even to ask if he could borrow some tools. Some things would just be pushing his luck too far, whatever his boss says about believing him now. But Mum seemed to want some kind of an explanation, and I wasn't going to remind her about what happened before, so I just muttered something about how it was probably the insurance stopping him.

Mum said, 'That's what Jonathan said, but really, why would that matter?'

I wasn't going to explain it to her. She was going off on one, and she can talk for England when the mood takes her. I kept my fiercest smile on. I wanted to tell her about the phone calls, but not when she was in one of those moods. I know what she'd be like, mouthing off. And she'd try to get me to stay with them, in the house, because don't I know I'm more than welcome, there's the room not being used and all I have to do is say the word, there's no shame in it, there's no sense in being alone and her stuck in a houseful of men. She'd like my company, that's what she says, but she means she'd like her little girl home again.

I don't know. I mean, she spent all our teenage years making out like she couldn't wait until we were gone and she could have peace and quiet and her choice on the telly every night, but the minute I'm gone, she wants me back. She wants me to revert back to a sweet little six-year-old, I'm sure that's it, a walking, talking doll who even agrees to wear frilly dresses on occasion. She wants me to be a grown-up version being fitted out for a wedding dress too, I bet.

Finally, Mum poured out some more tea and gave me a look that said she had something to say, and my heart gave a leap even though I knew she wasn't about to ask me what was bothering me so much. She said, 'I've been worried about Jonathan. He seems very down at the moment. Has he talked to you? Do you know what's going on?'

'Not really,' I said. 'He doesn't tell me much, you know.'

I felt bad saying that, even if it's true most of the time, because I'm worried too, a little. He came round last night, half-sloshed, straight from the Rose and Crown at chucking-out time, where he'd been since knocking off at the garage, I bet. He slumped down in my armchair and rolled a couple of spliffs, as if he's always round at my place, as if we're best mates, and we played the family game of circling the issue. I asked the necessary questions – how's work, how's Rachel – and got the usual replies – fine, okay. He was just a heavy lump, an object taking up space in my front room, demanding some sort of attention and not giving out any clues for me to start him talking. It's a long time since I've been able to second-guess his thoughts. I felt useless, nothing to start from and unable to advise him. By the time he stumbled out of the house promising me he would walk not drive, he had exchanged his silence for a promise not to tell Mum and Dad anything, because he didn't want to worry them, they wouldn't understand, nothing they could say would help anyway. He promised to talk to Rachel, tell her what was bothering him, and I guessed from the way he sighed that it was the usual problem, commitment: when's the wedding, when would they move in together, why didn't he have enough saved for the deposit when she was ready with her half and he only had to say the word.

Mum said, 'He's the one I worry about, you know. He just can't seem to get it together. If only he and Rachel could sort it out, set the date, start the ball rolling. You know I want to see one of you settled, and there's nothing on the horizon for you that way.'

I opened my mouth to say that that was okay, I didn't want anything, not yet, but she cut me off and said, 'I don't worry about you. You're an independent sort, always have been. Ever since you were a little kid in playgroup, insisting you could buckle your own shoes, remember that?' No time to confess that I can't remember, that I was three at the time, before she rattled on with, 'No, thank goodness there's no problems with you, it's just Jonathan we need to sort out, always the boys who cause the problems.'

I said, 'Well, that's men for you.'

'True enough,' she said, and poured out more tea from the pot, and then reached behind her, chair perilously balanced on the back legs, to bring the biscuit barrel over. She opened the lid, took out a custard cream and then pushed the barrel over to me. I put my hand in and pulled out a ginger snap, then pushed the lid back on as far as it would go.

Mum said, 'Yes, boys are always more trouble. I knew you'd be fine right from the start, right from when you first opened your eyes, but Jonathan was different. So shy. He used to follow you around everywhere when you were little. Remember that?' Before I could point out that I had been a toddler at the time, that my memories of that age come second-hand from her, she said, 'Yes, he'd follow you around, always watching you, like he couldn't believe you were real. And you used to get him to do whatever you wanted, remember that?'

I was tired of this game, tired of her trying to put us back into our baby selves. She has no idea how different things are now. I said, 'Oh, Mum, I'm sure lots of big brothers are fascinated by their baby sisters, there was nothing special about that.'

She looked at me as if she thought I was trying to say she was wrong, and for a moment I thought I'd said too much. But then she said, 'You're probably right.'

She was wandering off into memories of when we were little, I could see it. Sometimes I think she preferred it when we were that age, totally dependent on her, looking up at her as if she was a god or something, thinking she could solve everything, not able to spot the holes in the things she said.

I wanted to talk to her properly, but I couldn't see a way into telling her about the phone calls. And besides, what could she do? Would I really want her worrying about her little girl again? It's taken me long enough to convince her I can stand on my own two feet and to get out of that house without hurting her feelings too much — do I really want to undo all of that? Besides, she'd probably only brush my concerns aside anyway, tell me not to be so daft, because things like that happen but they never mean anything, it's probably kids playing games, or some friend doing a not-very-funny practical joke on me. She rattled on about next-door's daughter's new baby and how they had to incubate it because it was so little, its lungs barely able to breathe without help, and her whole face wrinkled with concern for this helpless little baby, and she said again and again how her thoughts were going out to the mother, trying to cope with all that stress and worry.

And in the end I stumbled away from the house after a heavy meal of leftover Shepherd's Pie, and I'd said nothing. I'd kept Jonathan's problems for him and said nothing about my own, and I was tired. I mean, really drained, my limbs were so heavy I could barely walk, and all I wanted to do was curl up under my duvet and sleep the rest of the day away.

Chapter Four

I sat in front of my computer with the chair pulled up close so that my lap was jammed out of view under the desk. I was supposed to be looking at the Marston Street project before meeting with Anthony that afternoon, but it was a quiet day in the office and I had Sophie's notebook open on my lap.

I knew I should get on with my work, resist the urge to look down and read. I could feel the paper under my fingers, roughened and dented by the impressions that her biro had made, stiffened by this unevenness. Behind me, the women I shared my office with were working quietly for once, too busy with the backlog they were trying to clear to pay me any attention. Even if they had bothered to look my way, I had the Marston Street folder open on my desk, and a word processing window open on my computer screen.

I looked at the words I had typed: Marston Street Project Application: Phase One Assessment. I selected the words and added bold and underline, then reconsidered and took the underline off. I centred the text and thought about changing the font from Times New Roman to Arial or Helvetica, but held off on making that decision.

Sophie had been writing in the notebook just before she left it on the bus. It occurred to me that she might well have written down what she was intending to do. If that was the case, if I kept reading I would probably find out where she had gone, and I would be able to tell people, and everyone would know whether she was safe. I could imagine it – all the people thanking me, Jamie shaking me by the hand, buying me a pint, inviting me to join his table, and all his friends smiling and welcoming me.

The notebook was a solid presence on my lap. I put my hand down and felt through the pages, my fingers running over the imprints of the writing, until finally I found the first smooth page. I glanced around the office, but I hadn't aroused any interest from anyone else, so I looked down. I felt almost excited as I turned the pages back to the start of the final entry.

'Pete,' a voice above me said, and I was so surprised that I jerked my knee upwards and bashed it on the underside of the desk with a loud thump, and the notebook dropped to the floor under my desk.

I looked up, trying to hide my confusion, feeling my knee ache and my face flush with blood. 'Anthony,' I said, 'I was—' but I stopped myself from explaining and forced a smile and rubbed my knee. 'You gave me a start.'

'Yeah, sorry,' he said, and grinned, and pulled up the nearest chair. 'Marston Street.'

'I was just looking at the papers,' I said.

'Yeah,' Anthony said. He wasn't looking directly at me, but was sitting forward in the chair with his legs wide apart and his elbows resting on his knees, smiling past me at one of the girls in the office. I didn't turn my head to find out which one. He said, 'You okay to meet a little earlier? Only, I've got to take my car in, I'd forgotten all about it. Clutch is slipping slightly,' he added, as if that would explain everything.

'Sure,' I said, 'no problem,' even though the report was nowhere near finished. If he wanted a rushed job that's what he would get, because I wasn't going to let him criticise me to Malcolm.

He nodded and stood up, still smiling across the office, then finally looked at me. 'Two o'clock, then?'

'Fine,' I said, sounding more positive than I felt, because he'd just wished away my lunch break. He walked away, back towards his office, and I heard the girls giggling in his wake. I got down on my hands and knees and reached under the desk for Sophie's notebook, then put it into my desk drawer. Outside it was a beautiful day, a bright, clear sky, but everything else, including Sophie, would have to wait until the day had officially finished.

Chapter Five

Alison was home before me, sitting at the dining table with her college folders open. As I went past her to put away the bread and milk I'd bought, she looked up at me and smiled, and I leaned down and kissed her on the top of the head. Her hair smelled fragrant, the sugary scent of her shampoo.

'Cup of tea?' I asked.

'Yes, thanks,' she said, and put her biro down and sat back, as if she had been working for a long time and needed a break.

I made the drinks and brought them through and sat at the table with her, putting the mugs down on a heatproof mat. 'So,' I said. 'How was your day?'

'Okay. Busy, you know.'

I nodded and sipped my drink. She told me about the latest missive from Head Office, and how annoyed she was, and the extra work it would mean. I started to tell her about Anthony rearranging the Marston Street meeting, and she tutted and shook her head.

'What?' I asked.

40

'You shouldn't let them take advantage of you.'

I was surprised by her tone. 'They don't.'

'You worked through lunch again, didn't you?'

'Yes, but it was my choice.' She was frowning at me. I said, 'Oh, come on. You know what it's like. I've got to show willing if I want the SPO's post.'

She was trying to wave the discussion away with her hands. 'Forget it. Forget I said anything.'

I couldn't tell why she was acting that way. I sat back and looked at her, at all the books and folders arranged around her. There wasn't much point in pressing her for an explanation, so I said, 'I should let you get on.'

'No, no,' she said, and her hand ran away from the folder she had been touching.

'You've got work to do,' I said, and started to get up.

When I was almost standing, she said, 'Did you clean my car out?'

She still had the same edge to her voice. I said, 'It needed doing. I know how busy you are.'

'Not that busy.' She sighed and sat back, away from her books, as if she was about to explain something to me. 'I wish you'd leave it alone. I like it that way.'

'What do you mean?'

'It's my space,' she said.

'But it needed doing,' I said. 'How could you prefer it that way? It was a pigsty.'

'You're exaggerating as usual.'

'I thought I was doing you a favour,' I said, but I couldn't keep the irritation out of my voice.

'Well, don't. I don't need favours. Maybe I'm not bloody perfect like you, but I happen to like it that way. I happen to like sprawling out. I can't do it in the house, so can't I at least have one place where I can? Is that too much to ask?'

She had worked herself up into an ugly frenzy. I looked at her face, trying to measure what I should say. I said, 'Well, I'm sorry,' but my tone betrayed me.

She must have realised how ridiculous, how unreasonable she was being, because she softened her tone and said, 'I just want one space for me, that's all.'

'Okay,' I said. 'Okay, I'm sorry, I won't touch your car ever again.'

I took my mug of tea over to the other end of the room and switched on the TV and sat down. I could tell that she had not yet returned to working and was looking at me, but I stared straight ahead at the local news, about a young boy suffering from leukaemia whose chrome scooter had been stolen from the back yard.

Alison said, 'Pete, don't be like that.'

'Like what?' I asked, sipping my drink, wondering what explanation she could come up with for being annoyed with me now.

'Going off in a huff. Honestly, you're so childish sometimes.'

'Me? You're the one who can't stand people tidying up after her.'

The news was interviewing the boy's mother, sitting on the edge of her sofa with her little girl on her knee while she explained how devastated Craig had been, and the little girl was winding her dirty hands into her mother's long hair. I tried not to think about how horrible that would be, those greasy little fingers working their way into everything.

Alison said, 'For God's sake, all I said was please don't clean the car out, I mean, why would anyone in their right mind be upset about that?'

'I'm not upset,' I said. She gave a sigh and when I glanced over she had gone back to looking through her folders, and even though she must have realised I was watching her, she kept her head down and didn't look at me.

I flicked through the channels with the remote until I found the national news. I wanted to concentrate on what was being said, but my whole body was tense, taut, reacting to every movement she made as if electricity sparked through the air between us. I felt the energy coiling up inside me, charging every nerve end, every muscle. So after a few minutes, I fetched my shoes from the hall and as I put them on I said, 'I'm going for a walk.'

'Fine,' she said, in an over-cheery voice. 'See you later, then.'

I had been intending to take Sophie's notebook with me, maybe find a quiet pub and sit and read it over a slow pint, but as I collected my jacket I realised I'd left the notebook at work in my desk drawer. But it was a nice evening for a walk, so I set off up Vernon Road and through the housing estate until I came to Bulwell Golf Course. It would be light for a couple of hours yet, and there were evening golfers walking in pairs up the long slope that led from the housing estate, past the Golden Balls pub with its benches looking out over the scrubby grass. In the distance I could see golfers taking swings, and children on bicycles going over the rough ground that ran up by the side of the course, and people taking dogs for a walk.

I've always liked the idea of a dog – a faithful companion by my side as I stride out through open spaces, a reason to be up and out early in the morning when the air is fresh and clean, before the day is muddied by the waking city. If I had a dog, I could have brought it out to the golf course, thrown sticks for it to fetch, waited for it to bound back to continue the game, struck up conversations with other dog owners. I could have been a familiar figure, known to the neighbours, recognised throughout the area. I would have liked that.

By the time I got near the top of the hill, there were streaks of orange starting to light the clouds as the sun sank lower in the sky. At the top of the hill, I turned and looked down the long slope I had climbed. The air was cool and fresh with an evening breeze, and the sound of traffic had retreated into a background hum. From there, the view stretched out over half the city, the houses crammed into streets in swirling patterns, the red brick punctuated with green where the parks and gardens were, the offices and blocks of flats rising above the city centre, and red-brick factories and warehouses and the castle atop its yellow rock.

I looked at the patterns made by the streets and the parks and the factories, and I thought, someone planned all of this. Someone sat down and decided that the housing estates stretching out to the edges of the city would follow this pattern, and they marked out on a piece of paper where the roads would go, drew in the parks and schools and shopping areas, allocated land for each house, oversaw the architectural styles of the estates. I can imagine how it must have felt, to plan out the estates and see the land being cleared, watch as the roads were laid out and the houses went up, red brick by red brick, house by house, street by street. And then the families moving in, and the slum clearances, and whole generations being brought up in streets laid out by someone's pen.

Sometimes I forget that the city has not always been here. I forget that under the tarmac and the bricks and the concrete there is just mud, that in the past the land we now call the city was just fields, and woodland, and floodplain, and pasture. Sometimes I forget that decisions were made, that people worked to create the streets and the buildings. Sometimes it seems that the city must have grown organically, spreading out like bacteria in a Petri dish, like a dark cancer eating into the countryside beyond.

The government says they're all for planning, for adopting strategies to use brownfield sites and safeguard the greenbelt, strategies to safeguard the future of whole areas dying with the manufacturing industry, utilising joined-up thinking to produce a holistic approach, joined-up solutions for joined-up problems, and thinking the unthinkable, and redirecting core services to meet new demands. And people trot out the phrases, the buzz-words, and hours, days, weeks, months are spent talking, and consultation is undertaken and analysed, and reports are produced and recommendations are adopted, and maybe I'm a cynic, but it seems that it is all a waste, it all just plugs up the timelines, hides the fact that it's not the planners in control, it's private finance – businesses buying up abandoned warehouses and factories, turning them into student flats or over-priced loft apartments, an explosion of cashing-in on the latest craze, and more flats going up than there can possibly be people to fill them.

I see the applications, the city centre awash with redevelopment, and the tram route a bombsite with the roads cordoned off, and everything rushing headlong for completion with nobody looking at the next step. Sometimes I think I'm the only one who sees the dangers. The city's economy is the fastest growing in the country, and yet it is the twelfth most deprived authority, low wages and low house prices, an education system on its knees. It seems to me that in the rush for completion someone forgot about the process. It cannot simply flow forward freely – change must be guided, directed, controlled, shepherded in the right direction, always looking at the detail, always looking at the process.

But I know I am out of step, living in the wrong generation. I've been left behind. Centralised planning is out of favour, not modern enough. Whatever the quangos say about participation and consultation, money talks, and walks all over anyone who doesn't embrace what it says.

I think that's the reason why Anthony got the promotion and I didn't. In fact, I'm certain of it. In the interview, when they asked me what I thought about current redevelopment strategies, I told them what I thought, and even as I saw their interest flicker away, I couldn't stop, I couldn't end my answer with a lame fudge, I had to plough on, and lament the rise in private projects and the fall in City-led projects. I know I talked about how good the tram could be, and how a twenty-first-century city needed to meet twenty-first-century transport demands, and how an integrated system with cross-ticketing and interchanges and well-designed routes could really get the city moving and cut down on emissions and contribute to the much-vaunted clean-air policy. But even this desperate attempt to key into the positive things being done in the age of private finance, even this could not turn the tide back in my favour.

When I walked out of the interview, sweating in my suit and about to loosen my tie, Anthony was sitting outside, already wearing the smile he was going to use for the interview, as if he'd painted it onto his face. I gave him an awkward smile and he gave me a look that meant he was weighing up how well my interview had gone from my appearance. It was common knowledge that we were the two serious candidates; there were a couple of externals going for the post as well, but with all the strategies underway, there was little doubt that they wanted someone who was already on board and up to speed. I knew as I walked away that he had got it; all he had to do was say what they wanted to hear, parrot all the right phrases, and he is too sharp a customer to let that sort of opportunity pass him by.

Later, after the appointment had been made, I heard that he had championed private finance, had sung the praises of the canalside redevelopment and the Lace Market renaissance and heralded the age of public–private partnership. He was on-message and I was harking back to an age that has been airbrushed out of local planning. Modernised away. How could a dinosaur like me ever have competed?

But I don't let that concern me too much. I know that my ideas may seem old-fashioned and unrealistic now, but local government thinking is a little like fashion – flared trousers may be out, but they will be recycled at some time, re-branded as retro-chic and brought back with a fanfare in some government consultation document, rediscovering core values, and when that happens, my wardrobe of ideas won't seem quite so out of place.

It's all about a process, about planning ahead

and thinking about the alternatives, identifying scenarios, building in contingencies, having an exit strategy.

I had reached the far end of the golf course, up to where the main road ran past and out towards the M1, so I turned and headed back down towards home. I hoped that Alison would have calmed down by the time I got home, but if she hadn't I would run myself a long, hot bath. Everything is a process. Alison sees us living together as a trial run for being married; deep down, I think she wants the whole white wedding and kids thing, the whole traditional caboodle. I know she thinks we've started the process already; I think her whole life has been rattling along towards that completion. And it seems like a sensible choice, a logical and progressive way to live.

I suppose the interesting part will be evaluating the alternatives that present themselves along the way. Keeping an open mind, because every process involves a learning curve. These things can't be rushed, the stages can't be jumped. But when I think of Sophie, when I think of the leap she has taken – it sends me cold, to think of stepping into the unknown, stepping away from everything that has gone before. Thinking the unthinkable – walking away from it all. I know I want to find out why, and how, and what she plans to do. The thought of it creeps into everything I do.

19 April

Played word bingo in the team meeting this morning. Julie, me and Amy, sitting together at a desk at the back of the crowd, jargon busting. Supposed to be making notes on the new call-queuing software, but we were holding out for Marion to use the winning buzz-phrase – 'customer-oriented voice-recognition computer interface', the future of telephone services according to *Call Centre* magazine. Of course, she didn't. But we had a giggle. We always do, part of the wind-up-Marion game.

Leanna asked again about switching desks. She's been on about it for weeks, claims the heating vent gives her a headache even though nobody else complains. I swear she just does it for attention. But Marion asked for volunteers to swap with her, and it suddenly didn't seem like such a bad idea. I've had it with the silent caller blocking up my extension, and Marion isn't doing anything about it. I swear she thinks I'm making it up just to skive off. So I called Leanna's bluff, and she looked so surprised, I'm sure she nearly fell off her chair. Marion looked gobsmacked too, and Julie called me a creep under her breath, but Leanna agreed to swap.

I figured this was how to find out if the caller was aiming at me or was after any old extension with a girl's voice on the end of the line. Maybe I'd be able to get on with some work and put it all behind me, and it might take me away from Julie but I need to meet my target this month to make my bonus.

So we swapped our stuff over, and Leanna had to make two trips for the mascots she keeps all over her desk – a sticky teddy on the side of her monitor, a couple of furry pokémons that sit on top of her in-tray. I swear she thinks they're cute, that they make her desk a home from home. Stuff like that just irritates me – people trying to convince themselves that they enjoy being at work. Pot plants and posters in clip frames, people eating breakfast at their desks – microwaved Weetabix left to go crusty in the bowl makes me feel ill – photos of kids and pets and partners blu-tacked to the sides of in-trays, postcards that say 'you don't have to be mad to work here but it helps', or 'feed me chocolate', or 'work is a four-letter word'. All that stuff irritates the hell out of me, and Leanna is the queen of office kitsch.

I was holding my breath all day for Leanna to get a call and freak on us. She would freak, too, and cry and make a fuss. I know it was cruel, I should have warned her at least, but I had to know whether it was me the caller wanted.

Nothing happened until just after lunch, the classic call time, when Leanna buzzed into my line and said she had a caller for me, and before I could ask who it was she'd patched them through and I could hear the static on the line. I was dead mad by then, ready to have a real go, call them all the names under the sun, but then they spoke, and it was only Mum, offering me a lift to Asda after work. I felt such a rush I thought I was going to hyperventilate and end up in a heap on the floor.

But maybe that'll be it. Maybe I managed to shake the caller off, they've realised I've freaked and a joke's a joke but they shouldn't take it any further. Maybe they got bored with never saying anything, just listening to me demanding to know who they are, or hanging up the moment I hear their silence. Whatever, I'm keeping my fingers crossed and hoping for the best.

Chapter Six

I put Sophie's notebook away in my desk drawer as the women came back into the office after lunch. They had all been to the pub together, I could tell, but I kept my head down so I didn't seem interested in what they had been up to. I had drawn a bingo grid on my notepad and I amused myself for a couple of minutes, filling in jargon and buzz-phrases, imagining Anthony and Malcolm talking, imagining how quickly I could have a full house from one of their conversations. It made me smile, because here I was, pushing the envelope, thinking outside the box, and they would be so surprised if they knew. I would have laughed out loud, but that would have drawn the women's attention towards me, and I didn't want that, it would have been awkward.

It's not that I want to go to the pub with them. I don't like to drink during the day – even the smallest glass of alcohol renders me incapable of accurate typing – and I don't see the point of sitting in a pub drinking coke or coffee and talking about work, I could do that much more effectively in the office. I

53

know they deliberately don't invite me, and Alison says that's rude, and I'm sure some people would be offended, but to me, it's a relief. I'm perfectly happy to be the only man sat silently in the corner. I'm perfectly happy for them to chat away about women's issues and to keep my ears closed when they start talking about their bodies. Of course, it would be pleasant to join in with easy banter, the way Anthony can, the way they talk to one another, but that isn't my character, I've never been comfortable with that sort of camaraderie. It seems so false, anyway – I don't believe that any of them would be friends if they didn't work together, and I'd rather be honest about that sort of thing.

When they all sat down and carried on chatting, it was plain to me that they wouldn't be starting work for a while. It isn't that I think we should always have our noses to the grindstone – on the contrary, a little amicable chat can release tension and so actually help people to work. It's just that their workloads always seem to be the slackest when mine is heaviest, and given a choice I would much prefer to work in silence.

There are some government departments, so I've been told, where silence is expected at work. I can imagine it – a library feel to the place, each person alone with their work and their thoughts. Places dealing with sensitive national secrets, I expect, or budget work where a miscalculation could plunge the country into a ten-year recession. I enjoy my share of responsibility, but that much would scare even me.

The women had pulled their chairs close together and were chatting about holidays. I glanced over at them. One was eating an apple and flicking through a holiday brochure open on her knees while the other four recounted their exploits in a variety of Mediterranean resorts. I couldn't concentrate on the Marston Street report that I should have been writing, so I decided to make some phone calls instead. The Land Registry, the Area Committee Co-ordinator, the developers' offices. I dialled the Land Registry. As the phone rang at the other end, one of the women behind me finished an anecdote and they all laughed, a sudden, loud roar that would have brought Malcolm down from his office if he'd been in. I didn't look round in case I was spotted and either drawn into the laughter or excluded from it. Sometimes I find it hard to tell which is preferable, which one implies more pity on the part of the women, and I resent being pitied by any of them.

On the other end of the phone a woman was saying irritably, 'Is anyone there?'

I had my hand over the mouthpiece, and I took it away quickly and opened my mouth to say yes, to apologise, but something stopped me.

'Hello, hello?' the woman said. 'If you're speaking I can't hear you.'

It was Anne-Marie, the woman I usually spoke to, the woman whose voice was usually so soft, so gentle. It was strange, hearing her voice like that. I wondered suddenly if this was how Sophie's caller felt, if this was how her voice struck him, if he was listening for that unexpected edge.

'You'll have to call back,' Anne-Marie said. 'I'm hanging up now.'

The line went dead. I hung up my extension and sat looking at the phone for a moment. Behind me, the women giggled over something else.

I dialled Anne-Marie again, quickly, and this time I spoke as soon as she had answered. 'Anne-Marie,' I said. 'It's Peter at City Planning.' She gave me a cheery hello, and I said, 'Sorry, I just called but my extension's playing up, I don't know, I couldn't hear you.'

'Oh, that's who it was,' she said, and we had a good laugh about it. I wasn't trying to say anything, to prove any kind of point, but maybe I was a little louder than I had intended to be, because when I hung up and glanced round I realised that the women had stopped chatting and were back at their own desks, starting work again.

I wanted to tell them that I hadn't meant anything by it, I hadn't been hinting that they should get back to work, but I realised that it would have been false, they would have seen right through that. So I simply turned back to my desk and picked up the phone to dial the next number on my list.

23 April

So who the hell is phoning me? And why ring me at home? It scares the hell out of me. If they know my work number and my home number, what else do they know about me? Is it someone I know? How could someone I know do this to me?

I'm going to buy an answerphone and screen every phone call. If I can hear who's calling before I decide whether or not to answer it, maybe they'll give up and stop phoning?

That first call at home was horrible. At least at work I'm surrounded by people, there's security on the door, there's no way someone can get to me, but here, here I'm completely on my own. As soon as I hung up I ran around the flat closing all the curtains, and double-checking that the door was locked. I'll have to get a big bolt to put across the door.

After I had closed all the curtains I sat there in the dark with the lights out, and I was so paranoid that I didn't even want to stand up in case they could see through my curtains somehow, and the phone kept ringing, and every time it stopped I thought it would be okay, and then it would start again. With all the curtains pulled and the lights out, everything just kind of closed in around me – it was like the rest of the world didn't exist any more, the only place left was that room, and the phone kept ringing, each ring like spindly fingers reaching in and poking around.

I went upstairs, ran up because the dark was terrifying me, I could see shadows jumping out and I had to run or I would have been stuck where I was, halfway up the stairs, not able to move, with darkness above and below me. I would have run a bath and lain there with my head under the water, but the thought of being naked while there was someone ringing me like that, while they're trying to scare me, I couldn't cope with that.

So I went to bed and pulled the duvet over my head, but I couldn't sleep, long after the phone had stopped ringing I couldn't sleep, because I kept thinking, this must be someone who knows who I am, who knows me, who else would bother? And who would do such a thing, how could someone know me and do this to me?

I don't know what to do if the answerphone doesn't work. I lie there in bed, wide awake, staring at the ceiling, and all I could think was that I can't stand this any more, and the last time I felt anything like this, I didn't stand it, I got up and left. Walked out. What's happened to me, that I feel like I can't do that now? I used to think I was such a strong person, independent, unafraid, ready for anything, tough enough to stand up for myself. But now I'm hiding under my bedclothes because the phone's ringing, and all the stuff that made me feel strong before, it's not there now.

Before, it seemed so simple. It was so easy to just pack a bag and walk away from everything. I thought it would all fall into place, I'd drift into a new life that would put itself together around me like a jigsaw. I'd be free of everything, away from Mum going on and Jonathan looking at me like I'd planned to wreck his life and all the classes I'd missed and exams I'd failed and the blokes I'd made a fool of myself over and all the stupid things I'd said and done just to prove I was up for a laugh. I don't think I could walk away now, not even with the way I'm feeling at this moment, not after spending so long trying to put things right. I'm too afraid that it will all fall apart. I'm too scared I'd be alone and broke, wandering around on my own, invisible to the world, completely lost in how big the world is. I don't want to be alone.

Sometimes I forget how relieved I was when Jonathan found me. Rescued me, that's what he called it, like I'd been in danger. But I was glad to see him, despite it all, despite him blaming me, despite him being one of the things I tried to escape.

He thinks that going to Arbor Low was some sort of message, but it wasn't, I swear it. What sort of message could it have been, anyway? He wasn't listening to me before I left — how could I have known if he'd get any kind of message? Maybe a while before, but not by then, the damage was done, we weren't close like we had been. The beginning of the end. Driving back in Dad's car, up the rutted track and worrying about Dad's suspension, he kept asking why, why, why, as if he didn't know, as if it had nothing to do with him. I was crying, and repeating that I was glad he had found me, and I was, really. He pulled off the road into the entrance to a farm, and he cut the engine and put his arms around me and gave me a long hug. And I didn't know what to do, I didn't know what I'd have to face when we got home, and he said it would be okay, he'd protect me, but he was wrong. He said people would forget, but nobody ever does.

Maybe that's how it is. Maybe nothing is ever okay, and things can't ever go back to how they were. Sometimes everything feels so tight, and I can't even breathe, and I think I'll be trapped like this for ever, like a fly in a jam jar with the lid screwed shut. Sometimes it feels as if there's this huge distance spreading out around me, and my life is somewhere just out of reach, waiting for me, if I can only get across that distance.

Chapter Seven

Alison had been to Homebase on the way back from work and picked up the paint we had chosen for the skirting boards in the through-lounge. I was tired when I got home; I had to shake myself back from wherever my mind had been wandering. But I managed to notice that Alison had already painted the skirting boards along the fireplace wall.

'That looks really good,' I said, and she beamed at me, brush poised over the can. 'I'll get changed and join you,' I said.

As I went back into the hall, someone knocked at the door. I pulled the lounge door shut behind me and opened the front door.

It was Jamie, looking apologetic, hands in the pockets of his oversized combat trousers. 'I wanted to ask you something,' he said. I was too surprised by his presence to know what to say. 'Sorry to disturb you,' he said, looking past me into the hall, and I realised he was hoping for an invitation to come in.

From the front room, Alison called out, 'Who is it, Pete?'

'It's okay,' I called back, and stepped out of the house, pulling the door shut behind me. 'How did you know where I lived?' I asked.

'I saw you getting off the bus.'

'You followed me?'

He shrugged.

'I know, I know,' I said, suddenly irritated. 'You're worried about Sophie.'

'Yeah, well, the police are investigating now. Doesn't give me much confidence.'

'The police? Do they think something's happened to her?'

He looked away down the street, a clumsy kid not wanting to face me. 'They say it's just routine. They say she must've just run off.'

'They said that she ran away?'

'Yeah, well, she did before, didn't she?' I nodded, and it seemed to encourage him that I already knew about that. 'Drove her family crazy,' he said.

'What happened?' I asked. 'She never told me.'

'Oh, I dunno. You know Sophie, she gets it all wrapped around her. Dropped out of her nursing course. Stayed away for a couple of weeks, then phoned Jonathan. Came back as if nothing had happened.'

I wasn't sure what to say next. Jamie glanced down at his feet. In the street a woman pushed a pushchair along the pavement, the wheels hissing on the tarmac. I said, 'Do you think she's done the same again?'

'Maybe.' He was looking round at the woman,

attracted by the sound. Then he looked back at me and seemed to have gained confidence. 'Will you phone the police? Tell them what you know?'

'I've told you, I don't know anything.'

He ignored me, fishing in his trouser pocket and finally pulling out a slightly creased police business card. 'This is the guy,' he said. 'Keep that, I've got loads.'

I took the card from him, about to protest again that I didn't know anything, but I could hear Alison moving about and I thought she was coming to see who was at the door. I said, 'I'll have a think if there's anything I can tell them.'

He shrugged, as if he was dissatisfied but didn't know what else to say. I put the card in my pocket and stepped back into the house, and he took the hint and turned to leave. As I closed the front door he turned to walk up the path, shoulders slightly hunched.

When I went back into the through-lounge, Alison was standing up, as if about to come to the front door. 'Who was that?' she asked.

'Just some guy doing a survey,' I said.

'What about?'

'Something about electricity suppliers.'

She seemed to accept that; at any rate, she sat down on the floor again and continued to gloss the skirting boards. I went upstairs slowly, pulling off my tie and undoing my shirt buttons.

I felt numb. I knew that I should contact the police, give them the notebook in case it could help.

I was exhausted, drained of all the energy I had felt on the bus, reading her words. She had wanted to get away – that pressure had to be released somehow, and it didn't seem right for me to be the one to bring her back to it. She had a right to privacy, to escape, if that was what she wanted.

If I gave the notebook to the police then there would be more people pushing their way into her life, poking through her thoughts, trampling over her words. She had come back before. She came back of her own free will, when she was good and ready. And I could protect her – I could be her cushion, a no-fly-zone. I had an image of her, hiding under the bedcovers in her flat, making a tent from the duvet and writing in her notebook by the light of a torch. Her face was a bright flare of orange as she lay on her stomach with her face close to the page. I knew how she felt as the phone rang, the silent caller pushing in through the darkness, hearing the fear in her voice, feeling the power he had over her emotions. I had a responsibility to her, a responsibility not to betray her trust, her confidence to anyone. I was her protector, her friend, her messenger, and when the time was right, when I knew the words she would want me to use, that was when I would tell people what she wanted them to know.

Sophie had known Arbor Low, with Jonathan, in childhood

25 April

The calls have stopped, now that the answerphone screens every call. I caught the silence once – maybe the caller was thrown, I don't know, but I have a full minute of silence, of the slightest sound of someone breathing, barely audible, before the receiver was put down and the caller didn't ring back. I sat there holding my breath for the entire length of the call. Part of me wanted to answer it, shout at whoever it was, because listening to that silence through the answerphone's speaker made it seem like the silence was in the room with me. The caller sitting in my front room breathing quietly, and I couldn't see them, the invisible man watching everything I do.

Now the calls have stopped, I can get on with things a little more. I feel better. I fill the flat with music – Jamie lent me some of his CDs, and I play them loud, because as long as I can't hear silence I know I'll be okay.

It's funny, I used to love silence. Being away from the city, away from all the traffic and the people and the noise, TVs behind other people's doors, kids screaming at each other in the street, drunks singing late at night, car alarms and burglar alarms and sirens and police helicopters.

I suppose that's why I loved going to Arbor Low so

much as a kid. I tried to explain it to Jamie once, when we went into the Peaks in his mate's car, but he didn't get it at all. He just wanted to find the nearest pub with a beer garden and enjoy the view from his seat. He said I was too serious, I should unwind more, kick back, go with the flow – as if I wasn't already feeling the effects of doing that, as if Jonathan didn't already blame me for all his troubles just because I'd kicked back, as if college wasn't about to throw me off the nursing course for being so unwound I was barely there at all.

But still, I persuaded them to go to Arbor Low with me, to the standing stones. I don't know why I took them there. Maybe it was a dress rehearsal for when I would go there alone? I don't think I could have just cleared off without a destination in mind. Back then, I just thought I wanted Jamie to feel the isolation of the place, to feel the wind and the space and the sky. But he called me a hippie tree-hugger and sat down on one of the stones and looked around as if he wasn't even impressed by the history of the place. I wanted to shake him, shout at him – really, what would he have been impressed by, what did he expect? I never said it was Stonehenge.

So I turned my back on him and stood on the top of the man-made hill and looked down towards the farmhouse. It was just the way I remembered it, seeing it from that distance, and I realised then just how much I was going to lose if Jonathan didn't stop blaming me, because I wanted him to think that those times might happen again, I wanted there to at least be the chance of all of us being in that house together, and all the laughs we had, and feeling like we belonged together. Behind me, Jamie and his mate were giggling away while they tried to roll a spliff in the breeze, and I was angry about that, I remember that. So I started walking down to the house, and I could sometimes still hear them laughing when the wind gusted. I wanted to tell them to shut up, because they were spoiling it, all the memories. But then, Jonathan and I had been the same, always laughing, like everything was one big joke, running around the fields and the farmyard and over all the stones, screeching at the wind and opening out our arms so our coats were like sails, and, later, creeping out after dark to drink smuggled rum and coke ready-mixed from a plastic bottle, sitting in the stone circle feeling brave and wild and protected. Jonathan would always pretend that he didn't want to, that he was scared of getting caught by Mum and Dad, but he'd always agree in the end, and he'd get a thrill from it, too, I just know he did.

When I got down to the farmhouse, though, it was all boarded up, every window, and I couldn't see inside. In the yard, the concrete was slimy with mud and going green where the water lay in dirty pools. One whole side of the house was speckled black and green with mould, and the roof tiles were slipping off the roof, and the lean-to where Jonathan and I made kites with Dad was collapsing in on itself, burying the bits of machinery rusting away underneath.

Then, it made me sad, seeing the place like that. But now, I think it was fitting, really, all that decay, it reflected everything. Was that why I went back again? I don't know. Maybe it was just the silence that I wanted, or maybe I just couldn't think of anywhere else?

The silence. It frightens me now, the thought of that dark house, and all the dark countryside, and the night so black when the stars were clouded over that it was like blindness, it was like there was nothing there to even be seen.

Jamie doesn't have any time for the countryside. We're city people, that's what he says, and I know he's right, I know I like street lights, and tarmac under my feet and the shops selling more than anyone could ever want and the pubs and clubs and cinemas. I love getting lost among the crowds of people out to experience it all.

But what if someone else has got lost in the crowd and thinks they've found me? What if the phone calls start again and don't stop, or I start getting other things, letters, or presents, or someone shouting at my windows or knocking on my door late at night? It scares me to think that maybe it isn't over yet. It scares me that I might not be able to hide away from it. I suppose the most frightening thing, the thing that scares me more than the dark, is the thought that maybe I'm not alone in the dark.

Chapter Eight

Anthony was waiting for me when I got back from
lunch. He was sitting in my chair with his feet up on
the low table that held the printer, his hands folded
behind his head as he laughed about something with
the women. That didn't annoy me so much as the
way they all broke off when I came in. Anthony
swung his legs round to let me past and into my corner, and the women turned back to their screens.

I stood at my desk and rifled through a few papers,
not looking at him. 'Yes, Anthony,' I said. 'What can
I do for you?'

'We need to talk about Marston Street.'

I turned to look at him. He wasn't smiling. 'Why?
I thought it was all going through fine.'

'It has gone through,' he said, then glanced towards
the women. 'Let's go to my office.'

I shrugged and said, 'Sure,' but I was irritated
by his tone. He might be an SPO now, but it's not
so long ago that he was a PO with me in the main
office. I don't like people who forget where they've
come from.

But I followed him down the corridor to his office. He was supposed to share it with another SPO, but the other had been seconded to the Tram Taskforce and he had sprawled out over both desks. Anthony's work always expanded to fill any available space. I could never understand how he got anything done, how he kept on top of anything, with all that chaos around him.

'Have a seat,' Anthony said, his back to me as he rooted through the pile of papers on the desk that was supposedly empty. I pulled up a chair and sat down. Anthony had been SPO for nearly six months now, but it looked like he hadn't yet finished unpacking. There were lever arch files stacked on top of each other on the shelves, a cardboard box of pens, and a stapler and a hole punch on the floor under the window, and the only things pinned to the noticeboards on the walls were the fire drill instructions and a list of extension numbers for various department staff, with other names and numbers scrawled in biro on the blank spaces.

'Ah, here we are,' Anthony said, uncovering a buff file with 'Marston Street Project Stage One' printed in my handwriting on the top right-hand corner.

I said, 'Is there anything the matter?'

'Well, yes, there is,' he said, and finally sat down and glanced at me. He seemed to be finding this awkward but I wasn't about to help him out. 'I thought you were dealing with all the searches on the land.'

'I did,' I said.

He scrunched up his lips into something that approached a wince. 'Well, I'm afraid you missed something. Covenant on the land, see?'

He was offering me a piece of paper from the file. I took it from him. He looked away, looking around the office as if he actually felt embarrassed about this. I read the details briefly, feeling a cold chill settle into a slightly sick feeling in my stomach. He was right, and I'd known he was right the moment he had started to explain. But I had checked – I had looked into it – I had looked into it and missed something vital. He had trusted me to be my usual meticulous reliable self, and I had let everybody down.

Anthony was looking at me now, waiting for a reaction. I wondered if his sympathetic expression was practised, like his interview smile.

I said, 'I don't know how this happened.'

He said, 'Don't worry too much about it, Pete. Everyone makes a mistake from time to time.'

He smiled, and I saw how white and straight his teeth were.

I took a deep breath, swallowed down the decision, said, 'Jesus, I'm sorry, Anthony, I really thought I'd covered all the bases.'

'That's why you need to use the checklist,' Anthony said.

I didn't bother saying that I had used it, that I always used it, that I'd ticked all the checks off as completed, that I'd thought everything was fine. Instead, I said, 'So, how much of a mess is it?'

'Oh, not too bad,' he said. 'I'll pull it from the

next committee, apologise to the developers, give us some time to sort it out.'

I nodded, not sure what to say.

'Don't you worry about it,' Anthony said. 'I'll sort it out from here. You've got enough PO's work to be getting on with.'

It was a dismissal of sorts, and it nearly killed me to mutter thanks. I should have spotted it, it was my mistake, and now I'd given Anthony the chance to rub salt into the wounds.

When I reached the door, Anthony said, almost off-handedly, 'Do you want to tell Malcolm or shall I?'

I turned back. He was sitting with the paperwork open in front of him, looking up at me with a neutral expression. I said, 'I'll do it.'

'Right-oh.'

I went out and pulled his office door shut with a loud click behind me. Malcolm's door was wide open but he was nowhere to be seen, so I decided to put it off until the next morning. I felt slightly sick, the kind of sickness that I felt when I woke in the middle of the night with the certainty that I had made a mistake, the kind of sickness that could make me panic when a deadline was looming, the sweat running out across my body with the thought of what I had to do.

I stumbled back to my desk and sat down, head in hands, looking down at the work I'd planned to do that afternoon. I had made the mistake, it was my fault. I couldn't look at other projects, I couldn't imagine how I could think about other pieces of work after this. I had to avoid dwelling on it, Alison always said I shouldn't worry so much about things like this. The mistake was made, there was nothing more I could do. I sat for a long moment, contemplating nothing, and then I reached down and opened my briefcase and took out Sophie's notebook. Nobody would notice if I dawdled one afternoon away – and at least this way I wouldn't make any more mistakes.

28 April

As usual, Mum's half right. The last house I went to
look at was nice enough — good-size rooms, a decent
sort of a kitchen, even a scrap of garden out the back,
and what do I expect for my money? I know I couldn't
afford a mortgage anywhere else in the country, not on
my wages, but still — I want that homecoming feeling
when I walk through the door.

And Mum says don't be so fussy because I'll change
it all anyway. She would say that. 'And,' she said, like
this was the clincher, 'you'll probably move again when
you get married.'

Every time I go to help her dye her hair, I think this
time she won't try to steamroller me into her point of
view. She says, 'You'll never get anything by being shy.'
She's never been the one for a quiet life.

But she did well, ten minutes at the kitchen table
with that gunk on her hair, already near the bottom of
the first pot of tea, before she started on me.

I told her again that a mortgage is the most expensive
decision a person makes, and I wasn't going to rush it.
I said, 'It's a big responsibility.'

She just looked at me and said, 'I'm sure having kids
is worse.'

That look doesn't throw me any more. I told her
again that I wasn't planning on kids, and I knew she

was going to launch into her prepared speech. How did I know what I would want in ten years, or when I met the Right Man, or when my biological clock started ticking down? I cut her off by saying it was all way into the future. She just smiled and said, 'Never say never,' like she knew what was going off in my head, and I know she thinks I'm weakening. She thinks it's a step towards changing my mind.

Mum was looking at Dad out in the garden, shirt sleeves rolled up as he dug the borders with a fork. She said, 'You spend too much time looking for perfection. You have to settle for the next best to perfect. Perfect doesn't exist.'

I sipped tea to stall my response. I didn't want to agree, but what could I say? I'm not a romantic, but Mum's alternative leaves me cold.

So Mum wheeled out the Dad speech. 'When I married your father it wasn't because it was perfect. I married him because I knew I could make it work. You have to work at life, Sophie.'

'I know,' I said.

So she trotted out the stuff about how she is glad she chose how she did, how she's glad she had me and Jonathan, how kids are hard work but worth it, how she hopes I'll find out for myself one day. She must have hours of prepared speeches stored in that brain of hers, neatly filed away. Work hard to get ahead. Pull yourself up because nobody's going to help you. Never give up on anything because you don't get anything for free. Work hard, get married, buy a house, bring up kids, retire and die. It doesn't matter what I do or say, I'm infected by their protestant work ethic, all twisted up with wayward-daughter's guilt. She believes everything she says, and I appreciate that, and I love them both, of course I do, but I have to say, if I had been in her situation I would have held out for more.

Mum asked me what was wrong with the house on George Street, but there was nothing much I could say. 'The second bedroom was a bit poky,' I managed.

'Most of them are. But it's nice and close to here.'

I knew what she really meant by that, so I tried bus routes, convenience for work, being near my friends, and the whole time she was playing the eye-contact game. So I said I didn't want to live along the tram construction route, and she said I was thinking short-term. And that's what it comes down to — she thinks this is it, she thinks three years is nothing when I'm deciding to be around here for the rest of my life. She thinks I'm marking out my territory, setting down my foundations. That thought makes me queasy. She used to say that all she wanted for me and Jonathan was that we were happy, what mothers always say. She said it so often I didn't think she was talking about compromise.

I said, 'I just don't want to make a mistake with that big a decision, that's all.'

'True,' she said, 'but you don't want to be so careful that the things you really want slide out of reach, now, do you?' I thought she was going to say something else, but then she looked at the clock on the cooker and said, 'Time's up.'

We sat there for a moment, just a split-moment of

knowing the tension had passed, and then we went back upstairs. I took the showerhead down from the hook and Mum took her blouse off and leaned over the bath. Through the cellophane gloves the lather frothed and grew under my fingers, white suds expanding into bubbles. My fingers sank into the soft twists of hair piled on top of her skull. I sprayed warm water against the foam, and the liquid ran creamy and spumey onto her neck.

I massaged her hair until the water ran clear, and I thought about when I had dyed her hair before; about the times she had dyed mine; about being a child sitting waist-deep in second-hand bathwater, waiting for Mum to pour shampoo onto her hands and rub it into my hair. The expectation of that moment! The slight chill of the shampoo as it touched my skin, then the pressure of Mum's fingers. Sitting there, I would watch the ripples run out over the bathwater, feeling it through my whole body, while she knelt beside the bath massaging my scalp, arms moving briskly, pulling the material of her blouse tight across her shoulders and her breasts. Then the cupped hand over my eyes as she washed the shampoo off, and the towel for me to step into, and the cuddle with the roughness of the towel, and laughing, both of us laughing about nothing.

Chapter Nine

We were redecorating the back bedroom, obliterating the last remaining signs of the previous owners of our house. Alison's idea was to make the room something between a study and a spare bedroom, with a fold-down futon-style sofa bed at one end and a desk and chair and shelves at the other end. She wanted a computer with all the trimmings to kit the place out properly.

Sometimes I do wonder what my life would be like if we hadn't got together. Is it possible that we have just settled, slipped into something because it's easy and expected? I don't like the idea of compromise, but the thought ran through my head as we worked.

And as we stripped off the vile yellow Humpty Dumpty wallpaper with the Mickey Mouse frieze, I have to confess to some feelings of regret. Not that we were getting rid of the paper, or that we were finally erasing the last imprint of the previous owners. I was quite happy with that – it was the final step in the process and the place would truly be ours at last. But I suppose there is always something a little sad in stripping a child's room back down to the bare plaster.

We had Trent FM on the radio and sang along to the songs we knew, Robbie Williams, assorted Spice Girls, Ricky Martin. I was up the stepladder with the scraper, putting the blade behind the seams and lifting paper and paint off in one heavy layer, while Alison followed behind with the steamer, pressing and scraping, the hiss and suck of the steam plate like a new bass rhythm behind the music.

Looking down at her from above was a strange sensation. She was wearing a tight little T-shirt and jeans, and when she leaned forward to scrape, her jeans gaped in the small of her back, revealing a patch of bare skin above the elastic of her knickers. I felt a slight thrill of guilt when I saw that gap, that exposed flesh, pale and smooth, leading away under her clothes. I couldn't see her face from above; her hair fell forward like curtains, and for a moment she could have been anyone. A stranger, a slim, beautiful stranger.

And it occurred to me that if we hadn't met when we did, if we hadn't had the courage to talk to one another when we met, it could have been someone else, a stranger I had never even met, down on her knees scraping slime from the stripped walls.

Or maybe I wouldn't have been here. Maybe she would have been down there still, but a different man would have been on top of the stepladder. It made me feel strange, thinking about another man looking down at Alison, another man pawing her when he felt like it, another man thinking about her body and what it was like to hold it, to touch it, to enter it. I could imagine his hands on her skin, and her hands running to meet his, and the little laugh she would give, and how she would surrender herself to him, allow him to explore her body, allow him to guide what she did.

I knew I shouldn't think like that, I knew Alison would have been furious if she could have heard what I was thinking, but sometimes these thoughts rear up through everyone's minds, I'm sure of it. I know it's irrational – a slight indent in the bed when I get home that must indicate the departure of a lover, the briefest scent of something – cigarette smoke, maybe – coming in through an open window and he must have been here. Alison chattering away about her day and I look for holes in her story, unexplained absences, untruths said to spare me, and me feeling terrible even as I think these things, because it would mean that everything she has ever said to me could be a lie.

Alison must have sensed that I was looking down at her, because she took the steam plate from the wall and glanced upwards. 'What's up?'

'Nothing,' I said. 'Just wanted a breather.'

The steam plate hissed out into the air, and she stood up and stretched out her limbs. I climbed down the ladder and did the same.

'Hard work,' she said, smiling at me.

I nodded. There were bits of paper and slimy

clumps of glue and pulp all over the floor, so I shook open one of the black sacks I'd brought up with me and started to fill it with the scraps. Alison stretched for a moment longer, then got down on her knees beside me.

'No, no,' I said. 'Have more of a break.'

'I'm fine,' she said, and started to collect up bits of paper. Her hands were already coated with the slime, her fingers papier-mâchéd. After a minute, she stood up again, picking bits of paper off her fingers, and said, 'I know, I'll make drinks.'

'Okay,' I said.

She went out, her feet running down the stairs. I switched the steamer off at the wall and the plate spluttered a few drops of cooling water onto the floor. She hadn't returned by the time I'd filled the first black sack, so I went back up the ladder and carried on scraping.

There is something therapeutic about scraping wallpaper. The rhythm of a mindless activity, I suppose, the feeling of the pull on the muscles, the slight ache in the wrist and the pressure flattening out the flesh on the fingers. I carried on scraping even after she had come back into the room and was standing drinking her coffee.

'Stop for a minute,' she said, and there was almost a plea in her voice.

I was surprised by that, but I climbed down the ladder again and picked up my mug of coffee from the floor. A scrap of paper had fallen into the drink; I pulled it out and dropped it into the open sack.

We had almost finished the longest wall and I said, 'It'll look good when it's done.'

She nodded her head, but I had the feeling she had wanted me to say something else. I didn't know what she wanted, so I just drank my coffee. There was yet another Robbie Williams track playing on the radio. Outside, our neighbour was standing in the garden while his toddler son tried to kick a football at him. I could hear our neighbour talking, calling out encouragement.

Alison was standing almost expectantly, leaning with one hand against the stripped wall, one socked foot on top of the other. I thought about kissing her, about whether that was what she wanted. Another man might have done that. Another man might have crossed the room and placed his hands against her hips and kissed her forcefully. Another man might have started throwing bits of paper at her, and she might have laughed, she might have lobbed wet, gunky balls of paper back. They would have had a mock fight, chased each other, laughing, grappling with one another, kneeling on the floor and scooping up handfuls of paper, rolling on the floor so the paper got caught up in their hair, until the fight became something breathless, became something else.

Alison looked away suddenly, as if she had read my thoughts in my eyes. 'Well,' she said, and flicked the steamer switch back on. 'Back to work, I guess.'

So I climbed back up the ladder and carried on scraping. We didn't speak. As my hands worked at the wall I felt with a new conviction that I had misunderstood something, I had misread what she was trying to say to me. Sometimes I can feel how close we are, I can feel how tangled our lives have become, I can feel the blurring where I end and she begins. At other times, we could be strangers, and when I look into her face I feel that I have never really looked before, I have never understood what I am seeing.

Later, lying in the bath, I thought about it some more, but I couldn't decide what it was that she had wanted from me. Did she turn away when she realised what I was thinking? Did it disgust her that I was thinking about sex – the sordidness of that thought, the awkwardness of the moment of deciding to approach?

There are a thousand permutations of how that moment could have developed, I know that. A thousand permutations, and I just settled for the one that was least awkward, least clumsy. I've never been very good at second-guessing. I don't want to appear a fool to Alison, to have her see me for the animal that lies beneath the skin.

30 April

Jamie came round again last night, sat himself down in
the armchair and proceeded to tell me that his band
has been offered a gig at the Running Horse. I think
he expected me to be impressed or something, but I've
been past there loads of times when the bands have been
playing, and not many of them seem like much cop to
me (music expert that I am), so I'm not as impressed
as I probably should be. I suppose it's good that he has
a dream that he's working towards, even if it obviously
isn't going to come to anything – I mean, if they were
going to be signed by some record company I reckon it
would have happened by now. Didn't say that to him,
of course – he's very intent on it, believes in the band
so much, and I wish him well, really I do.

He suddenly asked me why I'd got an answerphone.
The question surprised me, but I flannelled it, told
him I'd got it to answer my calls, what else would
it be for?

He said, 'Not to call-screen?'

'No,' I said, 'but I probably will.'

Then he said, 'You seem worried about something.
I thought maybe you were avoiding someone?'

I just laughed, like he was being daft. 'Only you,
and I failed there. You keep turning up on my doorstep.'

He grinned back and said, 'Yeah, well, you're prob-ably the only one I can talk into watching the band. It's not your sparkling company.'

'I'll only come if you buy me a pint,' I said. 'I'm skint till pay-day.'

'Bribing the fans,' he said, and put on a fake voice. 'That plan's just crazy enough to work.'

Then he couldn't resist any longer, and got on his knees next to the phone and started looking at the answerphone. The genetic attraction between men and technology – gets them every time.

'Very nice,' he said, and for a long horrible moment I thought he was going to play the tape, and the only message I hadn't deleted was the last message from the silent caller, which I'd found on the tape when I got in from work.

So I went over and took the machine from his hands and said, 'No fiddling, please, it's a delicate instrument.'

He shrugged and flopped back down in his seat, then said, 'We should record a message for the tape. My mate's housemates did a whole scene from *Reservoir Dogs*.'

'Which scene?'

'The one in the restaurant. The argument about tipping.'

'Cool,' I said, because he obviously thought it was.

'Seriously, though,' he said. 'I did Charlene and Nina's message. They reckoned it's better to have a man on the tape, so random weirdos don't think it's an all-female house.'

I felt my heart jumping. 'Why would a random weirdo phone me? I don't get crank calls.'

He was looking at me strangely, and I wondered what he had guessed, what I had said that had given it away. 'That's the thing about random weirdos,' he said. 'They're random.'

'Don't say that sort of stuff,' I said. 'You're just tempting fate.'

'Oh, come on,' he said, and tapped the coffee table. 'Touch wood it never happens, but you might as well be prepared. Not that I think it will, I mean it's hardly a problem any more. Too easy to trace the calls these days, surely?'

Yeah, I thought, unless they withhold the number. He was looking at me strangely again, and for a moment I was tempted to tell him about the calls, but I decided not to. He knew my work number and my home number, and he was sitting here talking to me about crank calls, and how did I know that he wasn't trying to double-bluff me, that he wasn't the caller after all?

He said, 'Are you okay? You seem freaked out.'

I said I was fine, and I was probably shorter than I meant to be with him. I did want to tell him about it because, after all, he is my closest friend, but then having someone as a closest friend doesn't always make them the best person to tell things to. I mean, Jamie's all very sympathetic, and I like him a lot, and he's good fun, but there are some things I can't talk to him about. I know that annoys him sometimes – after I ran away, he was very off, pleased that I was safe but off that I hadn't told him where I was going, or why. Even after all this time, I know he still thinks about that now and then, because when he thinks I'm not telling him something, he gets all very understanding and tries so hard to worm all my little secrets out of me.

He said, 'You would tell me if anything was wrong, wouldn't you?'

'You mean I won't just run off without telling you?'

He actually blushed, and then said, 'Yeah.'

'Okay,' I said. 'I promise I'll tell you before I run off.'

He laughed at that, and tried to hit me with the cushion from the back of the chair, but I put my hands up in time. Then, once he'd rearranged the cushion again, he said, 'But seriously, I saw your mum the other day. She said she was worried about you.'

I said, 'Last time I saw her she was worried about Jonathan. She always worries.'

'Yeah, I know, but you would tell me, wouldn't you?'

So I tried to reassure him, but I know he wasn't convinced, and I felt pretty bad about that. But after he left I thought about it, and then I started to get mad. Jamie thinks he knows everything about me, just because we go way back, but he doesn't know the half of it, he hasn't got a clue.

Then I started to think that it was strange that Jamie should come round and start talking about crank calls at all, and they say these weirdos get a buzz out of seeing their victim close up, out of seeing the effect they're having. Jamie knows my work number and my home number — it would fit. And he's got an enormous crush on me, he's had it for ever, anyone can see it, it's hardly news.

But then, I look at what the caller is doing. Making me suspect my oldest friend in all the world, making me think he's some kind of fruitcake, but surely I'd know if he was really like that? He wouldn't be able to keep that hidden, not from me, surely?

But I've kept enough hidden from him over the years, so maybe it is possible? Maybe we don't really know each other at all? I don't like that idea — I don't want to think there's some big gap in our friendship.

Would things have been different if I'd told Jamie what was going on back then? I doubt it — Jamie couldn't have changed anything, he couldn't have talked Jonathan round or squared anything for us. Maybe I just shouldn't have come back four years ago? Should have stayed away for good. It's easy to forget what it was like — Jonathan blaming me, and all the rows and the shouting, and Mum crying in the bathroom with the door not quite shut, and it got so even if we'd wanted to we couldn't have told anyone the truth.

Now, Jonathan acts like I just used it all as an excuse, like none of it really affected me, like I was just looking for a reason to go off on an adventure. He forgets what it was like, he forgets that I didn't just jack the nursing course in on a whim, I jumped before they pushed me off. He forgets how nasty he was to me, and how I put up with it because I felt so bad. He forgets that he pinned me up against the wall and told me it was all my fault, like I had power over him, like he had no choice but to do everything I said. He might have forgotten that, but I can still remember the wall hard up against my back, and the pressure of his arm against my throat, and his anger, and suddenly realising that he was stronger than me, I couldn't break free, I couldn't have stopped him if he'd wanted to hurt me.

But I came back. Despite it all, I came back, and I suppose I hoped things would be different, and they were, on the surface. And now, I've got too used to being in Nottingham, sticking to the same old routine, the job and the flat and Mum and Dad half a mile away and Jonathan around to sort out any problems and hanging around with mates I've had since primary school. I should be trying out new things, experimenting, diversifying, looking for new experiences. Instead, it's Sunday dinner with the family, and helping my mum or my aunts or my cousins with a wedding or a christening or a birthday party, and my dad coming round to do my DIY because I'm incapable, and Jonathan always around and watching me, like he's scared someone's going to leap out and drag me away by the hair, like he's got the right to check out every bloke I ever meet. I know they all mean well, I know they're being nice, but sometimes, in between all their attentions, I don't get a chance to breathe.

But I know why it is. I know why they're all so concerned. It's like a suicide watch that's grown into a habit nobody wants to confess to. They're scared that if they loosen their grip on me I'll slip away from them and disappear again. And instead of trying to wriggle free, I'm growing used to it, it's like it's always been this way, and I'm even looking for a house and a mortgage, I'm actually looking for another peg to hammer me down.

If I hadn't come back four years ago, if I'd stayed away until everyone thought I was dead and gave up looking, everything would be so different now. I could be anywhere, doing anything, living any kind of life I really wanted to.

Chapter Ten

Steve's birthday, and we had timed our arrival to be a fashionable twelve minutes late. We were meeting up in town, in a big chrome-and-wood café-come-pub just opened in what used to be a bank in the Market Square. One of those crowded, barn-like, brightly lit places, Ikea meets airport lounge.

The square was already filling with Friday night revellers, young men in polyester shirts and wet-look hair gel, women in skimpy dresses and high heels. Alison was wearing a new dress she had bought especially for tonight – she had commented cryptically that she didn't get many chances to dress up for a night out on the town. The dress was made from shiny silky cloth that floated down over her body, silvery blue in colour, and as I guided her by the elbow through the press of bodies in the pub, she kept tugging at the hemline and adjusting the shoulder straps.

We found Steve near the back, crowded in among work colleagues with the table stacked with pint glasses. They had all come out straight from the office, the young men crowded together with their elbows on the table, wiping their mouths with the backs of their hands as they drank. The women were at the next table, pulled up close, all in floaty, strappy dresses, sitting sedately with their legs crossed, their hands resting lightly on the table.

The music was of the loud, tinned variety. I leaned in and asked Alison what she wanted, and she eyed up the shorts and the alcopops on the girls' table before she made her choice. I managed to catch Steve's attention long enough to find out what he was drinking, and then I squeezed myself into the crowd around the bar.

When I got back with the drinks, Alison had found herself a seat between the two tables and I sat down between her and the boys. Alison sipped her drink and smiled politely at the girls.

One of the boys was talking enthusiastically about Robot Wars, and I guessed he was the workmate with the brother in engineering at Trent Uni. He had torn the top layer of paper off a beermat and was drawing with a biro on the white card beneath.

'It's going to be called The Spokesman,' he explained, and drew a long triangle pointing down with two large circles on either side. A large man at the far end said something I didn't quite catch, and they all laughed. I joined in politely.

There was a pause in conversation while he drew, so I said, 'I thought Steve said it would be called Sexorcet?'

The drawer glanced up at me and said, 'Steve said

they probably wouldn't allow that on tea-time telly. Not on BBC2, anyway.'

'Sexorcet?' one of the others said. 'Doesn't look much like a missile to me.'

The joker at the far end said, 'Paint it up a bit, it could look like a knob.'

'If that's what your knob's like you'd best get down the doctors' first thing Monday.'

'Mate, they've already got me in because it's such an awesome specimen.'

'Yeah, they can't believe it's attached to such a tosser.'

'S'right, the IVF clinic are offering me a contract for me sperm.'

Steve leaned over, across a stranger, punched me playfully and hard on the arm and said too loudly, 'How are you, mate? Glad you made it.' He smiled beyond me, his vision not focused, pissed already. 'And Alison too, great to see you.'

'Happy birthday,' we both said in unison.

'Aw, gissa kiss, then,' Steve said, obviously not to me, and I had to struggle out of the way while Alison simpered and giggled and gave him a kiss on the cheek that turned into a bear-hug and a play-wrestle until Alison pulled away, laughing.

The girls were having a quiet conversation, leaning in towards each other and giggling among themselves. I guessed they were talking about the boys; presumably dismissive, commenting on their laddishness, holding themselves up as more sophisticated, more adult. I escaped to the bar for the long wait to be served.

When I got back, Alison was deep in conversation with the woman next to her, nodding and smiling, heads together to catch each other's words over the volume of the music. A couple of the lads were pulling on their jackets and standing up, and the others were talking about motor racing. I eased myself closer to the girls' group.

Alison said, 'Pete, this is Helen. She works for the city, too.'

'Yeah? I thought everyone here worked with Steve.'

Helen smiled and said, 'That's my other half's role,' and signalled down the table towards one of the lads.

'Which department are you in?'

'Housing. Homelessness.' She had slightly crooked teeth and a smudge of too-pink lipstick had caught one of her top front teeth. 'I deal with rough sleepers.'

'Yeah? Are there a lot in Nottingham?'

Alison excused herself to the toilets while I listened to the problems of the rough sleepers; substance abuse, poor health, poor hygiene, depression. I nodded along with Helen's opinions about why there were so many drug problems (cause of homelessness; escape from being homeless) and young runaways (parents kick them out; care system in chaos; no benefits) and more government funding needed (thousands of properties standing empty; landlords exploiting the situation; council house sell-offs). I talked about all the applications I'd seen for luxury flats and lofts and apartments, and asked who was going to live in them, and made a plea for more centralised planning. I was relieved to discover that she didn't think my ideas were odd at all.

And all the time, I was thinking about Sophie, about what she would do if she had nowhere to go. I was agreeing with Helen, with this abstract description of how people could end up homeless through none of their own fault, and while we were talking, at the exact moment that the words came out of our mouths, Sophie could be going through the very same thing.

I had a sudden image of her, sitting in a shop doorway with an old sleeping bag around her legs, her army-surplus coat ragged and dirty, her dark hair lank and stringy and oily, her pale skin flecked with unhealthy blotches, her teeth crooked and stained.

'Well,' Helen said, pulling her arms into her coat and shrugging it on. 'Time to go.' I looked around and realised that last orders had been and gone, that the bouncers were starting to usher people towards the door.

The responsibility for getting Steve home had fallen to me and Alison. Waiting for the last bus sobered him up enough that he could stand unaided, swaying, the three of us the points on a triangle. We didn't speak. On the bus, with Steve ensconced in the seat in front of us, eyes closed and head nodding, I sought out Alison's hand with mine but she pulled away.

'You ignored me all night,' she said.

'No, I didn't,' I said, and then realised, and added,

'I mean, I didn't mean to. You were okay. Every time I looked round you were talking to someone.'

'I was bored,' she said. 'I didn't know anyone.'

There was the slightest hint of a wail in her voice. 'I didn't know anyone either,' I said.

She didn't say anything else, but held my hand and lay her head against my shoulder. I leaned my temple against the top of her head. She seemed to be tired, but I was wide awake, my brain alert and working quickly. I knew I wouldn't be able to sleep, not for a long time yet, not with all the things that could be happening to Sophie. How could I sleep easily in my bed when I didn't know where she was?

4 May

I should never have gone to look at that house. Edging
out of my price range and the wrong side of the city,
whatever the agent said about it being more Porchester
than St Anns. I would have turned away without looking, except Jamie was already banging on the door.

I should have guessed it was Marion Barker's house
before she opened the door. She's been trying to sell it
for so long, and I knew she lived over this part of the
city, and Sod's Law said I'd come across it sooner or
later. Slim information, though – she was as shocked
as I was when she opened the door.

'Sophie,' she said, and her expression got sterner,
like she was reacting on some deep instinct, putting
on a mask.

I said hello, and Jamie smiled at her, and then she
signalled for us to go past her, down the narrow hall
and into the front room. Brown velour furniture and
flowery wallpaper, china dogs mouthing yaps on the
mantelpiece, a green glass fish swimming across the top
of the television set.

Marion was nervous, her hands constantly running to
smooth down her hair. She was wearing flowery slippers
with pink fur trim, and occasionally she moved one foot
on top of the other as she talked. Replacement windows
twelve years ago, rewiring shortly after, a new boiler

97

three years ago, no problems with damp or the roof or subsidence.

Jamie and I followed her into the back room, fake-mahogany table and chairs, an imposing sideboard with a glass panel displaying a yellowing Coronation jug between Silver Jubilee and Royal Wedding mugs. The whole place was spotlessly clean, shiny with hygiene, even the sagging white kitchen units, and yet it was somehow lifeless, as if she'd bleached the atmosphere away.

Both bedrooms had the same stale feeling, the single beds covered in faded but ironed bedspreads, the dresser top in her room empty of all but a silver-backed hairbrush on a lace doily and a photograph in a silver frame that showed Marion sitting awkwardly in a family scene, the add-on to someone else's two-point-four kids, the maiden aunt. I tried not to meet Marion's eyes, because I had an image of her life – coming home late from work, eating a microwaved dinner in front of *Who Wants To Be A Millionaire?* before retiring to bed in a full-length winceyette nightdress.

Jamie took charge of the conversation while we drank tea from china cups with roses climbing towards the handles. He asked the questions; I couldn't even look at her as Marion answered in a level voice. It was a quiet neighbourhood, no real problems, the area's reputation was unjustified, she'd been here nearly twenty-five years but wanted a change, more of a garden, access to countryside.

Then she said, 'So, you're getting a place together, are you?'

Jamie was about to answer, but I touched his knee to stop him and said, 'Yes, that's right.'

Jamie looked at me with surprise, but Marion didn't seem to notice. She'd never married, she said, she'd never met quite the right person, she'd always been so busy, she was happy on her own.

She wished us luck at the door, and I suddenly wanted to take her hand and shake it, but I didn't know how to, so I smiled and thanked her and we went on our way.

Halfway down the street Jamie said, 'Why did you say we were together?'

I couldn't look at him, because I didn't have an explanation, it was just a spur of the moment thing. I said, 'It just seemed easier,' but I think he knew that wasn't the truth.

It wasn't that I wanted Marion to think my life was different from what it actually is. It wasn't even that I was embarrassed to be in Marion's house, letting her see into my life and poking my way around hers. Maybe I said it because I had such a clear image of where I might end up if I moved into her house. I could imagine myself sitting in that house alone, sitting up in a narrow bed reading romance novels, visiting other people's families as a guest every holiday. I don't want to live out my days in a cold old house, a maiden aunt, a spinster of the parish with a job marshalling targets in a call centre.

So Jamie and I retreated to the Arms for a couple of pints. We talked for ages, and none of his mates came in, and it was just like the old days. We ran round to the offie and got some carry-out, and went back to my place to keep drinking. Bad idea, work on a hangover and the phones so busy, but I didn't want to be on my own.

I had checked the answerphone when we came in through the door, and there were no new messages. No messages for three days, and I was even getting a little relaxed, thinking maybe the caller had given up, was going to leave me in peace now. But I felt uneasy, I have to say, and Jamie's company was a comfort, because what could the caller do with him here?

Jamie was halfway through some rambling anecdote about work when the phone rang. It was quarter past midnight – late, even for the caller. Jamie stopped mid-sentence and looked at me, and I sat looking at the phone for a moment, and then I knew that I didn't want Jamie to hear the caller's silence, and so I dashed to the phone and got to it just before the answerphone clicked in. I could feel the sweat sprouting out of all my pores, and my breath rattling in my throat, and I managed to gasp, 'Hello?' into the mouthpiece.

'Angie? Angie?' the voice on the other end of the line said. 'Angie, Stephanie had her baby, a girl—'

'You must have the wrong number,' I said, and the adrenaline stopped flowing through my blood, and my chest stopped heaving, and I was left cold and sweaty and clammy. I replaced the receiver and sat down again.

Jamie said, 'Are you okay? You look terrible.'

I nodded, and finished my can, and popped open another one. Jamie leaned in towards me sympathetically. I took a big swig of beer. 'I'm fine,' I said. 'It was just a wrong number.'

'You thought it was going to be someone else,' he said.

I shrugged, but there didn't seem any reason not to tell him, not now, not after all the drink we had consumed and the comfort I found in his presence. It didn't seem right to leave it just like that. So I took a deep breath and told him about the phone calls.

He listened, and frowned, and made sympathetic noises, and when I had finished he said, 'You should phone the police.'

'No,' I said, although I wasn't sure why. He pressed me, and finally I told him that I didn't want to make a big fuss about it, I was sure it would go away in the end. He wasn't convinced by that, but he's sensible enough not to push me when I won't tell him what's going on.

I said, 'You won't tell anyone about this, will you? I mean, Mum or Dad or Jonathan or any of your family? I don't want them to worry.'

'If you don't want me to, sure,' he said.

I sat there feeling the tears swelling in my throat and filling my eyes up, and he saw my face and said, 'Hey, hey,' and pulled me towards him and gave me a big hug. And I put my arms tight around him, and he held me tight, and it was so good being so close to him like that.

We separated again and he said, 'Who do you think's doing it?'

'I don't know,' I said. 'It must be someone I know, because they know my work extension and my home number.' I didn't add that it could be anyone, including him, someone I trusted really well, and that scared me more than the idea of a random stranger.

He said, 'Well, who? An old boyfriend?' I shook my head. 'Are you sure it's a man?'

'I think so.'

'Well, what men are there?'

I didn't answer, but I felt myself go cold. Because it could be Jonathan – it could be – after all, Jamie doesn't know about all the stuff four years ago, neither of us ever told anyone, at least I hope Jonathan didn't. That was our agreement – don't tell anyone – and my family is good at that kind of non-communication.

I said, 'I don't want to play this guessing game.'

'Okay,' he said. 'Okay, but you know you can trust me, don't you?'

'Yes,' I said, and my voice felt small and weak, and I hoped he wouldn't take the size of my voice as a sign of how much I trusted him.

He said, 'Oh, Sophie, you're my closest friend, you know how much I care about you.'

I nodded, and let him sit closer to me, because it did make me feel better. But I knew he was coming onto me. The oldest trick in the book, the sensitive listener with hands touching in sympathy. We were on the sofa together, me at one end with one leg folded under me, him twisting to face me. We weren't even that close to one another, and yet he thought that gave him the right – no, I don't mean that. I don't want to get angry, because he's one of my best friends, and we had drunk ourselves silly.

So I let him rest his hand on my leg as he talked, and

then we sat a lot closer, and all the time I was asking myself what I was doing. Then he put his arm around me, and I let him, and it felt so nice to be that close, to touch another human being. When we separated there was that horrible moment when I knew he was going to try to kiss me, and I didn't know until his lips touched mine that I didn't want it, that this wasn't it. I pulled away, turned away; he apologised, then stood up and put his coat on. I tried to tell him that it didn't matter, that we could carry on the way we had been, but he shook his head. Then he asked me to go out with him tomorrow, just as friends, but I'd already agreed to go to Mum and Dad's, and I felt guilty that I was relieved to have a genuine excuse. So I agreed to go out after that, just to make him feel better.

I've known for a long time that Jamie liked me that way; it would have been hard not to have noticed. Mum has picked up on it, and I know Jamie fulfils all her criteria. She'd like to see me settled, she says, whatever that means. It sounds so final, so rigid. I don't believe that there is one true love, I'm not a soppy romantic, but surely there has to be more than just getting on well with someone? Mum says it's a recipe for being left on the shelf – I used to laugh at that, because nobody believes that any more – but then, seeing Marion makes me wonder. Maybe Mum's onto something – maybe friendship is the best that's on offer? I just thought – I thought that if I ignored Jamie's feelings for long enough they would go away, and it would all slot together somehow. I guess I'm the stupid one after all.

Chapter Eleven

I woke to the sound of the car pulling up outside the house. The through-lounge had descended into dusk, bluish light bleaching the colours from the room, the TV glowing as the *EastEnders* credits rolled. I had dreamed about Sophie; dreamed of her in a dark street, alone, the city closing over her head like the flaps on a box. I struggled to bring myself back to this room.

The front door opened and shut, and there she was, standing above me, folders and files held to her chest.

I said, 'Sophie, I was getting worried.'

She flicked on the light and said, 'Who is Sophie?'

I blinked up at her, rubbed my eyes, said, 'Alison, Alison. I was worried.'

'Andrew and I worked late.'

'Andrew. I should have known,' I said, thinking of his smart suits and cartoon-character ties, his broad smile, all the time they spent together.

'What's that supposed to mean?'

I looked up at her, surprised. 'Nothing,' I said. 'I should have realised, that's all.'

She dumped her folders on the dining-room table and stayed there for a moment, her back to me, shoulders slightly hunched. I realised that I had Sophie's notebook open on my lap, and I closed it and slipped it behind me, down behind the cushions and out of sight. She hadn't moved. I thought about Andrew's hands, those manicured fingers, the soft flesh that was warm and damp when I shook his hand.

She said, 'You called me Sophie. Who is Sophie?'

'Did I say Sophie? I'm sorry, I fell asleep, I just woke up.'

She said, turning, 'Is something wrong?'

'What do you mean?' Studying her face, the creases around her eyes, her unsmiling mouth.

'You seem distant. You've been like this for ages.'

'I'm not distant,' I said, but the words felt disconnected and I added, 'Am I?'

She sat down next to me on the sofa. 'We used to talk about everything,' she said, 'but it doesn't feel like that any more.'

'I'm just tired,' I said.

'You're always tired.'

'There's a lot on at work. You know the pressure's on for the next SPO's job.' I hesitated. I knew I should tell her about the Marston Street project, that my mistake might cost me the next promotion, it might swing it in someone else's favour. Instead, I said, 'I'm not the only one who works hard.'

'I'm trying to get ahead.' Her voice was steady,

calm even, but those shadows beneath her eyebrows deepened with her frown.

'And I'm not?'

'That's not what I said.'

'But you're thinking it. Maybe things aren't going as quickly as I'd have liked.' I stopped, thinking again that I should tell her about the mistake I'd made. 'There's more to life,' I said. 'You're always working.'

She gave a little laugh. 'That's usually my line.'

'And you've been right,' I said. Behind me, the notebook's hard corner dug into my flesh. 'We need to create balance,' I said. 'We spend so much time working we never really get round to living. I don't want to feel alone.'

'You're not alone,' she said. She wasn't looking at me. 'We're both the same,' she said finally. 'We spend too much time on other things.'

'We have to try harder,' I said, 'make time.' I suddenly felt as if I was repeating phrases borrowed from someone else's vocabulary, someone else's life. But maybe that was what we needed? A jolt, a shock, an injection of alien DNA.

'We have this conversation over and over,' she said. 'It never gets us anywhere.'

'I know,' I said, and I suddenly wanted to get up, to leave this conversation behind. I wanted to get up, but the notebook was behind me, and I discovered that I couldn't move.

'I feel like we just talk in circles,' Alison said.

'So why do we bother?' I asked, and then, to try

and make peace, I added, 'We love each other, don't we? What else matters?'

She wasn't looking at me now. She had her hands in her lap, fingers massaging knuckles. She said, 'I'm the one making all the effort here, Peter.'

All the late nights, all the turnaround projects, all the phone calls when she stood cradling the phone. 'Yeah,' I said. 'With Andrew.'

Her hands clenched. 'I can't believe you just said that. You can't have meant that.'

'I'm sorry,' I said, but there was a tight knot inside me that wasn't sorry, a tight knot that wanted it to be so. I said, 'I'm sorry, I take that back. I'm just tired. I fell asleep and – it's been a long day.'

'For both of us,' she said.

I reached over and took hold of her hands, lay my head against her shoulder. She pulled one hand away and put her arm around me. I lay my head in her lap and she stroked my hair, and I felt the warmth of her body through her clothes. I could hear her breathe, and the regular beat of her heart. She leaned down and kissed me on the forehead, and I closed my eyes and felt her fingers touching me lightly on the cheek, tracing the shape of my ear, running along the line of my jaw. I felt so warm, cocooned against her belly, and her touch sent shivers like electricity along my spine. I curled there, as if drifting, floating as if suspended, brushed by her warmth.

8 May

Last night at Jamie's was one of those awkward getting-back-on-the-right-foot sort of evenings, clumsy silences and being ultra polite, at first, anyway. We watched TV with a couple of bottles of wine. I wasn't in the mood to go out and Jamie was skint, so we ended up watching some ridiculous beach-games show on Sky One, all bikinis and lager on the Costas.

By near the end of the second bottle of wine I was feeling more relaxed, sleepy even, and being away from my flat was such a relief. Except, then, I found myself looking at Jamie in the half-darkness of the room, and he was slumped right back in the sofa with his legs stretched out, holding his wine glass on his belly and laughing at the TV. The light from the TV was bluish and it made his skin look sicklier and paler than it usually does, and his chin was right down on his chest so I could see a bit of what would be a double chin developing. And I watched him watching TV, and for a moment I could see a whole life panning out in front of us; a whole life of me and him slumped in front of the TV with his double chin growing as the years passed. I could see him as a middle-aged man, still laughing at the TV, and me sitting patiently beside him, waiting for something to happen, and the years all counted down through the TV schedules. We'd be like my mum and dad, growing old without noticing that it was happening, and growing dull and used to each other, used to our life, used to knowing exactly what each day would be like before it even started. So used to all of it that we couldn't see the nasty stuff that goes off in the world, even if it was in our house, involving our kids, happening right under our noses.

Is that what being a responsible adult is all about? I feel like a kid still. Maybe getting older stops you seeing things? Maybe it's like snow-blindness?

It still surprises me that Mum and Dad believed whatever Jonathan told them, even with Jonathan's boss coming round the house, and threatening us with the police, and saying he'd give Jonathan his cards if he found out he was right. Mum and Dad were amazing, leaping to our defence, shouting at the bloke, telling him he'd got it all wrong, we were good kids, we wouldn't ever betray someone's trust that way.

And Mum actually said she was proud of us. Proud! We were both on our way, she said, we were doing the business, car mechanics and nurses were useful, were valued. It made me feel ten times worse, because I couldn't tell her I'd failed almost every module, I'd have to re-sit, and nobody knew, I couldn't even laugh it off at college because the others were all so into it, so full of how useful they were going to be. Did they laugh at me? Felt like it, when I walked into a classroom and they gave me their sympathetic smiles, and the women all wanted to mother me because I was such a kid next to them, and the men all tried to chat me up because every man fancies youth once in a while, it's part of the male growing-older ritual. All their earnest discussions, recounting the pointless office and factory and warehouse jobs they'd done for years before deciding on nursing, before deciding that they Cared, and somehow my Saturday job in Morrison's just made me feel more distant. Jamie was out every night partying, and Jonathan had one girl after another, and there I was, sitting in of an evening trying to understand my manuals. I suppose I was kidding myself, I was always going to return to type and stuff it up big time, and I didn't Care.

Jamie said, 'You're very quiet tonight. Are you okay?'

'Yeah,' I said. 'Of course. Just tired.'

'You still thinking about those phone calls? I don't know why you don't just call the police. They'd put a stop to it right away.'

'Not this conversation again,' I said. 'I'm not going to phone the police. They've stopped now, anyway. Haven't had one for nearly a week.'

'A week? Oh, well, that's all right then, I thought you were clutching at straws for a minute, but if it's been a full week . . .'

I hit him lightly on the arm and he played that I had hurt him. But I was relieved that he seemed to believe me. I said, 'I'm sure they've got bored by now.'

'A weirdo with a short attention span. That'll be right.'

I said, 'Are you deliberately trying to freak me out?'

'No,' he said, and adopted a more sympathetic tone. 'I just think you should get help. I could come over – I could stay over a few nights. Answer the phone for you, scare them off.'

110

'Yeah,' I said. 'You'd like that, wouldn't you?'

He looked hurt. 'Don't be like that, Sophie, you know what I said about—'

I waved it away. 'I know, I know. Least said soonest mended and all that.'

But yet again it was him who mentioned the phone calls. Sometimes I can be so naïve it frightens me – I'm so weak, and stupid, I can't even see what's going on under my nose. Because it makes perfect sense for Jamie to be the caller – he's there to comfort me, offer support and all that, and what if he's controlling it, what if he's controlling me just by picking up the phone? I feel like a puppet, and he's the one pulling all the strings.

He was building a spliff, sticking the Rizlas together while looking at the TV screen, and I wondered how I could have been so blind. It was stretching it too far to think some loony stranger had got my work and home phone numbers, but Jamie already had both. Jamie had a motive, too, however sick it was as a tactic.

I sat there for a while, listening to the TV voice-over describe how two of the contestants had ended up in the swimming pool, fully dressed, wrestling an inflatable crocodile. I felt pretty angry about it all, but I didn't want to confront Jamie, not then, not until I'd thought it all through. So I said, 'Maybe I should go. Work tomorrow and all that.'

'Oh, don't go just yet,' he said. 'Have some of this with me,' and passed me the spliff.

I took it and had a couple of drags and tried to decide what to do. I didn't want to be there but I didn't really want to go home. I didn't really want to be anywhere, to be honest. I would have liked to be nowhere — as if I was asleep, all my senses closed down and nobody paying me any attention, curled up and warm and knowing nothing.

I gave him the spliff back and started to put my shoes on.

He said, 'Wait up, I'll walk you back.' I started to protest, but he had already broken the lit end off the spliff and was putting the doggy remains into his cigarette packet to smoke later. 'It's late,' he said, 'and I'm not trying to freak you out, but you don't know what weirdos are out there. Let me walk you back, or I'll be worrying all night about whether you made it.'

So I let him, more because I never like the dark streets after midnight, they're too deserted, and the only people about are minicab drivers and drunken freaks staggering home. I can't stand that late-night friendliness, drunken enquiries about where I've been and have I had a good night and do I have a spare fag, and lone figures walking behind me, footsteps echoing mine, and that moment when I can't tell if someone's following me or if they're just on their way home and would be horrified, I mean really shocked, if they realised that the woman in front of them thought they might be an attacker. And the ones who walk fast and approach from behind, and the dilemma of whether to speed up to stay ahead of them, or to slow right down and let them past, and that horrible moment when they draw almost level and seem to stay in my blind spot longer than needed, and slowing right down until they finally go past, and trying not to look at them as they pass in case that sets something off, and the long relief and the feeling of foolishness that follows their passing.

So I let him walk me home, and we smoked some of the spliff as we walked, the blue smoke trailing behind us like a signal, and I started to think, because it's true, it's a statistical fact, that as a woman I'm safer walking home alone than getting a male friend to walk me. I mean, statistically, I'm more likely to be attacked by a friend than I am by a stranger hiding in an alley, and there I was with Jamie, and that meant I was in greater danger than if I'd told him to stay at home. I could have told him I'd phone him when I got home if he was that worried about whether I'd make it okay.

But then, there was that little bit of doubt, because how did I know who the caller was, what if it was some freak, waiting for me somewhere near home, or in the darkness of the yard behind the hairdressers', or maybe they'd broken in and were inside the flat, hiding in a cupboard until Jamie went? Or maybe it was Jamie, and this was all a pretext for him to get me home and then — but he wasn't like that, no, but nobody ever thought their attacker was like that, or they wouldn't have trusted them, and maybe the worst thing I could do would be to trust Jamie?

Jamie said, 'What are you thinking about?'

We were about halfway home, coming up past Vernon park, and there was no traffic about, not even minicabs, and the whole street seemed so silent, so dark, as if everyone was already asleep. No lights behind windows, no TVs playing as we passed the curtained front rooms.

I said, 'I was wondering who made those phone calls. I mean, it has to be someone I know, doesn't it? One of my friends.'

He didn't speak for a moment, and when he did speak he sounded as if he was concentrating very hard on the words he was choosing. 'Have you got any idea who it might be?'

'Someone I trust,' I said. 'The question is why?'

Again, he sounded as if he was choosing his words with care. I didn't look towards him. He said, 'What reasons do you think there might be?'

'I don't know,' I said. 'Someone who wants to freak me out. Someone who thinks I can be frightened into doing what they want.'

'And what do they want?'

'I don't know. Maybe they want me.'

'Want you?'

That encouraged me, wine and spliff suddenly convincing me that I was right. I said, 'Someone who's got a crush, maybe?'

He stopped walking, and I had to turn to face him. He said, 'I know what you're getting at. I can't believe you'd even think it.'

I said, 'How do you know what I'm getting at? Are you saying I'm right?'

He shook his head slowly, looking at me with a serious expression. 'I don't believe this,' he said. 'How could you think I'd do something like that?'

I could see my words had hurt him. I think I was getting close to something, maybe — and if he was the one, if it was him, he had to know that I was onto him, that I knew his game, that I could see the angles he was coming up with. But he looked so hurt, so confused. I said, 'Maybe I'm wrong. I don't know, I'm sorry, I didn't mean that.' But if he was manipulating me, then that was what he wanted, and I was playing into his hands again. I said, 'Forget it, I'm sorry.'

I started walking again, and after a moment I heard him follow me, and then he drew level with me. I didn't look at him at first, but after a moment when he still hadn't spoken, I glanced quickly at him. He was walking with his head down, looking at his feet, and his shoulders were a little hunched, and I felt bad about that, but if he was the one – if it was him, he would know I was onto him, and if he wasn't, surely he could understand, he could see beyond? I mean, that's part of friendship, isn't it, accepting when someone is in a mess and needs more understanding, more leeway than usual?

When we reached the hairdressers', I said, 'Do you want to come in for a bit?'

'No,' he said, not looking directly at me. 'No, I'll head straight back.'

'Okay,' I said. 'Thanks. See you later.'

'Sure,' he said, and turned away.

I went quickly up into my flat and into the front room, without switching on the light. From the window I could see the street, and Jamie was there still, bent over the spliff with his lighter in his hand, trying to get the flame to light. I watched him shaking the lighter and trying again, and finally he managed to light it, and then he went slowly down the street, smoking and slightly huddled, as if he was deep in thought.

Chapter Twelve

I put down the notebook and took another sip from my pint. It was almost half past eight and the Arms was crowded, but there was no sign of Jamie or any of his friends. I would have to leave soon if I wanted to get home before Alison, but I didn't want to move. I knew Alison would question me, would demand answers if I rolled in after her, but I was past caring. There were more important things to worry about than whether Alison knew where I was – Sophie was out on her own, and I had to speak to Jamie, and it really didn't matter that Alison would never understand.

The more I read of the notebook, the more concerned I found I was for Sophie's well-being. It wasn't just the things Helen had told me could happen to a runaway on the streets – although her voice did keep replaying itself in my head, running through my dreams, a catalogue of worst-case scenarios. No, whatever was possible, whatever could happen, I was sure that Sophie was stronger than that. She wouldn't walk into danger, she wouldn't allow herself to fall into those traps – at least, not under normal circumstances.

But these were not normal circumstances. I could imagine how she felt, how alone she was, with nobody to turn to, nobody to rely on. It could all have been so different. It was clear to me now that I should have made more of an effort before she disappeared. Social responsibility, to take care of those around us, and I had let her down. If I could rewind the tape and be standing at the bus stop with her again I knew what I would do. There had been so many opportunities, and I hadn't taken any of them – and because of that, I had to accept my own share of responsibility for whatever had happened to her.

And that meant that I had to act, starting with confronting Jamie about the phone calls, if he ever deigned to put in an appearance.

Starting with forgetting about Alison, and my own life, and my own responsibilities, because being caught up in the details of my own life is what stopped me from reaching out to Sophie in the first place, when it could have mattered, when it could have prevented whatever had happened to her since.

I was sitting at a table near the pool table, and I had a clear view of the whole bar. The table usually occupied by Jamie and his friends was empty; there was football on the TV, England playing somebody in a friendly, a World Cup practice match. The chairs had been pulled back into a rough semi-circle by a group of young men dressed in workboots and dusty trousers, one of them still wearing a neon vest. They were sitting back in their chairs, legs stretched out in front of them, pints of lager in their hands, total concentration. They were big men, solid from physical work, part of a clan. They wouldn't be worried about Alison getting home before them. They wouldn't feel guilt at being out without her. I felt how thin, how weak, how insignificant my presence was beside theirs. They had loud laughter, loud voices – I could hear their running commentary on the match from where I sat. They wouldn't be afraid to talk to someone at a bus stop, or to confront someone if they thought they'd acted badly.

If I was more like them, would that have made the difference? Would that have bridged the distance between me and Sophie, or would she have turned away from them as well?

It occurred to me that if I was someone else, if I was Steve, or Jamie, I would have pulled up a chair at the back of the group and joined in watching the game. I could have faked enough passion, bluffed an entry into their group with a few choice phrases. I could imagine that Steve would have known what to say, and Jamie wouldn't even have hesitated, and if Sophie had been with him she would have been just as enthusiastic about the game. I couldn't imagine Alison ever doing anything of the kind.

But then, Alison would have looked so vulnerable, sitting among those men with their easy confidence, their big bones and strong bodies. I found it hard to understand why Alison would be incapable of sitting comfortably among them. She would shrink into herself even more, draw away from them, set herself apart so they would see that she regarded herself as different. She would accentuate how little she felt she had in common with them, and then I would have to choose, I would be pulled that way too, and the men would see that. I could imagine it all, and it irritated me, because surely it was not so difficult to adopt a camouflage, just for the length of a game of football?

It disappointed me that Jamie hadn't come into the pub. I could imagine myself in that group of men, seeing Jamie walk through the doors, drawing myself up to my full height and challenging him. I would stand up tall and he would see the strength that I do have in my body, and the men would turn from the football to watch events unfold, and they would weigh the odds and declare me the favourite. If that happened, everyone would know, even if it was too late for Sophie to hear it for herself, and Jamie would have to back down, and he would be beaten, and he would concede that I was right, that he was no friend of Sophie, that he had never been her friend, that he had always had his own interests at heart.

And when – if – when Sophie returned, she would see who her real friend was, who had been the one really looking out for her interests. It would all be so clear to her – that I was the one protecting her, that I was the one without ulterior motives, without my own self-interest driving me forwards.

And if I had had the courage to start things with Sophie, I was sure that the situation would have arisen with her there to witness it. Maybe I would have known what was going on earlier, maybe she would have confided in me, and by challenging Jamie I could have stopped her feeling the need to run away.

Because Jamie had to be the one who was ultimately responsible, he had to be the one who drove Sophie away. When I picture her wandering the streets, a cold, lost soul wrapped up in her jacket, I can imagine how she feels, I can almost touch her emotions, it's like empathy, or ESP. I can see clearer than anyone else, clear into her life and her heart and her mind. Sometimes, when I'm dreaming, it's as if I can even hear her voice, calling to me, drawing me closer to her.

9 May

Of course, I was late to work this morning. Had to be, after a night like last night. I still wasn't dressed when the guy who always catches my bus arrived at the stop. I could set my watch by him, he's that precise, and I knew I was never going to make it.

And it's just bloody typical that I'd be late on a day when Marion's got it on her and looking for someone to blame. I was hoping she'd go easy on me, familiarity and all that now I've been to her house, but she gave me the evil eye right off. She didn't even give me time to put my coat and bag down, just called me straight into her office and closed the door.

Her office is like a time warp. The rest of us have got grey wood-effect desks that curve round, and all the partitions and filing cabinets and cupboards match, and it all looks dead nice and modern if you don't look too close at where the glue is coming unstuck and the wood effect is peeling off. But Marion's office looks like she's collecting the oldest furniture she can find — a dark brown teak-effect desk with steel legs, battleship-grey filing cabinets, shelving units all against one wall stacked high with lever arch folders with yellowed labels. She sits surrounded by all this stuff, and it used to be that it scared me, that it gave her some kind of seniority or something, as if she's been there for ever and can't be challenged, but today when I went in, it didn't scare me. It just reminded me of her house, her life.

I spun her a line about the bus not stopping for me, but she didn't buy it. Started going on that I'm always late, and I tried to tell her I wasn't late that often, and I always make up the time, but she wasn't listening to me. Started going on about my Attitude, and I could hear the capital A when she spoke, I swear. She said I was lackadaisical, and I wasn't meeting any of my targets, and I wasn't putting the proper emphasis on my work. I stood there and took it, like I was back at school, because what else could I have done? She was sat behind that monstrosity of a desk, a pencil in one hand tap-tapping out the words on a pile of papers. I opened my mouth to come back at her, but she held out one hand to stop me and said, 'Punctuality is what this office thrives on, Sophie. Accuracy is vital in this job, and if you are coming into work late then your whole attitude to accuracy has to be called into question, doesn't it?'

I wanted to say that this wasn't about punctuality or anything else, it was about her not liking me. She must have felt threatened now I'd been round to her house. I wanted to say that she was only doing this to me because I was prepared to stand up to her, and the others always back down and say nothing when push comes to shove. But I heard myself say, 'I am accurate. I've always been a good worker here.'

'When you first started here your attitude was very sloppy. We had to have talks about it before, remember?'

'Yes, I remember,' I said, because how could I forget being hauled into the office and Mr Bennett from upstairs coming down to issue me with my warning because I'd been pissing about ringing other people's extensions. It wasn't just me, of course not, but I was the one caught, I was the one Marion made a beeline for. I said, 'That was three years ago. I'm a lot more responsible now.'

'Are you? It seems to me that you are sliding back into old habits.'

And then she was going on about what I was like before, how I never did what I was told, how I was lazy and skived whenever I could, and what was I supposed to say? I wanted to tell her things are different now, I'm different, but she wasn't going to listen to me. She's got it all fixed in her mind and nothing I say will ever change what she thinks about me.

Then Marion said, 'There have been complaints that you haven't been completing your turns on the rota.'

That got me mad, I mean, I always do my shift, and if anyone has a problem they should have the bottle to come to me and say it to my face, instead of creeping off behind my back and telling Marion like we're kids or something.

Marion said, 'You left early a couple of Fridays ago when you should have been covering enquiries.'

I told her I swapped with Leanna, did her Tuesday for her, but Marion acted like she didn't believe me, and I wanted to scream at her but I knew she wouldn't listen. She didn't even break stride at this cannonball through her argument. She said, 'I am talking about a general problem with your work.'

Then she was pulling out bits of paper, like she'd been preparing for this, and started reading off all the times I'd missed my targets. Demanding to know why I hadn't been answering all my calls. And her voice was drilling right into me, all these times I hadn't been pulling my weight, and I couldn't flannel her with stuff about difficult cases, and she wouldn't buy that I was freaked out by the silent caller, not when he hasn't phoned me at work since I swapped desks with Leanna.

It's crazy, because anyone else would have understood what I was going through, they would have been at least a little sympathetic. I wanted to throw myself on her mercy, break down, admit I was trying to hide, admit I wasn't pulling my weight, admit I was scared all the time, because every call I answered might be him. But I knew she wouldn't give a toss about that. I knew from the hard look in her eye, and the way she'd got her jaw clamped shut. She'd just say I should phone the police if it's a problem, but I can't do that, she just doesn't understand. I had to fight back tears, but it wasn't that I was upset by her, she doesn't scare me, it's just that nothing is easy any more, nothing ever seems to work out for me, and I'm so sick of it.

Marion was going on about how I had to concentrate on my work and not daydream, and I wanted to say I wasn't daydreaming, I wasn't doing anything of the sort. She was going on about forgetting about anything else while you're at work, like it's possible to shove your life in the desk drawer when you get to work and forget about it until shift end. She was going on about separating home and work life, and I couldn't take it any more, I couldn't listen to any more of her insane ramblings, I felt like I was going to explode.

So I said, 'If you had a life outside work you'd know how stupid that sounds.'

And then I knew I shouldn't have said it, I wanted to scramble and grab the words back out of the air, but they were said, I couldn't rewind, I couldn't rub them out.

Marion stood up over me, rose up like she really was mad, spitting mad, roaring, and she looked twice as big and I was really scared, I mean, I wanted to get out of there. I was apologising like crazy, but she wasn't listening, and then she was yelling at me – how dare I say that, how dare I make assumptions, who did I think I was – and I couldn't just stand there and take it, not off a witch like her, not off some old dragon like that, so I started yelling back, yelling that she never listens to me, she never believes me, she never lets me get on with my job, always marching up and down the office, always breathing down my neck, she's never liked me, she's had it in for me right from the beginning.

There was nothing I could do to stop it, and I could feel all the tears coming, and I knew if I stayed there any longer I'd lose it completely, so I got out. I ran out of her office and through the main office, a blur of faces all looking at me, and I ran out through the main door and down the stairs and out onto the street at the back of the building.

Once I was there, I stopped. I was gasping, choking on my tears. I couldn't breathe properly. My chest was tight, hurting like hell. People passing in the street were looking at me. I sank down with my back against the building and I tried to get my breath back.

After a bit, when I was struggling to light a cigarette with shaking hands, Julie came out and found me. She told me they'd all heard the row in the office, but Marion was acting like nothing had happened. I gave Julie a cigarette. She started describing the others' reactions, and pretty soon she'd got me giggling, but I still felt like I was going to cry. Julie asked me what was going on, but I never told her. I didn't want to tell anyone about the phone calls. It just makes me feel so vulnerable, like I'm walking around naked, like someone else is controlling what I do, and it freaks me out.

Julie told me I had to go and speak to Marion, and I knew she was right. I felt like if I didn't go back in right then, I never would. So Julie linked her arm with mine, and we went back upstairs. Everyone was pretending not to look at me. I left Julie at her desk and went towards Marion, in her office with the door open, looking through paperwork. She must have seen me coming, but she kept her head down, didn't look up until I knocked on the open door.

'Come in,' she said, and even forced something like a smile.

I went in and shut the door. I felt terrible. Stupid more than anything else. I started to speak before she had a chance to, and said, 'I'm really sorry, I didn't mean any of that, really.'

She looked at me for a moment, and I thought she was going to have another go, and I would have turned and walked straight out, or burst into tears, if she had. But then she told me to sit down, and she even sounded friendly, and that made the whole thing even worse.

She said, 'I'm sorry that you took any of that personally, Sophie. It wasn't meant to be personal. If you're having problems outside work, you should let me know.'

I had felt all the tears flooding back, but then I thought, I don't want to tell her anything, she just wouldn't understand. She'd look down on me, and I'd get labelled unbalanced or something, and then what would happen? I'd never get to be Team Leader — not that I want to be — but what would she put if I asked her for a reference for another job? She's got a low enough opinion of me as it is. I don't want her knowing my own private business. So I told her some porkie about Mum being ill, and she was all sweetness and light after that, and she said she could understand that my thoughts were elsewhere, and I shouldn't worry about the targets, and if I needed time off I only had to ask. I felt like such a louse by then, but there was nothing I could say.

When I got to my desk and switched on my computer, I felt the start of a headache growing behind my eyes, and it was all I could do to stop myself from crying, because I just knew right off what a horrible sort of day it was going to be.

Marion might be all sympathetic to me now, but one day she'll use all this against me, I just know it. She loves throwing old times back in my face. I know I wasn't very mature back then, I really wasn't very responsible when I started working here. That much has been told me over and over from all sorts of places. But what am I supposed to do about that? I can't erase the past, and nobody else seems to want to either. I know I should have taken this job more seriously when I first started, just like I should never have packed in the nursing course, or persuaded Jonathan to lie, or run off and not told my family where I had gone. I was younger then — we learn from experience, surely that's what it means to be human? But nobody ever seems to want to let me move on from what's happened in the past, and so I'm stuck with it.

And what can I do? Part of me just wants to pack up and leave. Walk out, on the job at least. I could do that — I've done it before, after all. But last time was different — last time there was stuff I could just walk out on. And it worked, sort of. I didn't have Jonathan blaming me for every little thing that went wrong, telling me it was my fault that he might lose his job, or that nobody believed the lies he was telling, or that he couldn't live with himself with the way Mum and Dad were acting about it all. As if I forced him to go along with the plan. As if the plan wasn't to get him off the hook in the first place. As if I was over the moon about it, enjoying every minute. He didn't even notice the state I was in, and how bad I felt about it all, and how there wasn't any way back for me either. He didn't even seem to care that I couldn't do my nursing course, that it was all too much, because all he could see was what was happening to him.

But things are different now. Am I more sensible? I don't know. I want to quit my job, but what if I did? How could I pay the rent on the flat, or tell my parents what I'd done? I just had to get on with it, even though it was the last thing I wanted to do. And the day just got worse and worse. A string of idiots on the phone, yelling about problems with their bills that were not my fault. One of the temps going home sick so that we were one person down as the day got busier. Marion walking round the office with the Target Book as if she carried the weight of life and death in her hands. And all the time I was thinking, who was it? Which one of my so-called mates told Marion that I wasn't pulling my weight? Which one of them wants to drop me in it, as if I stand a snowball in hell's chance of getting the vacant Team Leader's post anyway? But there wasn't any sign, there was nothing I could put my finger on to work out who was trying to stitch me up.

Chapter Thirteen

I told Malcolm I had a dentists' appointment and knocked off work a couple of hours early. I wasn't sure what time Sophie's shift finished work, but I wanted to be there when they did come out.

The call centre was the only business left in a large sixties office block looking out over Parliament Street and into the Market Square. The entrance to the offices was at the back; the front of the ground floor housed a greasy spoon café and a shop selling out-dated women's clothing, polyester and elastic-waisted. I cut up the alley that ran along the side of the shops and hung around, trying my hardest to look inconspicuous, at the large, dark goods entrance to the Forte hotel across the road. The whole street reeked of the sixties; there was nothing that wasn't ugly, flat concrete façades towering up, colours dulled by decades of exhaust fumes. I kicked my feet against the tarmac and waited for the familiar red-and-white striped shirts to appear.

I was worried about how I was going to approach

the people as they came out; Sophie's notebook made it sound as if they would be on alert for all sorts of weirdos. But when the time came, it was remarkably easy. The first person out was a thick-set middle-aged woman, who stopped outside the entrance to fish around in a family-sized handbag and pull out cigarettes. I dashed across the road and put on my brightest smile.

'Excuse me,' I said. 'I was looking for Leanna. I've got a message for her from a friend.'

The woman looked me up and down and obviously decided I wasn't a freak, or a mass-murderer, or an angry customer. There was a crowd of red-and-white shirts coming through the glass doors together, see-ya and ta-raring, and the woman turned her head and shouted, 'Hey, Leanna, someone here for you.'

A slim, slight, cropped-blonde girl extracted herself from the group and came over. The middle-aged woman thrust her head in my direction and wandered away. Leanna looked at me.

I said, 'I'm a friend of Sophie Taylor's.'

'Oh aye?' she said.

'Yeah. I'm trying to track her down.'

She glanced away and said, 'Well, nobody's heard from her. We've had the police round and everything.'

'Yes,' I said. 'They're taking it pretty seriously.'

She frowned. 'They don't think anything really serious has happened, do they?' Before I could reply she continued, 'Only it is dead weird, isn't it? I mean, her going off and that, without telling anyone?'

'Yes,' I said. 'Very strange. That's why I want to find her.'

'She'll be okay, though,' Leanna said. 'I mean, she always falls on her feet.'

I considered telling her some of the things Helen had said could happen to a runaway on the streets, so that she could see why I was worried, why I was so keen to find Sophie before any of those things could happen. But Leanna didn't sound very confident that Sophie would be fine, whatever she actually said – she seemed to want some sort of reassurance from me, so I just said, 'Oh, I'm sure. I just want to check she really is okay, that's all.'

She glanced around her, nodding goodbye to the last of the stragglers as they left the building. Then she said, 'So how could you find her if the police can't?'

'They don't know her like we do,' I said. I tried a gamble. 'She mentioned you to me, said she liked you, that's why I thought you might be able to help.'

She frowned as if puzzled, but her face had brightened a little. 'She said that?'

'Yes. And I think you might know something, I mean, something you don't realise is important, and together we might be able to work it out.'

She let out a little giggle.

I said, 'Do you want to go for a drink? Just a quick one?' I touched her elbow, and she let me walk her towards the Tap and Tumbler down the street.

'I don't know,' she said, stopping, looking at me with uncertainty.

'I won't keep you long,' I said, guiding her on. I felt strangely confident that she would do as I wanted. 'I'm talking to all her friends, but none of them knows much about what was happening at work.'

We reached the pub door. She sighed, and hesitated, and looked at me again.

'You really think I can help?' she asked.

'Yes,' I said. 'Really.'

She rolled her eyes, then pushed open the pub door and led me in. It was dark after the brightness outside, and for a moment all I could see was the blinking of the fruit machine against the far wall and the pale orange lights above the bar. Leanna went straight to a seat by the window and peeled off her coat as she sat down. There was a young couple in the far corner, talking listlessly, but otherwise the place was empty.

'What would you like?' I asked.

'Half a lager top,' she said. 'And some cheese and onion crisps. I'm starving.'

I went to the bar and gave the order, glancing back at her surreptitiously. She was sitting with her elbows on the table, running one hand through her hair. I paid for our drinks and carried them over. She sat up straight, immediately broke open the bag of crisps and started to eat them. I spent a moment settling myself into the chair and taking a sip from my half of bitter.

Then I said, 'Did Sophie say anything to you that might have got you thinking? Anything that didn't seem odd then but might do now?'

'No,' she said. 'She didn't say a thing.' Then she smiled and said, 'I mean, nothing odd. I mean, she was her usual self.'

'How long have you worked together?'

'I don't know. She started a little after me, that was – wait a minute.' She thought about it. 'Must be just short of four years.'

'And you've always been in her section?'

'Yeah, sure.'

'Did Sophie mention to you that she was getting strange phone calls at work?'

'We all get those,' she said, sitting back, fingering some crisps as if she couldn't decide whether to stuff them all into her mouth at once. 'One time I had a heavy breather,' she said. 'And Amy had to get an injunction out against one nutter.' Then her expression fell. 'Oh – you don't think? No, that can't have happened, can it? I mean, the police don't think that, do they?'

'Oh no,' I said, exuding all the casual confidence I could. I had hoped to be able to share some of my fears, but it was plain to me that Leanna was the wrong person for that role. 'Nothing like that. But they do think she might have had some odd phone calls, and that she might have mentioned them to someone at work, someone she trusted.'

'Me?' Leanna said, and frowned, and thought. 'No, she never said a thing.'

I took a small sip from my drink before speaking
again. She had hardly touched her drink and it was
an effort to keep my pace to hers. 'How about
when you swapped desks with her? Did she say
anything then?'

'No,' Leanna said, then seemed to realise something. 'You think that's why she swapped? But I was
the one who asked, she was doing me a favour.' Then
she hesitated, and glanced up at me. 'No, I should
have known she wouldn't do something just to help
me out.'

I was surprised by the resentment behind her tone.
I said, 'Why?'

She gave a little, sour laugh. 'I'm not stupid, you
know. Sophie thinks I am, but Sophie's wrong.
Sophie always thinks she's being so generous when
she talks to me, like I need her charity or something.
Leanna no-mates.' She took a large sip of her drink
and added, 'You were lying when you said she likes
me, weren't you?' Before I could deny it, she said,
'Don't try to fool me, I know she doesn't like me.
But I'm not so paranoid that I think she actually
dislikes me. I'm nothing to her, that's all. Miss
high-and-mighty always acting like she can do what
she wants and bogger everybody else. Manipulative,
that's what she is. She always looks right through me
like I'm not even there, unless she wants something.
Selfish cow.'

Her face had contorted into something quite ugly,
and I wondered what had happened to make her so
bitter. I had the sudden urge to slap her across the

cheek, make her eyes smart and jolt her back from whatever spiteful place she had crawled into. But she glanced at me then, and must have read something in my expression, because she said, 'Oh, come on, if you're a friend of hers you must have seen that side of her.' I didn't reply, so she continued, 'The only people who can't see it are those daft enough to fall for her rebel act.'

'Her rebel act?'

'Yeah, you know. Always playing up like she's the wild child. She can be a good laugh, in small doses. Good entertainment value. All the others love her for that. Except Marion.'

'That's your supervisor?'

'Yeah. Marion always says Sophie doesn't work hard enough, but whatever I think about Sophie, that isn't true. She always pulls her weight. Marion just doesn't like her, but I don't know why.'

'Maybe because she's so popular,' I said.

To my surprise, Leanna said, 'Yeah, I always thought that, too. But Sophie reckons it's to do with when she first started working there. Sophie was a right handful back then. Angry, like she didn't want to be there at all. I'm surprised she didn't walk out sooner, to be honest.'

I took another sip from my drink, looking at the glass to avoid making eye contact. It was hard to see how Leanna could have misunderstood Sophie so badly. I said, 'After you swapped desks with Sophie, did you get any strange phone calls?'

'No,' she said.

'And there's nobody at work who might have been trying to wind her up?'

'No,' she said. 'Not that I can think of. Anyway, Marion would have spotted it in the logs. She's always on the look-out for people chatting instead of working.'

I forced myself to smile. 'Tough supervisor.'

'Yeah, but fair. Always fair.'

It occurred to me that the person who had told Marion that Sophie wasn't pulling her weight was probably sitting in front of me. The jealous co-worker, lonely and dejected in the face of Sophie's obvious popularity, spreading her own vicious version of who Sophie is, using Marion's antipathy towards Sophie for her own spiteful ends. I could feel something like anger mounting inside me, that petty jealousy could have contributed to why Sophie had decided to run away.

Leanna said, 'I've really got to go now.'

I looked up. She had finished her drink and was standing up, ready to walk away. I realised I'd been quiet for too long. I said, 'Thank you for talking to me.'

She shrugged, as if aware that she hadn't been much use, and then she said, 'That's okay. I hope you find her. What did you say your name was?'

'I didn't,' I said, but she was waiting. I had a momentary surge of panic about what I could say, but I took a chance and said, 'It's Jamie.'

'Oh,' she said. 'Oh,' and sat down again. 'She mentioned you.' And then she blushed.

'What did she say?'

She blushed again. 'I don't know if I should tell you.'

'Please,' I said. 'I won't be upset, I promise. She probably told me herself anyway, you know what Sophie's like.'

'Okay,' she said, reluctance in her voice, but she was leaning towards me across the table. 'She said you've got a big crush on her.'

'And what did she think about it?'

She only hesitated for a moment. 'I know you probably won't believe me,' she said. 'She laughed about you with the others. Julie and Amy. She used to tell them everything you did, and take the piss, and they'd all have a good laugh. The little puppy-dog, that's what she calls you.' She stopped, and then gave me a brave little smile. 'I'm sorry, I probably shouldn't have told you that. But it's better you know what kind of person she is.'

'I see,' I said.

'She said you're too nice. A wimp. The boy next door.'

I nodded.

She frowned at me. 'You're not what I expected,' she said.

'No? What did you expect?'

'Someone, I don't know. Younger.'

I just shrugged.

Leanna stood up again. 'I'm sorry,' she said. Then, 'I've got to go.'

I wasn't sure which bit she was sorry about. She

seemed to be so cruel, so devious – and yet, that apology confused me. There was no nasty edge to her words, not the way I'd heard other people talk. It was more as if she was hitting back for some wrong she thought had been done to her. I found that, despite the things she had said, I actually did feel a little sorry for her.

She had left by then, the door banging shut behind her. I considered having another drink and reading some more from the notebook, but I was tired. There was a sour taste in my mouth. I wanted a chance for Leanna's words to fade from my mind. I felt almost dirty, for having listened to Leanna, for having lied to her, too, and more than anything I wanted to get home and get myself clean.

11 May

Jonathan and Jamie both turned up at my flat last night. Both of them crowding into my living room with offerings of booze and cigarettes, falling over each other to entertain me. Pathetic.

I think it was planned, them both being there. Not that I think they rang each other up and plotted behind my back – they don't like each other well enough for anything like that. Jonathan thinks Jamie's a pretentious waster, pissing around pretending to be a musician to hide that all he does is serve on the till in Selectadisc. Fine words coming from Jonathan, who can't even get it together to move out of Mum and Dad's house, even though he is twenty-seven and practically married to Rachel already. But then, Jamie gives as good as he gets, describes Jonathan as a know-it-all know-nothing, Jonny no-mates with his no mates around him, talking big until it comes to it, all mouth and no trousers. It's a miracle I survived a night of those two in the same room.

But then, to each other's faces they're nice as pie. People say girls can be two-faced, but that's nothing compared to these two, sat in my living room all grins and matey jokes, like they're actually glad to see each other. Which is why I think it was probably planned, the result of a chance meeting in the street or, more likely, the Arms, a few pints while they cook up a plan because they think I'm feeling low or something like that.

At first I thought Jamie must have told Jonathan about the phone calls, and I would have given him a right mouthful if he had. A secret's a secret, and I don't want Jonathan turning all caveman and barking off about protecting me. I don't need protecting by anybody, especially not Jonathan. The way he talks, you'd think he's the one who's got his life planned down to the final detail.

But then, when Jamie went to the offie for more booze, Jonathan finally got to the point. Mum was worried. That made me laugh – she tells me she's worried about Jonathan, and then tells him she's worried about me. Cut out the middle man and she'd be up to speed on everything if she tried being direct.

Or maybe it's all some sort of plan cooked up by Mum, a way of making us talk to one another when in all honesty I think we'd be happier if we never saw each other again. Mum thinks the big fall-out was sibling squabbles, and pushing us together, playing us off against each other, will get us to be close again. She has no idea how far off the mark she actually is, and I'm sure that can only be a good thing.

I told Jonathan there was nothing to worry about, and he narrowed his eyes to show that he didn't believe me. I thought he was going to push it, and if he had I'd have told him where to go, but he changed his mind and just offered me a cigarette. When I leaned in to get a light off him, his hands were shaking.

I straightened up and took a deep draw on the cigarette and looked at him. He was in a state, I could see that, but when I asked him what was wrong, he just sat back and said, 'Nothing,' and held his cigarette up to his mouth so I couldn't see his face.

I said, 'Oh, c'mon, what is it? Rachel? Mum and Dad? Work?'

He let out a too-heavy sigh and shrugged and said, 'It's nothing. Just work. People being arseholes, you know?'

'Sure,' I said, and waited for more, but he didn't say anything. So I said, 'Is your boss still being a bastard?'

'Oh, no change there,' he said. 'You'd think he'd have got over it by now.'

I grinned at that, but I could see it was bothering him. Before I could press for more, he said, 'So, c'mon, tell me what's up.'

'Nothing,' I said. He wasn't going to buy that, so I said, 'Oh, you know, life, work, all that crap.'

He looked at me for a long moment, as if he was puzzled by something. 'It's more than that,' he said.

I didn't want him to go off into some rant about what I should do, what I was doing wrong with my life, as if he was completely sorted and never did anything daft, so I said, 'No, honestly, I've just been tired. Not sleeping well. It'll pass.'

'You're turning into a hermit,' he said. 'You've hardly been out.'

I knew then he'd definitely been talking to Jamie, and I had to hide how annoyed I was about that, because he wouldn't understand. I wanted to tell him that just because he's my big brother it doesn't mean he can control everything I do, it doesn't work that way, it never has. But if I did say that, he'd just tell me someone's got to look out for me, as if I'm incapable, and I didn't want to get into that, not when we were getting on so well.

But then Jamie came thumping back up the stairs, and whatever we might have said was gone in an instant. I was relieved that Jamie was back, but a part of me was irritated, too, and I know that that was wrong of me.

But still, I was relieved when they finally both left. I watched them from the window – they were both drunk, walking away together up the street, swaying in towards each other as they went. My head was spinning slightly from all the beer, and I didn't want to go to bed, so I sat up for a while, the TV on though I wasn't following whatever was on, I was just letting the colours play out in front of my eyes and the sound fill up the emptiness of the room.

I drifted off, and it was about an hour later that the phone started ringing. Nearly 2 a.m. It had got cold in the living room, but I didn't want to go to bed and leave the phone ringing, so I sat where I was and waited for the answerphone to click in. I half thought it might be Jonathan, apologising for something or finally wanting to talk, but when the machine played through the announcement and sounded the beep, it was followed by silence. I let the silence play – it could only have been a few seconds, fifteen maybe, but I was holding my breath in my throat, and then I couldn't stand it any longer, I released my breath and sucked in more, and picked up the receiver and started to shout at the silence. I don't even know what I was shouting – to leave me alone, to stop interfering in my life, to let me be, creep, pervert, freak, weirdo, fucking bastard. The person on the other end hung up at that, finally, but I didn't for a second think they were gone for good.

So I went to bed and tried to sleep, but I was too wired, too much adrenaline singing through my veins, and I was finding it hard to breathe. As if there was suddenly no air in my lungs, and my chest got tighter with it, and I was dizzy with all the thoughts screaming around in my brain, and I wanted to get free from it all.

Sometimes, I feel like this is never going to stop. The caller will keep ringing, and every time he rings he'll be crawling further under my skin, and he'll never let me find out who he is because that would end it all right there and then, and at the moment he can see what he's doing to me, he's up close to it, and he can run away and play his anonymous little games.

No, the only way it will stop is if I do what I did last time. Out in the open, breathing in all that air, sucking it into my lungs, and nothing there but all that space, nothing but space and wind and hills and sheep bleating in the fields. I know most people run away to London, hope to get sucked right into the heart of the city, swallowed up whole by it. I'd feel lost down there, sucked in and choking on it, lost among all those people, every one a stranger.

For me, it has to be the open countryside, standing

on the top of the granite rocks with my lungs expanding, feeling the wind make sails with my clothes, looking down into a steep valley with rocks smashed to pieces at its foot, and birds floating on the air below me so I can see the tops of their wings spread out as they drift.

And I wouldn't have to worry about phones ringing, and work sliding beyond my control, and the lies people spread, and losing my job and my flat and any hope of a home, having to move back in with Mum and Dad, back to my childhood bedroom, failed again, squabbling with Jonathan, Mum and Dad so disappointed, no privacy, smoking out of the bedroom window with the curtains shielding the room from the smoke, because no cigarettes under my roof thank you very much, and going round to Jamie's to smoke spliff and creeping back into the house so Mum and Dad don't smell what I've been up to.

Except, maybe I wouldn't even be able to do that, maybe Jamie wouldn't want me coming around any more. Maybe just at the moment when I need him to be there, I've driven him away and he won't want me around him any more. I want to apologise to him, tell him I never meant what I said, and I know he's my friend, and even, if it was the only way to keep him as a friend, maybe I should even let him kiss me, let him think that I want him in the way that he wants me.

The other option would be to do what I did before and hide out among the hills. Would Jonathan try to rescue me again? Sometimes he seems like a different person to the one I used to know.

Chapter Fourteen

I didn't really want to go to the Arms for my regular game of pool with Steve. It was Alison's night at college again and I would have been more than happy to stay at home alone. I could have run a hot bath and spent time just lying there with the water lapping over me, reading Sophie's words.

But when I got home from work, Alison was there, picking up a folder she'd forgotten to take with her that morning. She was roaming around the house looking for the folder, resisting asking me if I'd seen it because she was always having to do that, and when I went upstairs to change out of my suit she came and leaned in the bedroom doorway.

'You're out with Steve tonight, aren't you?' she said.

'Yes,' I said, and forced a yawn and a stretch. 'Mind you, I'm so tired I might give it a miss.'

'I think you should go,' she said.

I looked across at her then. She had picked up the folder from on top of the dressing table, where she'd left it that morning, and was flicking through the pages, a frown of concentration on her face.

I said, 'I've got some paperwork I need to go through for a meeting tomorrow.'

'That can wait, can't it?' She pulled a piece of paper out of a plastic wallet in the folder and looked at it, but I had a feeling it was only so she didn't have to look at me. 'They don't pay you enough to bring your work home with you.'

'Yeah, well,' I said. 'I'm committed to the job, aren't I?'

She glanced at me, as surprised by my tone as I was.

I took the edge out of my voice. 'If I want the next SPO's post I've got to put the hours in.'

She just nodded her head, trying to slide the piece of paper back into its plastic sleeve. I wondered if she thought I was being nasty, hard, but I wasn't sure what I could say to undo the words. So I started to unknot my tie and said, 'What's on at college tonight?'

'I don't know,' she said. 'Something about managing investment portfolios.'

'Totally riveting stuff, then,' I said, and she smiled, and I knew by the smile that it was okay again.

She said, 'You should meet Steve, though. Do you good to get out. Stop moping around the house.'

She wasn't going to drop the subject, but I reminded myself that it wasn't really her fault – I hadn't told her about Sophie's disappearance, or that I had found the notebook, so she couldn't be expected to know how much I was starting to find out. I was sure that if I did tell her, she would be pleased that I was concerned, would probably offer to help me in my search. But I didn't want to drag her into it, not when she was so busy all the time. It was better all round if I kept the situation to myself and didn't share Sophie's notebook with anyone, not just yet.

I wished her luck as she headed off to her class. I lay on my back on the bed with my arms stretched out and listened to her car pull away. When the sound of the engine had died the house was very quiet. I was comfortable there, sleepy, and I might have stayed there all evening if Steve hadn't phoned to check I was still okay for our game.

I did consider cancelling, citing paperwork as my excuse, but the house was very quiet with Alison gone. I found myself craving the warmth, the noise, the atmosphere of the pub, all the people out for a nice evening, Steve wisecracking and me playing his straight man, pretending to be wound up by his jibes. It would make a nice break, not to think about the Marston Street project, or the SPO's post, or whether somebody would stitch me up the way Anthony had done.

It's strange how quickly a place can become familiar – Steve and I had only adopted the Arms and its pool table as our regular meeting place about four months before, but already the pub was as familiar as my own front room. When I went in and heard the music playing through its usual repertoire on the compilation tape and smelled the cigarette smoke in the dusty air, and my eyes adjusted to the gloom with the fruit machine lights winking and running their full display of colours, I felt a sense of relief, of welcome, of homecoming. The usual old men were at the bar, having one of those conversations that revolve around which pub used to be where, owned by which brewery and changed to whatever name now. I nodded and smiled my way through to the bar, ordered myself a pint of Classic and found a table near the pool table to wait for Steve.

Jamie and his friends weren't in yet, and that was a relief to me. Part of me wanted to talk to Jamie, to confront him about the phone calls, to demand whether he was the one who had driven Sophie away, but having Steve hovering in the background would have made it all too awkward. I don't know what I would have done if Jamie had admitted to it – I couldn't imagine that possibility even arising. But even if he denied it, I suspected that his guilt would shine through, and if he cared for Sophie as much as he claimed to, then I could imagine that his feelings of guilt had to be hammering away at him every time he thought of her. Of course, that could be the reason why he was so desperate to find out what had happened to her – if he had betrayed her, as Sophie said he had, then who else could take responsibility for her disappearance?

Steve arrived a few minutes after me. He fetched himself a pint from the bar and I started to rack up the first game. Nobody ever seemed to want to play pool on the nights we were there, as if the familiarity I felt for the place was extending itself out to us, and we were being absorbed into its fabric. As we played our first game, I wondered whether Sophie had ever felt this way, about this place, or about any place. I liked to think that she had been a part of the fabric of the Arms just as much as Steve and I were – it was another point of connection between us, another sign of how important we had become to each other's existence.

My mind was swimming with all of these thoughts, and after I lost the first game disastrously, Steve nudged my arm and said, 'Are you okay, mate?'

I made an effort to pull myself back to the game. I realised I'd barely spoken to Steve since he arrived; I didn't even really know what he'd been talking to me about.

I said, 'Sure, I'm fine. I'm sorry, I'm just a bit distracted, that's all.'

He was bent over the table to break, and I couldn't see his expression. He sent the cue ball down the table and the other balls clattered out across the back end. One yellow dropped down into a corner pocket, and he looked up at me before lining up another shot. 'Something to do with Alison?' he asked. 'You can tell me what's going on.'

I watched the next yellow roll to the edge of the cushion to cover another pocket. Steve stood back and looked at me expectantly, so I leaned down and sent the cue ball rattling into a group of balls in the centre of the table. The balls spun out and knocked Steve's carefully positioned yellow out of harm's way.

'What makes you think it's to do with Alison?' I asked.

'So there is something going on?'

'No,' I said.

He said, 'If something's bothering you, talk to someone. Talk to me. Don't bottle it up.'

'Have you been talking to Alison?'

'No,' he said, but he took his eyes off me, sipped at his pint, then leaned down to play another shot. 'Not really,' he said. 'She's worried about you, Pete, otherwise she wouldn't have said anything. But you know what Alison's like – I'm sure she's just got it all wrapped around her head.'

'Why?' I asked. 'What did she say?'

He had played a poor shot, leaving me a straight pot to the side pocket. I waited, not wanting to look away from him just yet. He said, 'She just said you were quiet. Distracted. She said there was something on your mind that you wouldn't talk about.'

'And she wanted you to find out what this great distraction was?'

I felt as if the pressure was building up inside me, but he just frowned, ignoring my tone, and said, 'No, nothing like that. She just asked if you'd said anything.'

I played my shot while I considered that. The red dropped into the pocket with a satisfying thud, and I said, 'What the hell does she think, that I wouldn't tell her if there's something up?'

'I knew you'd take it this way,' he said. 'I told her. There's no talking to you, Pete, that's your problem.'

'That's not true,' I said, and I could feel something like a wail rising in my voice. I stopped it where it was, swallowed it down. 'I tell Alison everything,' I said.

I missed the next pot, and Steve walked around the table, examining all the angles.

'There's nothing to talk about,' I said. 'There's nothing wrong, I'm just tired, that's all. A lot to do at work, you know how it is.'

'Sure,' he said. 'Sure, I hear you.'

But I knew he didn't believe me. I tried to imagine how they had come to this conclusion, what I had done to make Alison think there was something going on, but I couldn't put my finger on it. And they must have been talking behind my back – surreptitious phone calls when I wasn't around, discussing me, talking about whatever they thought I was doing wrong as if they had some sort of right, some sort of proprietorial control over my life. It made me flush up inside, that Alison would have spoken to someone else about our private life, that Steve would have listened and gone along with a plan that she suggested. Alison didn't even particularly like Steve – she had hated his birthday party, after all – and yet they had talked to each other behind my back.

We played a couple more games in near silence, both of us avoiding unnecessary talk. Steve seemed to be irritated, and that annoyed me, because he was the one trying to force his way into my private business. I had a right to keep things to myself if I wanted to – Alison didn't have an automatic right to know everything I did or said or thought, and if she didn't, then Steve certainly didn't either.

We stopped at four games and Steve sat down while I went to get the next round in. I hadn't yet been served when the door opened and a cool breeze rushed across the back of my neck. I turned my head, and saw that it was Alison coming into the pub, shaking rain off her umbrella. She saw me at the bar and came over.

I said, 'I thought you were at class all evening?'

'That's a fine way to greet me,' she said, and laughed. I forced a smile too. 'The tutor had baby-sitting problems so we finished early.'

I nodded. She was waiting expectantly, so I said, 'What do you want?'

'Half a lager, thanks,' she said, looking around for Steve.

'I'll bring them over,' I said, and she nodded and headed over to Steve, who was smiling at her. Planned, I thought, she left early deliberately just to find out what Steve had wormed out of me. They were chatting as soon as she had shrugged off her coat and sat down. Steve was shaking his head slightly, and then Alison glanced up and across at me and I turned my head away quickly.

But when I looked away, I saw that Jamie was in his usual corner with his usual crowd. I hadn't seen him come in, but he must have been watching me, because he raised his hand and started to come over. I looked back at Alison and Steve, but they were still talking. Part of me wanted to cut Jamie dead, to walk off and leave him, but I knew that he would only follow me over to the table, so I fixed a smile and ordered our drinks and waited for him to reach me.

His hair was wet with rain that hung in large drops on his dreadlocks. He ran a hand through it, as if he was conscious of how he looked, and said, 'Did you phone that copper?'

'No,' I said. 'There didn't seem to be much point. There's nothing I can tell them, I've told you that already.'

'But they want to talk to all of her friends, just to see if she said anything at all.'

I collected my change from the barman and glanced back at Alison and Steve. Alison was getting up from her seat to give me a hand with the drinks. I said, 'Look, I can't talk now. Give me your phone number and I'll give you a ring.'

He hesitated, but then fished around in the thigh pocket of his army-surplus trousers and produced a biro and yet another police business card. He leaned on the bar and started to write, slow cramped letters and numbers. Alison was saying something to Steve, laughing and pushing her chair out of the way to stand up fully.

'Please phone the police,' Jamie said.

Alison was starting to come over now. 'I keep telling you that I can't tell them anything new.'

'I don't mean anything,' Jamie said, as if I'd stung him. 'I just wanted Sophie to be okay. The police are getting worried now.'

'Okay, okay,' I said. 'I'll phone them.'

I took the card from him and shoved it in my pocket, and started to collect up the drinks.

'If you give me your number I can get them to call you,' Jamie said.

'No,' I said. 'It's okay, I'll do it.'

Alison was at my side now, smiling at Jamie. 'Need a hand?' she asked.

'I'm just coming,' I said, and passed her half of lager to her. She turned back towards Steve.

Jamie stopped me with his hand. 'Please do phone,' he said, and I nodded and carried the drinks back to our table.

When we had sat down, Alison said, 'Who was that?'

She seemed to be using a deliberately casual tone. I adopted the same tone and said, 'Oh, just some bloke I've seen in here a few times.'

'Who did he want you to call?'

The same casual tone. I glanced back across the bar, where Jamie had rejoined his group of friends. 'Nobody,' I said. 'It's nothing.'

'It didn't look like nothing.'

A frown was growing across her face. Steve had looked away. I felt the tension and knew I had to say something, so I said, 'A woman's gone missing, run away, and he thinks I might know something about it, but I don't. That's all.'

'She's still missing?' Steve said.

'What woman?' Alison asked, looking at Steve.

'It's nothing,' I said quickly. 'She's done a bunk, that's all. She used to get the same bus as me every morning.'

Alison's frown was growing.

'I don't really know her,' I said. 'It's just the police want to check—'

'The police?' It was both of them.

'It's just routine,' I said.

Alison said, 'Why do they think you can help?'

'They don't,' I said. 'That guy does, but I can't, I mean, we just caught the same bus, that's all.'

Alison sipped her drink as she digested my words. I looked at my pint, at the paler cloudiness settling through into the darker beer, but I suddenly wasn't thirsty. I wanted to turn the conversation away from this topic but I didn't know how to, and Jamie had said the police were getting concerned, and if they were concerned then could something have really happened to Sophie? Did they know something that I didn't? Were they scouring the countryside for her as we sat there talking?

Alison said, 'What would make a grown adult run away? That's the sort of thing a kid would do, not an adult.'

'Maybe she's not right in the head,' Steve said.

I wanted to object to that – I wanted to say that Sophie was perfectly rational, and was entitled to do whatever she thought she had to – but it would have caused more problems, so I kept quiet.

Steve said, 'Maybe she's in debt? People run away from bad debt all the time.'

'Who knows,' Alison said. 'Personally, I'd talk to someone, get help, I mean, nothing can be that bad, can it?'

I kept my head down, turning my glass round in my hand, not wanting to make eye contact with either of them. I found it hard to understand how they could have so little concern, so little empathy for Sophie and the predicament she was in. I felt that I was the only one with any real idea of what was going on – even Jamie seemed to be more concerned about where she was than why she had gone at all.

'Not everyone's like that,' Steve said, and then I found that they were both looking at me, and I wondered why, whether they could hear my thoughts somehow, whether I was that transparent.

'What?' I asked, but they just shook their heads, string puppets acting out the same emotions, the same responses. A perfect couple; they deserved each other. I looked back round at Jamie with his friends, and I remembered suddenly that Sophie had never liked the Arms, didn't much like Jamie's friends. Had she felt the same as I did now, sitting in this pub with tension like humidity in the air, feeling the tension with every molecule of her body, and Jamie having no idea what anything really meant?

I turned back to Alison and Steve. Sophie would have carried on, she wouldn't have let anyone know what was going on unless she wanted them to, she would have hidden it all so well that nobody would have been able to guess. It didn't really matter that Steve and Alison had been plotting behind my back, that Steve had betrayed our friendship by agreeing to Alison's plan. If anything, that just made my situation easier – at least now I knew where I stood, I knew how far I could trust both of them.

So I sat drinking my pint, pretending to laugh at Steve's jokes, pretending not to notice that Alison was laughing harder than was necessary, and that Steve was aiming his attentions her way. I felt a cruel coldness growing inside me as I watched them, but I drank my drink and gave my smiles and hoped that I could get through it all unscathed until I could lie in bed and surrender to sleep and dreaming.

I knew I had to play it cool or it would set Alison's antenna up and scanning. After we had said goodbye to Steve at the corner where our journeys home parted company, I kept her busy with questions about how her day had been. She was a little more reticent than usual; on most occasions, she would jump at the opportunity to be lyrical about her job, and management structures, and the complications faced by customers whose endowment policies didn't cover the mortgage at the end of the term, or the stupid things people said when they didn't really understand investments or how interest was worked out or what the tie-in clauses on their mortgage were.

When we got home, I went straight into the kitchen to put the kettle on for a late-night cup of tea, and she followed me in there with a time-to-talk expression.

She said, 'I want to know what's been going on.'

I was at the tap, filling the kettle, so she couldn't see my expression. I gave a little laugh and said, 'What do you mean? There's nothing going on.'

'I don't believe you.'

I turned the tap off and took the kettle back to the plug. 'But that's the truth,' I said. 'There's nothing else I can say.'

'There's something about this woman,' she said. 'Why didn't you tell me about her?'

'There's nothing to tell,' I said. 'I don't even know her.'

Alison leaned back against the work surface and folded her arms across her stomach, looking down at her feet.

I said, 'I don't have to tell you every little thing, do I?'

She recoiled slightly at my tone, and I regretted the way I had spoken. 'You don't seem to tell me anything any more,' she said. 'You never used to be this secretive.'

I shook my head, stepped towards her. 'I'm sorry,' I said. 'But there's nothing wrong, honestly. I've just been a bit distracted lately.'

I put out my arms, wanting to hold her, but she pulled away.

'Don't,' she said.

'Why not?'

She turned away. 'I never wanted to be in a relationship where the other person was lying to me.'

'I'm not lying,' I said. 'You can't think that, surely?'

She shrugged, still not turning back. 'If you don't want to touch me then you shouldn't pretend.'

'But nothing's changed,' I said. I couldn't understand what was happening – whatever I felt at the moment, we had always been in love – there was nobody else for either of us. And yet, as I stood there looking at her, as I summoned up the courage to convince her of this, there was a coldness creeping into me, as if I were looking at a stranger. When I looked at her, when I thought about love – when I thought about sex – all I seemed to think of was Sophie.

Alison was saying something, and I forced myself to concentrate. Her voice was uncertain, quavering slightly. She said, 'I can't stand not knowing. You always tell me everything. That's what we do – we share everything. It's got something to do with this woman, I know it has.'

I put my arms around her, wrapped her up tight. I said, 'It's got nothing to do with her. I've never even spoken to her. I don't know her at all, I just catch the same bus as her. Alison, I love you.' She jerked away at my words, but then she turned to face me, and I smiled at her and touched her lips with my lips. She didn't pull away. I kissed her harder. She responded, and I felt the closeness of her heartbeat and the swell of her chest as she breathed, and that she was here, that she loved me, that we were together and loved each other. In that moment it even seemed to be enough.

Chapter Fifteen

I did phone Jamie, the following day. Alison was out at some works' do, a birthday bash or someone leaving, I couldn't remember which. I cried off with paperwork; I told Alison that there was a big deadline coming up, but the truth was, the stack of papers on the Marston Street project had come back and I wanted to check that I hadn't made any other mistakes.

I read all the way through the papers, sitting at the dining-room table with a mug of tea by my side. It was a warm evening and I could see into the back garden where birds were hopping around in the long grass. Somewhere nearby, in another back garden, there were people sitting outside; the low sound of their voices and the occasional bursts of laughter carried over the walls and fences. I tried to work out where this social gathering was taking place, but the sounds bounced and echoed off the houses so it seemed that they were all around me, that I was the silent centre of their circle.

After a while, I pushed the papers aside and

listened to the voices, but I couldn't make out what was being said. The Marston Project seemed so unimportant when there was life going on all around me, when so many people were doing so many different things. I considered phoning Steve; it was just the night for a pint at the Golden Ball, sitting at the tables out front overlooking the golf course. But I didn't really want to talk to him, after the way he had betrayed me to Alison. There was a knot of anger inside me that tightened when I thought of how he had behaved.

So I phoned Jamie instead.

He sounded surprised to hear from me, but said immediately, 'Did you phone the police?'

I considered lying about that, but it didn't seem wise. 'No,' I said. 'Not yet. I wanted to talk to you first. Can I come round and see you?'

He hesitated, but his curiosity must have got the better of him and he said, 'Yeah, do,' and gave me the address.

After I had hung up, I sat for a while on the sofa, trying to calm the anticipation that was jumping through my nerves. The evening was gathering in around me. The neighbours must have gone indoors, or adjourned to a pub, because it was quiet now. I felt completely still, and when I closed my eyes I imagined that I could feel individual particles of air brushing against my skin.

I knew that the sensible thing to do would be to take Sophie's notebook to Jamie, explain that I didn't know her very well, step out of my involvement in

Sophie's life. It hadn't yet gone so far that it was out of my reach – like the Marston Street project, I had a chance to turn the situation around. But Jamie – before I handed the notebook over, I had to know whether Jamie had betrayed her, whether he had been the one making all those phone calls. Something was holding me back from handing it over to him – an instinct, perhaps. Even after I had put the notebook in my jacket pocket and gone to the front door to set off, I found I couldn't cross the threshold. I stood there with the front door open, looking out at the street, stood there with my hand in my pocket touching the notebook, until finally I told myself that I didn't have to end it all now. It depended on Jamie, on what he said when I talked to him, on whether he would say much to me at all.

Jamie lived about half a mile away, in the few narrow streets of terraces squeezed between the drive-thru McDonald's and the old textile factories and warehouses, now mostly closed. His street had houses on one side and the high walls of an old factory on the other side, the same dark red brick, windows behind wire mesh blocked up from the inside with cardboard. The windows of the houses were blocked, too, with heavy nets and curtains that were twenty years out of style, pulled across window-panes going black with exhaust fumes from the main roads running along either end of the street.

I pushed the notebook further into my pocket and took a deep breath as I reached Jamie's door. Old wood in regulation blue, and curtains shutting out the world like every other house. I knocked and waited.

He opened the door quickly and ushered me inside. The door opened directly into the front room, as I had known it would. A radio played pop hits further inside the house, but he had already shut the door leading into the rest of the house. The décor was cheap-rented; a dark brown velour sofa, a grey armchair that didn't match, posters blu-tacked to the faded beige wallpaper (*Pulp Fiction*, *The Usual Suspects*, *Trainspotting* – student stuff from five years earlier), an ugly metal fire under an uglier wooden mantelpiece.

Jamie stood in the centre of the room, his arms folded across his chest, as if he was daring me to speak first. I headed for the armchair against the back wall and, as I sat down, said, 'So, is there any news?'

'No,' he said, turning to face me. Then he unfolded his arms and perched himself on the edge of the sofa. 'I was hoping you had something to tell me.'

The notebook was pressing itself against my thigh in my pocket. I ignored it and said, 'No, I haven't heard from her since the day she went missing. Have the police come up with anything?'

He shrugged. 'They say she must have run away. She's on CCTV at the railway station.'

I was relieved by that. The only clue I could have offered and they knew about it already. If I wanted to walk away, I could. Now was the time.

I said, 'Where was she going?'

'They didn't tell me,' he said, but I had the feeling he was lying about that.

'So, the police aren't going to enquire too much more, then?' I asked.

He had slumped right down in the sofa, but looked at me. 'Sounds like you don't want them to,' he said. 'Why is that?'

'That's not it at all,' I said.

He sat forward. 'Who are you? Sophie never mentioned you to me.'

'She told me a lot about you,' I said.

'So what do you think has happened to her, then?'

There was a sullen sort of challenge in his voice. I said, 'If she's run away then maybe we should leave her. Maybe she doesn't want to be found.'

'But I worry about her.'

'I know you do.'

He started picking at the skin around his fingernails. 'She might do something daft.'

'She might be happier,' I said.

I had noticed some photographs in cheap frames on the mantelpiece, and now I got up and went over to have a look. Some were lad shots – drunken late-night poses, four lads in T-shirts and combat pants draped across each other on the sofa, beer cans and full ashtrays in evidence on the floor. A couple were lad shots with Sophie in the centre, laughing as she looked up at the camera, in the middle of playing at pushing the lads away.

I said, 'You've known Sophie a long time?'

'We went to school together.'

I picked up one of the shots including Sophie. Her top had ridden up slightly as she had twisted, and one hand was tugging it down again even as she laughed. 'You like her a lot,' I said.

He came over to where I was, took the picture from me and put it back on the mantelpiece. 'She's my friend,' he said.

'But you wanted more?'

He was close up to me now, and I could see right into his dark eyes. His breath was slightly sour, his skin shiny, slightly blotched around his nose. 'She isn't interested that way,' he said, and then added, 'What's it to you?'

There was resentment in his voice, and I wondered what kind of friendship could have made him so resentful. 'I was just wondering why she ran away,' I said mildly.

'You know nothing about it,' he said.

He hadn't moved, and I could hear his breathing, feel the warmth of his body, but I felt that I couldn't move either, I couldn't step back for space. I said, 'Maybe she had a reason to leave.'

'What are you suggesting?'

'You know what I'm suggesting,' I said. 'She told me about the phone calls she was getting.'

If he was surprised that I knew, he didn't show it. 'Those stopped weeks before she went,' he said.

'No they didn't.' I had the sudden urge to pull the notebook out of my pocket and show him the evidence, Sophie's own words, but I resisted the temptation.

'She told me they did,' he said.

I opened out my hands in a kind of shrug.

'You're saying they had something to do with it?'

I had to laugh at that. 'How could they not? Maybe they drove her over the edge?' He was flustered by that, I could see it. I pushed on. 'Do you feel guilty about that?' I asked, and he almost jerked at the words.

'Are you trying to say that it was me?'

I shrugged again.

He didn't say anything for a moment, looking into my face, but I didn't flinch away from his gaze. Then he said, 'Get out.' He strode across the room, towards the front door, then turned to face me. 'You didn't come here to help,' he said, and his hand went to the lock and he started to turn the mechanism.

'I just want to find out what happened,' I said, not moving.

'Why? You hardly know her. She never mentioned you.' His hand dropped away from the lock. 'Who are you, anyway? What's your connection?'

I could feel myself growing angry now. I said, 'You think you know everything about Sophie? You think she told you everything?' I could feel the notebook in my pocket, and my confidence grew. 'She told me about you,' I said. 'About what happened after you went to look at that house together.'

His eyes widened. 'She didn't—'

'She told me she doesn't feel that way about you.'

'So what? She knew, I knew, what does it matter?'

'So maybe you think she left because of you?

Maybe she left because she couldn't handle being around you, so she went to find someone she could be around.'

'That's rubbish,' he said, almost shouting.

'She couldn't handle the phone calls.'

'That wasn't me,' he said, and ran a hand through his hair, and looked at me again. 'Jesus, that was probably you, wasn't it? That's how you know all this stuff. It was you all along.'

I laughed at that. 'Don't be ridiculous,' I said. But it was strange, I almost believed that he hadn't made the phone calls, that he wasn't the one behind all of this. And if that was true, then who could it have been?

Jamie came towards me again, but stopped further away than he had been. 'You know where she is,' he said.

If Jamie hadn't made the phone calls, then there was someone else in the game, another player to watch, and I didn't even know who it was. My head was spinning with all the thoughts running through my brain.

'If you were a real friend you'd know yourself,' I said. 'You wouldn't need me to tell you.'

'So where is she?' he demanded.

The heat of my anger was passing. I looked back at the photograph, at the shine in her eyes and the laughter, her head thrown back with the laughter, and that hand, pulling down at her top.

Jamie had come closer. 'So, where is she?' he repeated.

I turned to him. 'I don't know,' I said. 'Really, I don't. I wouldn't be here if I did.'

He said, 'So tell me what you do know.'

'Nothing,' I said. 'Just what I've told you, nothing more.' He seemed to be struggling for what to say next, so I said quickly, 'I've got to go.'

I stumbled my way to the door and struggled with the lock, and then I was back out in the street again. Jamie called after me, trying to persuade me to stay, but I walked quickly, hoping he wouldn't follow. I knew I had messed up; I had got myself more deeply involved in whatever was going on, I hadn't managed to pull free at all. But despite that, I felt oddly pleased with myself. I had told Jamie the truth, I had demanded to know what was happening, and although I realised I had been wrong about Jamie making the phone calls, I felt that I was getting closer to something. As I walked, the notebook pressed against my hip, and I put my hand in my pocket and touched the smooth cardboard cover, and I realised that if I could find out for sure who was behind the phone calls, if I could fit that final piece in the puzzle, then the whole picture would suddenly come clear.

13 May

Mum's birthday. I usually end up enjoying our family get-togethers, but Mum's birthday always has the nightmare that me and Jonathan do all the work so that Mum can talk to her guests. It's kind of a family tradition, the only way we can make Mum be the star of the show instead of the caterer. It's not that I mind doing the work – I actually like seeing everyone enjoy the food, and getting praise for it, too – it's having to work with Jonathan, who's usually mardy about something.

And, of course, he'd had a row with Rachel. Rachel was covering it up, all sweetness and light in the front room with Mum, and that meant that I got it in the neck from Jonathan, starting in the car on the way back from Asda. He's such a tight-wad, I swear, going on at me like I'd done something wrong just because I wouldn't get the cheapest of everything. I told him sometimes you have to pay for the quality, but he went on like I was blowing a lottery jackpot in one go.

So he huffed and puffed, and when we got out of the car park and onto the slip-road, he tried to put the car into gear but he was in such a mood that he missed, and the gearbox crunched, and now they've started the tram roadworks it's a nightmare getting anywhere. They've blocked off half the road, and the traffic was backed up all the way along, and he just sat there fuming and struggling to get the gear, while all the cars queued up past us and no bogger would let us out. Finally, we did manage to get onto Radford Road, and crawled along up past the police station, and Jonathan was still fuming, I mean if it had been a cartoon there would have been steam coming out of his ears.

Then he said, 'All I'm saying is you have no responsibility, Sophie. You never have had.'

'Why? Because I spent a few quid more than you wanted to? Get a life, Jonathan.'

He was staring at the road and gripping the wheel like this was some kind of white-knuckle ride, refusing even to glance at me. I started to rifle through his tape collection, and he tutted away, and I put Travis in the tape player and turned the volume up a little.

It was a hot day and all the windows were wound down to allow some sort of air to circulate, though hardly anything was stirring and the air was thick with exhaust fumes and the heat rising from all the other cars. He reached over and turned the music down, so I could hardly hear it over the sound of the engines.

'I wanted to hear that,' I said.

'Well, I need to concentrate.'

'We're not even moving,' I said. 'It's hardly a Grand Prix circuit, is it?'

He still wasn't looking at me, but I could see a frown even from where I was sitting. He said, 'You're just so bloody selfish, Sophie.'

'No I'm not,' I said. But I didn't turn the music up again. When it was obvious that he wasn't going to say anything more, I said, 'What makes you say that now?'

171

'You just are. You always have been.'

He really pisses me off when he makes statements like that. I said, 'I suppose you've always been Mummy's thoughtful little angel, eh?'

'Piss off. You know what I'm talking about.'

'Yes I do, and I don't want to have it thrown back in my face all the time.'

He did look at me then, his face flushed red. 'It's okay for you, isn't it? You weren't here for Mum's birthday four years ago, all the worry you put them through, and Mum crying her eyes out because you never rang.'

'I know,' I said. 'I know it was wrong. Don't you think I know that?' He didn't say anything more, nudging the car through the gap between parked cars and the barriers around the roadworks. I said, 'I don't know how long I have to keep saying sorry.'

'Sorry doesn't make it all better, you know. You have to work at it.'

'Yeah? And what the hell do you think I've been doing for the last four years? Sitting around on my arse? I've done everything I can to make it better. I've spent the last four years trying to prove what a good little girl I am. What else am I supposed to do?'

He didn't reply.

I said, 'No, Jonathan, I want to hear your answer. I don't know how you've got the face to blame me. You're the only one who won't let me put this behind me and get on with my life.'

There were temporary traffic lights at the mini roundabout and as we pulled to a stop Jonathan put on the handbrake with a vigorous tug and turned to face me. 'You might think that all that stuff can be forgotten, but you weren't here when Mum and Dad were worried sick, and the police were round, and they were phoning everyone they thought might know where you were. They thought something had happened to you, Sophie. You should have heard Mum. She was so sure that you would have phoned, she thought you were lying dead somewhere. When you didn't phone on her birthday, it was like they gave up hope. They thought you were dead, for Christ's sake. How could you do that to them?'

I couldn't look at him. I stared ahead, out at the men in their neon vests digging through the tarmac with their drills. A JCB shovelled the dirt into an open-topped truck. I wanted to shout at Jonathan, shout that he couldn't put all the blame on me, he had to shoulder some of the responsibility himself. Instead, I said, 'You know as well as I do what the situation was.'

'Yeah, right,' he said.

I said, 'You can cover it up as long as you want, Jonathan. You can say what you like. At least I don't pretend nothing happened.'

'Huh,' he said, bitter, straight from his throat. The lights had changed and he put his foot on the accelerator and made the engine roar. The woman driving the car in front turned and glared at us before she drove off.

I said, 'Don't you think I wish it never happened?'

The road ahead of us was now almost empty of

traffic and he sped up as we went past the old Shippo's brewery. After a moment, he eased his foot off the pedal and said, 'See, that's your trouble. You talk like it was a disease or something, totally out of your hands, and that's just bullshit. You're just a selfish little cow who never thinks about other people's feelings.'

'What, like yours, you mean?'

He didn't reply to that.

I said, 'Yeah, because you're mister innocent, mister considerate. You never do anything wrong. Don't come the high and mighty with me, Jonathan, we both know it isn't true.'

'You should watch what you say,' he said, and I knew he was furious, and I was a little scared by that. But he didn't say any more, and we drove on in silence. We turned over the railway line and headed out along Western Boulevard towards the house. He was driving way too fast, idiot speed.

I said, 'I don't really care what you think. I've tried to put things right. You're the one who won't let things lie. You like bringing it up to remind everyone that you're the blue-eyed boy who never causes trouble, but that's not true, is it?' He didn't reply, so I added, 'God, you're pathetic.'

We had turned onto the next road and he accelerated again. He was still going too fast when we reached the turning into Mum and Dad's road, and the wheels slipped and skidded a little as we turned. I didn't say a word, and then we were in the house, and hugging Mum, and Rachel was helping to unload shopping from the car.

When they had carried most of the shopping in, and Jonathan and I were fetching the last bags, I said, 'We should try to get along, so Mum doesn't notice.'

'Sure,' he said, with a grim sort of smile. 'I don't want to ruin Mum's birthday.'

I would have loved to have come back at him over that one, but I let it ride. Rachel helped us with all the preparation, and with shooing Mum out whenever she tried to invade the kitchen, but if Rachel noticed any atmosphere between me and Jonathan she didn't say anything. Maybe the atmosphere between those two was so bad that she didn't notice any change.

At any rate, we got all the food prepared, and by the time my uncles and aunts arrived and the youngest cousins were running around the house showing off like mad and playing fire engines, I was ready to relax with a drink. And we had a nice sort of afternoon, perched on the armchairs with plates of food on our laps, watching Dad and the uncles getting pissed, and the aunts all talking like they hadn't seen each other for decades, and Mum sitting in the middle of it all with a Cheshire cat grin across her face.

Afterwards, Aunty Carol offered to watch the kids and we all headed up to the Coach and Horses for a drink – all the women on gin and tonic except me, scandalising them all as usual with a pint of bitter. The usual jokes about it putting hairs on my chest, and then the usual challenge for everyone to play pool. I wasn't in the mood for pool, so I sat with Mum and Rachel and watched the action from a distance.

Mum was going on in a slightly drunken manner

about how much she was enjoying the day, and Rachel and I just smiled and let her rabbit. I don't get to see much of Rachel these days, what with Jonathan being such a pig at times, so when Mum wandered off to the loos I wanted to talk to her. But I didn't really know where to begin, so I sipped my pint and smiled shyly, and then finally took the plunge and asked whether things were okay between her and Jonathan.

She forced a smile, then said, 'Oh, well, you know what Jonathan can be like.'

I was almost tempted to say, yeah, obnoxious, brutish, nasty, full of himself, spiteful, arrogant. But I didn't.

She said, 'I don't know, it just seems like his thoughts are somewhere else all the time. He's out drinking most nights. I never know when I'm going to see him.' Then she looked at me, almost as if I could resolve everything for her, save her relationship. 'Do you know what's going on? I know you two are close.'

'Not really,' I said. 'We're not that close any more.'

'Why not?' she asked. Big blue eyes looking at me, like I could tell her. The best kept secret in Nottingham.

I said, 'Oh, you know, I'm not that interested in cars.' She smiled at that, so I pressed on. 'Have you tried talking to him?'

'Of course I have,' she said. 'He won't listen to me. Says I'm talking nonsense. But it's not normal, is it? I mean, he's drunk nearly every night, and when he isn't drunk he's just driving around in his car till one or two in the morning. He's not right in the head, I'm sure. It's like he's not with me, even when he is. His mind's always somewhere else, but he swears there's nothing going on.' She frowned, and glanced across at the pool players then leaned in towards me. 'You don't think he's seeing someone else, do you?'

'No,' I said. 'Of course not.'

I think I managed to convince her that he might be a pig, but he was at least a faithful pig. He had got her into a right old state, and I had the feeling that there was more going on than she would tell me. But before I could push for any more details, Mum was back, and Dad was bringing more drinks over to our table.

Mum was wearing a new blouse that Dad had given her, and when he had gone back to the game of pool she laughed and told us that she'd pointed it out to him in the Victoria Centre last time they'd been in there. 'That's a tip for you,' she said. 'Never let a man buy you clothes unless you've told him exactly which thing you want. One year I didn't do that and I ended up with some foul polyester thing, disgusting, had to take it back and change it for something else.'

We all laughed, and I said, 'When was that? I don't remember that.' But the moment I'd said it, I knew why I didn't remember that. Mum must have seen from my expression that I'd twigged which birthday she was talking about – even Rachel seemed to know, because she stopped smiling and looked away.

I could have kicked myself. The whole day had gone by without any reminding little digs at me, and I'd hoped maybe it was finally being forgotten, but then I had to open my big gob and drop myself right in it.

Mum looked at me for a moment, long enough to tell me that I'd been thoughtless again, bringing back unhappy memories, and then she turned to Rachel and said, 'So, how are the plans for the house coming along?'

Rachel told her some bold lies about how there was a delay in sorting out her and Jonathan's mortgage, and Mum just nodded her head and swallowed it whole. Jonathan must have primed Rachel well on what to say to get round Mum. It made me mad, to think that once again Jonathan would come out in a good light when behind it all he was no more perfect than I was, and in many ways was worse than me.

So Mum turned to me and said, 'That's all we want for you, that you settle down happily.'

I forced a laugh and said, 'You mean with a husband and kids and a house and a job?'

'Why not? Is that so terrible? I mean, you've got a job, and you'll have a house soon, if you ever find one you like. There's a next logical step after all that.'

I felt this sense of rising panic, as if my whole life was being planned out for me just like that. I said, 'But what if I don't want that?'

'Why wouldn't you want that?' Mum asked, and I looked at her face and I thought about all the trouble I had caused her over the years. Rachel was frowning at me, communicating that I should just keep Mum happy, say what she wanted to hear, so I laughed it all off and said yes, of course, that would come sometime, when I met the right man, when I was ready for it.

But I felt like such a liar, and it didn't help that

Rachel and Jonathan were lying too. I mean, it suddenly seemed like the only communication between the generations came about through lies. Is that normal? Is that how every other family survives? They might all think that Jonathan is so much more responsible than me, but they're wrong, he's just a better liar, better at coping than I am. And all of that makes me sad, because I don't want to lie to anyone, but maybe that's the only way we get to live the way we want to?

Chapter Sixteen

They had changed the bus routes now that the tram construction work had started in earnest. Most of my regulars switched to an earlier bus and I was surrounded by strangers every morning. It had crept up on me; I had barely noticed the gradual drop away in my regulars until I realised one day that most of them had gone. But I didn't mind, I wasn't even tempted to switch with them, in case one morning Sophie reappeared at the bus stop and I had the chance to really get to know her.

It was four weeks to the day since she disappeared. Four weeks that stretched back through my memory as something much longer, much greater. Four weeks and no word from her to anyone.

I went to my desk every morning in the same way, past the Tram Taskforce office, and usually the door was closed, but this time I looked in through the open door and saw them all standing around with mugs of coffee, papers and rolled-up plans and books and leaflets stacked on the table in the centre of the room. It was exciting, to be so close to the plans, the schemes, the route-maps and flow-charts on the walls; the energy of real change, of real developments taking place. I hesitated there, looking in, but one of the planners glanced across at me, so I smiled and nodded and walked on to my desk.

My department was busy too, of course, with all the competing plans for city centre leisure complexes and all the developments in the Lace Market and along the canalside. Anthony was deeply embroiled in the row over relief road compulsory purchases. I kept my head down; after the Marston Street fiasco, I was relieved to be left to checking facts and figures on the backlog of domestic planning applications.

I was trying to make sense of some architects' plans for a warehouse conversion to flats when Malcolm called me into his office. It wasn't much of an office for someone of his status, most people agreed with that; a cubbyhole lined with shelves of box files on which were glued peeling yellow labels, things like 'Meadows Clearance' and 'Hyson Green Redevelopment', all the old schemes from when he had started, when city planning really did shape the city. Malcolm, crumpling now into the gentle obesity of late middle-age, was apt to refer back to those days with the kind of fondness I could not envisage ever feeling for my own work.

Malcolm saw where I was looking and said, 'It's quite something to think back to all the changes I've seen.'

'It must be,' I said.

'You'll think the same in twenty years, looking back on now,' he said.

I inclined my head slightly and smiled, but I was thinking that all I would be able to say was that I saw it happen. Malcolm was in there when it counted.

Malcolm looked up at the files again. 'Yes, those were exciting times all right.'

'Quite a role to have,' I said, 'shaping the city.'

He raised his eyebrows. 'Never pictured you as a glory-seeker, Pete.'

I shrugged. 'There's more to this job than checking application forms.'

'There should be,' he said, looking at me with an expression I couldn't interpret. 'There used to be, anyway. It's all private finance now, all the big schemes, anyway. No, we've seen the last of the great city planners. Those days won't come back again.'

I shrugged again and looked away, not wanting to acknowledge that I was thirty years too late to do the things I'd been trained to do.

Malcolm sank back in his chair, twirling a biro around his fingers. 'I wanted to check how you're going on the backlog of applications.'

'Fine,' I said. 'Most are pretty straightforward. A fair few conversions from commercial for student housing – do we know how we stand on the Housing Act?'

'Legal are still working on it.'

He wasn't really interested, I could see that. But we chatted briefly about whether the Council would be brave enough to challenge the Barnes versus Sheffield City Council precedent, and the glut of applications from developers cashing in on the trend for city-centre living, and the rumours that the canalside redevelopments were even attracting London commuters now Midland Mainline had improved the service.

Finally, Malcolm got round to saying what he meant. 'Some people have commented that your work doesn't seem quite as – well, as careful as in the past.'

'Yes, I know, I can only apologise. The Marston Street thing – I know, I should have picked up on the—'

'Mistakes happen,' he said, waving that aside. 'It was salvageable. I just wanted to be sure that things weren't – that you aren't getting snowed under while your section is short-staffed. I know you're down two POs. Personnel assure me the posts are being pink-formed as we speak.'

I said quickly, 'Everything's fine, honestly. I have been tired lately, the tail-end of a bug probably, but there's nothing to worry about.'

Malcolm looked relieved. 'Good,' he said. 'The problems we've got with sickness.' Then he smiled and said briskly, 'Anyway, that leads me onto something I wanted to talk to you about. As you know, Anthony has been seconded onto the Tram Taskforce for the six months of the initial works. He's clearing his workload now to make way for the secondment.'

'That's right,' I said, feeling myself growing green with the thought.

'Obviously, while he's away we need someone to cover his responsibilities here. You've got your Diploma so you're the obvious candidate. How would you feel about being seconded as SPO for six months, see how you like it?'

'That would be fine,' I said, feeling a rush of excitement.

Malcolm smiled. 'I'll have to clear it with Personnel, of course, but I'll get back to you as soon as I hear anything, okay?'

'Sure,' I said. 'Thanks a lot, Malcolm.'

Then I was back in the corridor, feeling the impact of the news as I found my way back to my desk. I was due this; it was mine by rights, and finally it had happened. I sat at my desk, looking at the pile of work on it, and the folders I should be opening, and the new mail stacked in my in-tray. Then I imagined myself as SPO, going out on site visits, attending meetings, talking to architects and developers, being asked for my views.

After all the work I had put in, Alison would be pleased. I picked up the phone and started to punch her number into the keypad, but then I stopped and hung up again. Alison had been going on about SPO posts more than I had – and sure, the extra money would be nice, but that was hardly the central issue. I could imagine pound signs in her eyes, insisting we booked a holiday, somewhere foreign and hot, planning how to spend the money when I was the one who had to worry about actually doing the job.

I sat looking at the phone, and then I turned and

looked around the office, at all the women behind me who were chatting quietly as they worked. I felt that I should tell them what Malcolm had said, but I didn't know how to begin. Clear my throat and make an announcement? Cross the office to tell them as a group? Pick them off individually, casually, in the kitchenette while waiting for the kettle to boil?

I turned back and looked at my desk, at the piles of paperwork and the files stacked against the wall, at my computer screen where a blank report template looked back at me. I realised that I was sweating, although it was not a hot day. Because what would happen if I couldn't do the job? This was my chance, but what if I blew it? I could imagine sitting in a meeting, being asked what my opinion was, all those faces looking at me, Malcolm waiting to hear what I would say, the Councillors fixing their eyes on me, expecting an expert view, the secretary with her pen poised over the minute book.

This was my one chance, and I could feel myself starting to shake. I looked at my hand, held it out flat, palm down, and watched the vibrations running along my fingers. The Marston Street mistake was not a one-off, I knew that. I just wasn't capable of taking on that sort of role, that sort of responsibility.

I got up shakily, went along the corridor and down the stairs, out past reception, out to the wooden bench where the smokers usually congregated. I sat down on the bench and tried to draw in breath, tried to draw the cool air down into my lungs. Who was I kidding, even thinking about it?

The sensible thing to do would be to go back inside, knock on Malcolm's door, tell him I had reconsidered. I imagined myself standing there, trying to explain. I could tell him that I didn't feel ready yet, that I needed another year, maybe two, as PO. I could tell him that the office couldn't cope without me, we were two POs down already and the backlog was piling up.

But I knew he wouldn't buy that. He would see straight through that. He would see right through to the truth, that I was never going to be ready. And then I would be stuck as a PO for the rest of my life, stuck in the same corner of the same office, doing the same dreary tasks day after day, watching everyone else get their advancements, watching Anthony rise through the grades to take Malcolm's job when he retired.

My breath seemed to be constricted in my chest. I leaned forwards, elbows on knees, blew and sucked air in and out of my lungs. I felt trapped, hemmed in from all sides. What would Alison say if she knew? What would Steve say? And how would Sophie react if I told her?

But Sophie at least would understand. Alison would criticise, would tell me I was being stupid; Steve would shake his head in incredulity; they would be on the phone to one another, cooking up schemes to get me to take the job. But Sophie wouldn't do that. Sophie would never hang around and let herself become trapped – she would do something about it, she would break free of it somehow.

And I shouldn't feel trapped. When I returned to my desk and started going through the motions of registering applications on the database, I realised that there was no need to feel tied to this place, this office, this job. I was never going to make a difference, never going to change anything. I was just a small cog in a big machine, so who would miss me if I wasn't even there?

On the bus on the way home, I closed my eyes and tried to calm the thoughts that ran through my head. I had been happy – I could remember being happy. There had been Alison, the house, my job, the chance of SPO. There had been no reason to think – but I felt as if my eyes had been opened for the first time. And it was Sophie who had opened them for me – her voice, her words, the passion she must have felt to get up and leave, just like that, without a word to anyone.

It was hot on the bus, airless. I watched the streets pass me by, all the lives that crowded together in those streets. From the top deck, I was level with the first-floor windows of the flats in converted houses and above the shops and takeaways that lined the roads out through the inner city. Most of the windows had heavy nets or curtains or blinds preventing people from seeing in, but occasionally I caught a glimpse of white walls and sofas covered in throws and plants in pots on the windowsills. It was like a glimpse into other worlds, a view of other people's secret lives, and I was surprised that I had never really paid any attention before, I had never really looked beyond the bricks, through the glass, at the lives that lay beyond.

I felt a burst of energy, of enthusiasm, as I got off the bus. I stood there at the side of the road, looking up at Sophie's windows, thinking of all the times I had looked at those windows but never actually seen inside. There was the opening to the passage at the side of the hairdressers' just in front of me, and there was nobody around, nobody to see. My pulse grew faster; I could feel my heart pumping against my chest; it was difficult to breathe as I walked down the dark, narrow passage. Then I was in the back yard, the sun-glared concrete yard with its disintegrating sofa, stacks of old bricks, the remains of an outhouse with the wooden door hanging at an angle.

I pulled up the flap on Sophie's letterbox, put my fingers through the brushes of the draught excluder, felt along the other side, but there was no key on a string. I ran my fingers along the ledge above the doorframe but there was nothing but black grime, the crackling torso of dried-out flies, the broken skeletons of leaves. I turned around and faced the glare of the concrete yard, and I closed my eyes, feeling dizzy, feeling myself sway against all of that reflected light.

I tried to sink myself back into the words that Sophie had said to me. I knew them; I had read them over and over. I could sink myself back into that voice, as if I was shrinking down inside my mind, inside the centre of my brain, and letting Sophie's words flood in to fill the void. I felt the heat of the sun on my face and I opened out my hands palm-up to take more of that heat. When I opened my eyes again the colours had dissolved into bluish light, and I was walking in a violet haze. I was certain that there would be a spare key somewhere – I could feel it, as if Sophie had left one there deliberately for me to find.

I thought of what Alison or Steve would do if they could see me now, and I almost laughed out loud. I thought of Malcolm in his office, thinking up ways to take the job offer back, and Anthony rubbing his hands with glee, and how shocked Jamie would be if he only knew the truth, and how shocked everyone would be if they had any idea at all what was running through my head. Peter the rock, cracking at last, high on words, high on a voice, tripping on the discovery of the key to Sophie's flat.

And there it was, in my hand. I had found the hiding place in the old outhouse, tucked into a ledge, just as I knew I would, just as Sophie must have intended. She wanted me to help her. It was a message, that I was right to keep looking for her, that she wanted me to find out what had happened to her, and all I had to do was open that door and step inside.

I didn't want to alert anyone in the hairdressers' shop, so I put the key in the lock and turned it slowly. The lock clicked but the door opened without a sound. I stepped inside and closed it behind me. The air in the flat was cooler than outside, but I could barely breathe, the coolness sending a chill across my skin. I was in a small entranceway; steep stairs led up to the flat, covered in an old grey carpet peeling away from the grips in places. There was a small pile of mail stacked on the bottom stair; I moved to it and looked through, a mixture of white and brown envelopes, all bills. I looked up at the top of the stairs, high above me, then I slipped my shoes off and left them with my briefcase next to the pile of mail, and started to creep up the stairs.

I placed my feet carefully, edging up to avoid any creaking. I could hardly breathe; the air seemed to be thick with dust, as if the place had been abandoned long ago. At the top of the stairs, there was a landing with two doors leading off and more stairs going up. I stood listening for a moment, then opened the first door. A small kitchen, old white units against one wall, a window looking down into the yard. There was a cereal bowl in the sink, filled with water, filmy with old milk. The tap dripped slowly into it, each drop sending ripples outwards across the surface, the sound counting out my heartbeats into the empty flat.

I went onto the landing again and opened the other door. The living room. The curtains were open and light shone through the nets, playing with the dust in the air. White walls, a nasty red plastic sofa half-covered by an ethnic throw, an armchair that was cousin to the sofa in the yard, a small coffee table strewn with letters and papers. My socked feet felt the ridges of the cord carpet as I crossed carefully to the far wall, to the mantelpiece above the gas fire. There was a photograph in a fake-tortoiseshell frame, a family portrait in front of a grey farmhouse.

I took the photograph back over to the sofa and sat down. Sat where Sophie might have sat, looking more closely at the photo. She was smiling, her mouth slightly open as if she had just finished speaking, her mother and father looking at her, a tall blond man who had to be Jonathan standing a little behind her. He was frowning into the camera, his eyes darkened by shadow.

I turned the frame over and unclipped it. The thing fell apart as soon as I had; I cradled it in my hands and placed it down on the table. I took the photograph out and looked at it again, then turned it over. It was dated a little over five years ago, in Sophie's handwriting, and underneath the date she had written the place. Arbor Low Farm. I put the picture into my jacket pocket, with her notebook, where it would be safe.

I went over to the bookcase by the window. Her telephone and answering machine were on top, and I touched the telephone receiver and tried to imagine her in this room, listening to its ring, standing over it, not daring to pick it up to hear silence on the other end. Then I pressed the eject button on the answering machine, but there was no tape inside.

I ran my fingers along the spines of the books on the bookcase. Cheap novels, a dictionary, a collection of nursing handbooks. It surprised me that she had kept those after giving up on the course. I pulled

one out at random and flicked through the pages.
Instructions with line drawings, how to take blood
samples, stitch cuts, dress wounds. I put the book
back and returned to the sofa.

There were papers, letters, bank statements strewn
at all angles on the coffee table, as if they had been
emptied straight out of a drawer. I started to sort
through them, to tidy them into piles. Details of
houses with estate agents' photographs, a rent book
for the flat showing a week left until the rent was
due again, her passport with a younger face frowning
at me from the photograph page. Her parents were
listed as next of kin in the back – I sat there for a
while before taking her notebook from my pocket
and copying the contact details into the back.

Upstairs was a small bathroom, the bath edged
with shampoos and cleansing gels and scented crys-
tals, a plastic shower nozzle wrapped around the
taps. Sophie's toothbrush was still in a plastic cup
on the basin, a purple brush with the bristles bent
down on one side.

I pushed open the bedroom door and went in
slowly. The curtains were still drawn but the light
came through them, a blue light that washed over the
unmade double bed, the bottom sheet pulled away
from the mattress in some disturbed dream. I opened
her wardrobe and stood looking at the clothes, the
spare workshirts, the blouses and sweaters, the jeans
folded over the bottom rungs of the coat-hangers.
I put out my hand and touched the soft cloth of a
well-worn sweatshirt, and it was as if she was still in

the room, and when I put my face into the cloth the smell of soap powder and her warm body filled my nostrils.

I climbed into her bed and pulled the duvet over me, and I could smell her scent on the sheets and the pillowcase. I lay my head down and closed my eyes and imagined her warmth there beside me. I could almost feel her presence, her shape indenting the mattress, drawing me closer to her body.

And she had wanted me to be this close to her. Why else would she have left a key for me? Why else would she have left her notebook with me? She wanted my proximity, she wanted me to break down the loneliness she felt.

And if only she had been there – if only I could reach out my hand to touch her, run my fingers across her face, between the strands of her hair – if our bodies pressed together, if her arms encircled me. I could feel her touch, her hands travelling over my body, pushing in under my clothes, undoing my clothes, until my skin was hot against the cool sheets. I felt that all I had to do was to succumb, to allow her to manipulate me, to melt into her caresses. In that moment, I felt that there was nothing that could separate us, and my breath caught in my throat even as I told her how much I wanted her.

My hands shook as I fumbled to get dressed again. I felt slightly sick, but I didn't want to move from under the warm covers. It was very light in the room and I could hear traffic in the street and people talking as they walked along the pavements. I turned onto my side and lay looking up at the ceiling that she must have stared at, night after night. I could imagine lying there, listening to the phone ringing downstairs, listening to the rings and thinking about the person who was calling.

On her bedside table there was half a packet of cigarettes, Marlboro Lights, the gold and white box crumpled at the corners. I opened the box and took out a cigarette, feeling the strangeness of its shape between my fingers and then between my lips. I lit it with her disposable lighter. The first intake was dusty, dry, clogged my mouth with the brown taste, tickled in my throat and lungs. The paper crackled and burned deep orange as I drew the smoke in.

I took the photograph and the notebook from my jacket pocket and lay there smoking and looking at them. I felt warm, cocooned in the bed. I had been resisting reading the final entry, not wanting her words to stop, but now, here, in this bed, it seemed like the right time. I had so much more than just her notebook now. So I opened it at the last entry and listened to the calm air and the hush of the cars passing by, and I started to read.

17 May

There are days that start with the dread that it's all going to be too much. A day that will eat right into me, right through me. Sitting on the bus going to work, and all I think of are rocks and hard places, frying pans and fire. Everyone wants a piece of me, everyone is a suspect for something.

I'm already late for work, and that means Marion will call me into her office again, and somewhere someone will notice and grin, loving it, because they're trying to use me to leapfrog past us all. I'll know who it is when they're made up to Team Leader, Head Snitch, brown-nose to the bosses, the double agent for upstairs. I'll know who it is and despise them, just like they obviously despise me. And I'll have to stop myself from collaring them outside, if my job means anything to me at all.

I can see exactly what today's going to be like. It won't matter that I want to keep my head down, that I want to plough through the work so the day goes quicker; I can feel a migraine growing in the centre of my brain, and the headpiece is going to hurt my ears, and every call will drill in through my skull and my ear drums and feed the migraine until it spreads. And every bit of static on the line will sound like someone breathing quietly, and that will make my heart jump out of my chest until they speak, a billing enquiry or a direct debit question or a desperate plea for more time to pay, no, don't cut us off, I've got three young kids, the cheque's in the post, I can pay in cash on Friday, the cheque won't bounce this time, the bank screwed up and I don't know what to do. A million excuses, and most of them feasible, believable, maybe even true.

I want to talk to Jamie, but every time I phone him his housemates answer instead; he's at a band rehearsal, he's doing a stocktake at work, he's visiting his mother, he's nowhere to be seen. Maybe they're telling the truth, maybe he has always been this busy and I never noticed, or maybe he's standing next to the person as they speak, shaking his head and cutting the air with his hands, telling them to lie to me. I always thought I could say anything to a real friend, they'd absorb it, take it, understand it, but there has to be a limit and maybe I crossed it before I even knew I'd reached it. He probably tried to tell me, but I didn't listen.

I want to tell him that I know it wasn't him making the phone calls. I want to say sorry for ever thinking that it was. I think I owe him that much.

I want to tell him that I'm tired of it all, I need to wipe it all clean, draw a line under it, start again.

Sometimes, I wish I could have a head injury. Nothing too bad, no paralysis, no loss of cognitive powers. A simple bump on the head that would put me out cold and wipe all my memories. Overwrite the files, de-frag and clean up the hard drive. Then they could power me up again and I'd be good as new, no stalling, no crashes, no system errors.

But for that to work I'd have to wipe everybody else's memories, too. Collective amnesia. Cancel out everything, year zero for all of us.

I don't really know why I answered the phone last night. I knew who it was – I think I've developed a sixth sense for when the silent caller will ring. But I couldn't stand it any longer, I couldn't stand having to second-guess what was going on. So I answered the call, and I met his silence with my own, and we listened to each other breathe, listening for what seemed like hours.

So I asked him. I asked him, 'Why are you doing this?' And then, 'Have I done something to upset you? Are you trying to punish me?' And then, 'Are you trying to tell me something?' And his breathing changed, as if he was trying to hold it in, as if he was crying and trying not to let me know.

So I said, 'Why are you crying? Why are you upset?'

He was trying so hard to stifle it, but I heard his tears. I don't know why, familiarity perhaps, a shared history, a blood tie, but I knew from that tiniest sound that it was Jonathan.

I was surprisingly calm, I've got to say. I always pictured that moment as one when I'd lose it completely, off the scale, telling them what I would do, how I'd plague them and curse them and make their life hell for what they did to mine. But not Jonathan. I couldn't do that to Jonathan.

So I said, 'I know who this is. I know who I'm talking to. Why are you doing this to me?'

He took a sharp intake of breath, but I wasn't sure if it was because I'd rumbled him or because he was stifling his tears.

So I said, 'It is you, isn't it? Why are you doing this? Don't you know how much you're scaring me?'

I didn't expect him to suddenly start talking. I wasn't expecting him to explain it all, but I did expect something, some sort of acknowledgement that I was right, or wrong. But all I got back was silence.

So I said, 'Is it because of what happened? You said there was trouble at work. Are you scared I'm going to tell someone? I won't, you know that. I know how important this is. Mum and Dad'd never forgive you, I know, not after the way they defended you. And Rachel. I know all that, don't you think I realise that?'

Nothing but the sound of his breathing.

I said, 'I don't understand why it's such a big deal. I don't understand why this is messing with your head. Talk to me, please.'

Nothing.

I said, 'I know you didn't mean all the stuff you said back then. There's no point feeling bad about it. I know you wouldn't hurt me, just like I wouldn't ever betray you, I wouldn't cause trouble. Please, just tell me that it's going to be okay.'

I sat listening to his breathing, waiting for a reply, willing him to reply, but after a minute he just hung up. I had the feeling that he wasn't going to call back, not now I knew it was him. But I don't feel any better for knowing. I don't know what he expects me to do. I haven't told anyone what happened, but he still acts like

198

I'm going to betray him at any minute. And that makes me mad, because doesn't he remember how worried he was, and how much he frightened me? I know he didn't mean it, but doesn't that tell him how much I'll do to protect him? If I was going to drop him in it I'd have done it then, when he was losing it and I thought he'd crack up. He's so straight-down-the-line, so rigid, so desperate to please everyone, I know he doesn't want anyone to know what we did, but doesn't he realise it would be just as bad for me if I ever told? Doesn't he think Mum and Dad would be doubly hurt if they knew we'd both been lying and they'd been so desperate to defend us?

But he's got this idea that I always get away with stuff. He thinks that because Mum and Dad never mention how much I hurt them when I ran away, that must mean I'm off the hook. He doesn't get it at all. I'm the one everyone's got such a downer on, I'm the one who's always got to apologise for stuff I've done. How much sympathy can I have for Jonathan, when I'm the one who always gets it in the neck anyway?

But then, he is my brother. He's the one who came and found me when it all got too much before. Sometimes I think he must regret that — sometimes I catch him looking at me, and I reckon he must wish he never came and found me at Arbor Low.

And what if he hadn't? Would things have been different for him if he'd left me there? If I go away then his problem goes away, at least that's what he thinks. There's nobody else to tell people what he got up to. Jonathan could settle down with Rachel, buy their house, have their kids, give my parents the grandkids they're so desperate for, save up and open a garage of his own maybe. And I could fade into the background, and over time, after a while, maybe they wouldn't even think about me any more. Everyone would go on with their lives as if I never even happened.

And if that isn't what Jonathan wants, then he'll know where to find me. He'll know that the choice is his. He'll know that it's up to him whether he wants to come and bring me back home again.

But it is all such a mess. Is that the only way out? Isn't there something else I can do? I want to talk to Jonathan, but I'm scared. I'm scared that I'm wrong, like I was with Jamie. I'm scared that just asking Jonathan will cause more problems than it would solve. I'm scared that if I am wrong then everything will continue just the way it is, and all the pressure building up until I explode, until I really lose it. I'm scared that I don't have any control over anything that happens. I'm scared that if I go, Jonathan won't come to find me.

But I can't just do nothing. I can't just let things drift. I have to take that chance – and at least I'll know, at least I won't be wondering any more.

Chapter Seventeen

I walked around the streets for a long time before I went home. I don't know what I had really expected – some great insight, perhaps, or an explanation, a resolution. I felt strangely flat. I didn't have any answers, but I wanted to understand. I had been so close to Sophie through the notebook, and I felt almost cheated that I still didn't understand what had happened.

Because why would Jonathan make those phone calls? He already had access to Sophie, he could go round to her flat any time he wanted. She was his sister, for God's sake, he had more intimate access to her life than anybody else. I would have loved to be in that position, so close to her, so completely trusted by her.

Part of me wanted to march straight round to Jamie's house and demand to know what he knew. He was as concerned for Sophie's safety as I was – if I explained what I knew, I was sure that he would work with me. But I didn't know how I could explain it – how could I tell him what I knew without mentioning the notebook? Whatever happened, I couldn't let him have that notebook, I knew that was the last thing Sophie would want.

So I could find Jonathan, confront him, tell him what I knew and force him to fill in the gaps. But even as I thought that, I could feel the adrenaline starting to pump in my veins, and my hands started to shake, and a cold shiver ran through my whole body. If Jonathan was responsible, if he had hurt Sophie in some way, then I knew I couldn't trust myself to confront him. I don't know what I would say, what I would do, if he had hurt her.

I went home. Alison was in the bath, preparing for a Friday night out with her girlfriends. I sat downstairs on the sofa, listening to the roaring in the pipes as the tank filled up again. I had to do something, I knew that. If something had happened to Sophie I would never forgive myself if I stood by and said nothing about what I knew.

I still had the notebook in my pocket. Usually, feeling it press against my hip was a source of comfort, but not any more. I took it out and looked at it, then turned to the back where I had copied out Sophie's parents' details. I knew that Sophie probably wouldn't want me to talk to them, but I was growing impatient with Sophie's wishes. She had laid a big responsibility at my door, one that I wasn't sure I could handle. If I spoke to her parents it could all be taken away from me, and I wouldn't be dragged into whatever it was that had happened. I could have my own life back, instead of being pulled further into hers.

Before I could talk myself out of it, I carried the phone out of the hall and shut the living-room door behind me. The telephone wire stretched just far enough to sit at the end of the sofa, but from there I could at least hear if Alison started to come down the stairs. I dialled the number.

Sophie's mother answered, quickly, as if she was expecting a call. I hadn't really planned what I was going to say and for a moment I didn't speak, but then she said, 'Hello,' again, a question rising through her tone, so I spoke quickly.

'I'm a friend of Sophie's,' I said. 'I – I just wondered if you'd heard anything from her.'

Her voice came back with a rush of hope. 'No, no, we haven't – have you?'

'No,' I said. I licked my lips, tried to find the right words. 'Do you have any idea why she left?'

'No,' she said, guarded. 'Do you?'

The moment of truth. I took a deep breath, tried to think how I could phrase this. Tell her to ask Jonathan what had happened, or tell her about the phone calls Sophie had been receiving? I could tell her what I knew and then hang up, and nobody would need know how involved I had become.

I had opened my mouth to speak, but I didn't have any words, I didn't know what to say. Sophie hadn't told her parents what was going on, she hadn't wanted to hurt them – did I really have the right to tell them for her? She wanted to protect them, and her mother's concern came through in her voice, and what could I actually tell them anyway? I said, 'No, not really. Have the police found anything out?'

'No,' she said. 'Not a trace since she caught the train to Derby.'

Derby. Arbor Low, I thought. She's gone back to Arbor Low.

'Who are you, anyway?' Sophie's mother was asking. I tried to stammer out that I was just a friend, but she was asking again, 'What's your name? How do you know Sophie? How did you get this number?'

'I'm just a friend,' I said. 'Just a friend. I'm sorry to have bothered you.'

I replaced the receiver quickly, cutting off her voice, cutting off whatever she was trying to ask me next. I realised that I was sweating again, my heart racing. I took the phone back into the hall and stood at the bottom of the stairs listening to Alison getting out of the bath. She would go out soon, and I would be able to think about how I could pass on what I knew without getting dragged down deeper.

Chapter Eighteen

There was a garbled message on the answerphone when I got up the next morning, Alison with loud music thumping in the background, shouting that she was staying at a friend's house. I made a cup of tea and drank it in the kitchen. The police arrived when I was taking the vacuum cleaner out of the cupboard under the stairs.

I led them into the through-lounge and fetched myself a Marlboro Light from the pack on the sideboard. I was surprised at how calm I felt, seeing them come into the house. There were two of them, in plain clothes, wearing dark suits under their flashermacs that made them look more like sales reps than police. I was relieved about that; I didn't want the neighbours to start asking Alison why the police had been round.

McAllister and Joseph. They both wore moustaches that seemed more regimented than was strictly necessary, but since my only previous knowledge of CID came from watching *The Bill*, I wasn't sure whether I should be surprised by that. McAllister was the senior one and marked that with an extra two stones of weight, mainly on his stomach. When he sat down on the sofa he was slightly out of breath, while the other one looked on with what could have been disgust, or possibly contempt. Joseph was standing in front of the fireplace, casting his eye over the pictures on the mantelpiece. He picked up a photo of Alison and me on holiday in Corfu and showed it to me.

'Who's the girl?' he asked. 'The missis?'

'My partner, Alison,' I said, suddenly feeling uncomfortable. I had started to sweat again; I placed the cigarette in the saucer on the arm of the chair and pushed my hands down between the sides of the chair and my legs, in case they started to shake.

If Joseph had seen what I was doing, he didn't comment on it, but said, 'Been together long?'

'Lived together for four years,' I said.

'Going to get married?'

He had picked up the picture of Alison's niece and was turning it over as if he was more interested in the frame. I said, 'We haven't really talked about it,' but I was too distracted by his fumblings to pay much heed to my own words.

McAllister said, 'Anyway, you must be wondering why we're here.'

I looked over at him. He had taken a white cotton handkerchief from his jacket pocket and was rubbing his mouth with it. He cleared his throat, crumpled the handkerchief across his lips, then looked at me expectantly.

I tried not to show how disgusting I had thought

that was. The handkerchief travelled back to his pocket. I said, 'I imagine it has something to do with Sophie Taylor.'

Joseph was looking at the ornaments on the mantelpiece. The glass dolphin we'd brought back from Corfu, the porcelain ballerina that had come with Alison when we moved in together. I wanted to leap up and take the things away from him, stop his greasy fingers from wandering over more of our possessions.

McAllister said, 'What makes you say that?'

'Because there's no other reason for you to be here.' I watched Joseph reach for the glass pot-pourri dish that Alison's sister had bought us, and I couldn't stop myself, I had to get up and cross the room and take it out of his hands. 'Careful with that,' I said. 'The lid'll fall off.'

Joseph didn't say anything, but sat on the sofa next to McAllister and took out a small notepad. McAllister allowed himself some sort of smirk, which I guessed was intended to be a sign of friendliness. I decided to interpret it that way, anyway. He said, 'Yes, we are investigating Sophie's disappearance.'

I think he was expecting me to say something, but I could feel a wobble rising in my throat, and the sweat gathering in the small of my back and under my arms. I wondered if they could tell, if they had noticed. My cigarette had burned half down, so I picked it up and tapped the ash off and drew in a little smoke. It made me cough slightly.

Joseph said, 'You should give up.'

I forced a smile, but stubbed the cigarette out. My mouth tasted dry, ashy.

McAllister said, 'You seem nervous.'

'Nervous?' I said, a little too quickly, then laughed. 'No, no. Touch of flu maybe, or hayfever.'

They both looked at me. I brushed a hand across my hair and forced a smile.

McAllister said, 'You telephoned Mrs Taylor yesterday.'

'Yes,' I said. 'How – how did you know that was me?'

'She dialled 1471. She told us the conversation seemed – odd.'

'Odd?'

'That's what she said. Why did you call them, Mr Williams?'

'I wanted to know how things were going. I probably shouldn't have done, I know. I realised it was a mistake.'

'Why a mistake?'

'Because I couldn't help. Because she wanted some news and I didn't have any,' I said. 'So, is there any news?'

McAllister said, 'It seems like she's just run away.' His voice was casual, but I couldn't help feeling that he was being casual deliberately. 'She's done it before, you know.'

'Yes,' I said. 'I knew that.'

McAllister leaned forward and said, 'That's right. You've been talking to Jamie Forester.'

'Yes,' I said, feeling a cold chill run through me.

I resisted the temptation to rub my hair again. 'He gave me a number to call, but I'm sorry, I'm afraid I never—'

'That's all right,' McAllister said. 'We know people are very busy. Where is it you work?'

'The city planning department,' I said. 'I don't really know Sophie, not really. We just caught the same bus every morning, that's all.'

'But you phoned her parents, so you must know her pretty well.'

'I was worried, that's all. You hear of such terrible things happening to people these days. The world's a violent place.'

'Very true.' McAllister's voice was smooth, sickly like chocolate. 'But if you hardly knew Sophie, why did you tell her parents she was an old friend of yours?'

'Did I? Well, I couldn't very well tell them I barely knew Sophie, could I?'

Joseph seemed to find that funny, but stifled his laugh into a cough and looked down at the notes he was making when McAllister glanced across at him.

I said, 'Does it matter? I was worried, that's all. I thought they wouldn't tell me anything if they knew I didn't know her very well.' I knew I should shut up; their expressions told me I wasn't helping my case, but now that I had started to speak I realised it was going to be difficult to stop. 'We might not have been bosom buddies, but I happen to think it's important to care about what happens to other people, there're too many people who just ignore everything going on around them as it is.'

'Sure, sure,' McAllister said, and sat back again. 'Of course, she's probably fine, most missing persons are, after all. But we have to check. You understand. It's routine.'

I nodded my head, and then felt that I was nodding too vigorously, and stopped. 'So you think she's fine.'

He opened out his hands to indicate he didn't know.

'I'm sure she's fine,' I said.

Joseph said, 'Well, sometimes people do stupid things in the heat of the moment.'

'Not Sophie,' I said.

'You'd be surprised,' Joseph said.

I said, 'Sophie wouldn't do anything like that. She wouldn't let anything get her down that much.'

'So you do know her quite well, then?' McAllister asked.

'No, not really,' I said.

'Where did you get her parents' phone number from?' This was Joseph.

'Directory enquiries,' I said. I was feeling very uncomfortable now – I had the feeling that they weren't convinced by anything I was saying. I said, 'Look, if you've got a question to ask, then just ask me. Don't pussyfoot around like this.'

'There's no need to be so defensive,' Joseph said. 'We aren't here to accuse, or demand answers, or anything like that.'

McAllister said, 'The problem I have, Mr Williams, is that none of Sophie's friends seem to know who you are. Nobody had even heard of you until Jamie Forester bumped into you outside Sophie's flat, on the day she disappeared. Now, do you see why we think you might know something?'

I said carefully, 'I can see what you're saying. But there's nothing strange about it, I promise you.' I thought about the notebook, suddenly wishing I had destroyed it, so that there was no chance that I would weaken and give it to them, so that there was no chance of them finding it. I tried to work out what I should say, how I should act to convince them that there was nothing suspicious about me, but I didn't know what to do. Everything I thought of that I could say just sounded more and more incredible, and I knew they wouldn't believe the truth. I said, 'She dropped her swipecard. Her security card to get in through the office door. I wanted to return it to her.'

'So where is this card now?'

'In the other room. I just chucked it in a drawer, to give it back when I saw her.'

'You didn't consider taking it to her workplace? Or handing it in to the police?'

'No,' I said. 'I thought it might get Sophie in trouble if they knew she'd lost it. Left it behind on the bus. I didn't want her to get into trouble.'

McAllister said, 'That was very considerate of you,' but he meant something entirely different with his tone of voice. 'Perhaps you could fetch it for us?'

'Sure,' I said. 'No problem.'

Joseph followed me into the kitchen and stood in the doorway while I opened up the drawer. I had tucked it right away at the back so that Alison wouldn't find it, and now I had to push my hand inside the mess of bits and pieces to try to locate it. Joseph started some inane chatter about the plants growing into a jungle in the garden, and I answered him as best I could while I looked for the card. I would have to sort the drawers out later, once they had left. Finally my fingers closed around the card and I pulled it out and gave it to Joseph.

When we went back into the front room McAllister was on his feet, doing his own inspection of the ornaments. He took the swipecard from Joseph, turned it over, examined it, but there was nothing he could learn from it, it wasn't about to jump up and tell him where Sophie had gone. He put it in his pocket and glanced at Joseph before saying, 'Well, thank you for the time, Mr Williams.'

I followed them to the front door, feeling the relief sweeping through me. 'If there's anything I can do, please don't hesitate,' I said, regretting the words immediately.

But McAllister simply smiled and said, 'Thank you, Mr Williams. We'll be in touch if we think of anything.' There was a slight sneer in his voice, a momentary unpleasantness that cut right into me. But I forced a smile and he added, 'I'm sure she'll turn up right as rain. You know she ran away once before?'

He seemed unaware that he had already said that once, but I was brought up on Columbo, I knew better than to underestimate a policeman in a tacky mac. I said, 'Yes. Jamie told me.'

McAllister didn't say anything else, just nodded. Joseph was already at the front gate, struggling with the latch. I watched until he got the gate open and they both went out onto the street. McAllister spent time carefully closing the gate behind him, glancing up at me as he did so.

I shut the door and went back into the through-lounge. I could smell the cigarette smoke, and the sofa cushions still bore the imprint of the two police-men. I opened the top window to change the air, and plumped up the cushions, and straightened the furniture. One of them had left the slight trace of a muddy footprint on the carpet and I dragged my toes over it until it merged into the pile. The ornaments and photographs on the mantelpiece were out of place, so I fetched a duster and wiped down the surface, then placed each item back where it should go. The glass pot-pourri dish was last, but as I went to put it back my hands started to shake, and as I tried to put the dish down it slipped out of my hands. I watched it fall towards the tiled hearth, and the lid fell free, and all the pot-pourri tumbled out, reddish brown petals and leaves dancing out through the air. I tried to reach for the dish, and my hands grappled with the air, and the dish smashed against the tiles, and I dropped to my knees, looking down at the shards of glass in among the petals. I must have been like that for seconds, or minutes, I couldn't tell which. The dish was broken, there was nothing I could do to put that right.

And then Alison was back in the house, coming into the front room, seeing me kneeling there.

'God,' she said. 'God, what's happened?'

Looking into my face. Dropping her coat on the sofa and crossing the room to me.

I said, 'It was an accident. I dropped it. I didn't mean to.'

She knelt down beside me and started to pick up the larger fragments of glass. I saw the crystal pattern of the dish cut into the pieces that she held.

I said, 'I'm sorry,' and then, I didn't know why, I couldn't explain it, I started to cry. No graceful, silent tears; these were big gulping sobs, snot-choked, filling my throat, running from my eyes, thickening in my nostrils. My hands were shaking; my whole body was shaking.

'It's okay,' Alison said. 'It doesn't matter. It's only a dish.'

And then she put her arms around me, and I buried my head in her chest, on the soft uppers of her breasts, wetting her blouse, snotty tears all soaking into the material, and she held me tight there, warm, enclosed by her arms and her breasts. I took deep breaths, let her warm scent, the warm air off her body fill my lungs. The tears started to dry on my face, and finally she released me, and I ran the balls of my fists into my eyes, and wiped my cheeks on my sleeves.

Then I felt foolish, and had to look at her and away

from her, but she wasn't laughing, she wasn't angry, she seemed concerned.

'I'm sorry,' I said. 'I don't know what came over me.'

She didn't speak, still kneeling there, looking at me.

I said, 'It's nothing, I'm sorry, just a little wobble. Ignore it. Ignore me. I'm sorry.'

'Don't be,' she said, and her voice was gentle. 'Don't apologise.'

I stood up awkwardly and went into the kitchen to fetch the dustpan and brush. When I came back she was standing, the glass cupped in her hands. I got down on my knees and swept the mess up, and then held out the pan for the fragments she was holding. She hesitated for a moment then dropped them into the pan.

When I had disposed of the glass and put the dustpan and brush away, I went back into the room. She was sitting on the sofa.

I said, 'Did you have a nice night?'

'Yes,' she said, distracted. 'We went to The Rig after the pub, had a boogie. Are you okay?'

'Fine,' I said, and forced a smile.

'There's something on your mind, isn't there?'

'No,' I said. I sat down in the armchair, flopped down. I wanted to smoke another cigarette. I picked up the box and looked at it, reading the health warnings, the tar and nicotine content, the quality guarantee. Alison was frowning, so I put the box down again.

'There is something wrong,' she said. 'Why have you started smoking all of a sudden?'

'Because I want to,' I said, and then felt euphoric, a wave of euphoria all through me, and I laughed. 'Why the hell not? Loads of people do.' And to demonstrate what I meant, I took one out of the box and put it between my lips, laughing still.

She came over to the armchair and pulled the cigarette out of my mouth. 'You're acting weird,' she said. 'What's up with you?'

I could tell she was starting to get annoyed, but I couldn't help laughing. I wondered how she would react if she knew the police had been round, if I told her that the police thought I was up to something too.

But she hid her irritation well, and knelt down next to the chair, and when she spoke her voice was gentle again. 'Are you going to tell me what's going on?'

The euphoria was evaporating, too quickly, sinking right through my system. I felt tears rising to the surface again and I looked away. I knew I owed her some sort of explanation. I said, 'Oh, I don't know. It's just everything. Maybe I'm stressed out. Maybe I'm cracking up. Do you think I'm cracking up?'

She considered that, frowning. 'I don't know. Is it something at work?'

'Maybe,' I said. I hesitated, but I wasn't sure why. 'They offered me a promotion to SPO. Just temporarily,' I added, as she started to react.

'But that's wonderful,' she said, then must have seen something in my expression, because she dampened her enthusiasm and said, 'Isn't it?'

I just shrugged.

'Is that what this is all about? I thought you'd have been pleased.' Before I could respond to that she said, 'When did they offer this?'

'Yesterday.'

I thought she was going to demand to know why I hadn't told her sooner, but she didn't. Instead, she said, 'It's obviously bothering you. Tell me what you're thinking.'

I thought again about Joseph and McAllister, here in the house, touching everything, leaving their mark on everything. I couldn't see how I could tell her about that, how I could even begin to explain it to her. And the strange thing was, I wasn't even sure that I wanted to. I said, 'Oh, I suppose I'm just worried about it. Stressed that I won't be able to do the job after all. It's a lot more responsibility.'

'It's more money, too,' Alison said. 'That'll help. We could do with that. But it is what you want, isn't it? I remember how disappointed you were when Anthony got the promotion over you. Now you've got a chance to show that you're the right person for the job, for the next post that comes up.'

'Yes, that's true,' I said, trying to muster some enthusiasm.

'You do want this job, don't you?' Alison asked. 'I mean, I know I keep going on about the money, but it doesn't matter, not if it's not what you want to do.'

'It is what I want,' I said. 'At least, it's what I've been looking for. I'm just nervous that I'll screw it up, I suppose.'

'Everyone gets nervous when they get a promotion,' she said. She took my hand in hers, her small, slim fingers caressing mine. My hands were much bigger than hers, redder, the skin blotchy. I felt strangely detached from her, as if it wasn't my hand she was massaging, as if it wasn't Alison touching me like that.

I pulled my hand away. 'Anthony never seemed nervous.'

She frowned. 'There's a difference between how people seem and how people are. Anyway, Anthony's an arrogant fool, you said so yourself.' She said the words really quickly, as if she wanted to get them out of the way. 'Peter, what's really going on? You seem really distant.'

I knew she wanted me to say that it was about us. That I felt that things were slipping away from us. To explain that I felt so cold inside. But I didn't think that it had anything to do with her, to do with us. This was something separate. I said, 'I'm sorry, I don't mean to be like that. I'm just preoccupied, I suppose.'

For a moment, I thought she was going to say something more, but she didn't, she just nodded and stood up. She had her back to me, and paused in the doorway. 'You should talk to me more,' she said. 'That's why I'm here.'

I started to say that I was sorry again, but she had gone out into the hall. I heard her feet on the stairs. I picked up the cigarette from the chair arm and lit it, but it tasted disgusting, so I stubbed it out.

Chapter Nineteen

That Monday morning was the first time since she had disappeared that I didn't find myself hoping that Sophie would be back, rushing down the passage at the side of the hairdressers', running to catch the bus. I felt almost liberated that I wasn't holding my breath until the doors clattered shut and the bus jerked away up the road.

It was ridiculous, that I had allowed myself to become embroiled in her life. I felt ridiculous, a grown man with a teenage crush; she had blown me off course, taken my eyes off the important things in my life. My job, paying the bills, the house, Alison.

When we first met, there was nothing I wouldn't do for Alison. My days revolved around her – my thoughts flooded with her presence – my stomach scrunched and rolled at any reminder of her existence. She made me dizzy with the concept of us being together. I could barely function when I wasn't with her, and I would wait for her outside her work, a bunch of flowers in my hands, and we would sit together on the bus, and that was when my day would really start, talking on the bus, listening to how her day had been without me.

But all of that excitement faded. It sank into domesticity, somewhere between the shopping and the washing up. It was in danger of being killed off finally because of me, and because of Sophie.

All through Monday, I was trying to work things out in my own mind. There was still time to resurrect the relationship with Alison – I felt that she had not given up, she had not decided that it was all over between us. I had put us in jeopardy, but there was still time to pull it back. I had a vision of us, a candlelit meal, a balcony looking out over an evening sea, the sun sinking down to be extinguished by the waves. There would be soft music, violins, and I would go down on one knee and offer her a ring, and she would take it, and the moonlight would dance in her eyes as she said yes, and then we would kiss.

The thing with Sophie, it was just a brief infatuation, a fascination with the mystery. I was just a sucker for the romance of disappearing into the night. True, she had played on that, she had hooked me and reeled me in, but I was not going to allow her to come between Alison and me.

And the notebook – I was starting to hate the sight of that notebook, the way the corners curled and showed the cardboard under the glossy cover, the way she hadn't even bothered to take care of it. Her handwriting was a mess, and the biro made deep impressions in the paper and stopped the pages from sitting flush with one another. And what did it really say? A lot of immature whining, some remnants of teen angst, a few sour suspicions breaking friendships apart. Leanna was right, Jonathan was right – Sophie only ever thought about herself, and I had allowed that to affect my life.

It was clear to me that I had to end my involvement with Sophie once and for all. I wasn't like Sophie, I couldn't just walk away from my obligations. This time, I had to finish it properly.

I smoked a cigarette while I walked towards Sophie's parents' street. Their house was at the end of a long cul-de-sac of red-brick forties semis. I concentrated my efforts as I went up their street. All I had to do was walk up their driveway, push the notebook through the letterbox and stride calmly away. No fuss, no bother, just a resolution that there would be no turning back from.

It was a quiet street. I watched for faces pressed up to the edges of the net curtains, the resident spies keeping an eye on comings and goings, but the street seemed to be empty. There was someone cleaning out the inside of a car at the far end of the close; I could see blue jeans kneeling by the open back door, the person's torso hidden inside the car. As I got nearer, I felt myself starting to sweat, and the shaking began in my hands. I felt as if I could predict that something was going to happen, a sick lurch that warned me, but I kept going.

Once I had pushed that diary through that door, it was over. I would go back to being Peter Williams,

Senior Planning Officer (temporary secondment) for Nottingham City Council, and I would ask Alison to marry me, and we would settle down and have children and I would continue to advance through the pay scale, and Alison would qualify to advise on endowment investments, and we would move out of our suburb and into a nicer one – with a private garden, and a nice view, and good schools for the kids to ensure their future. It was all so simple – there was no choice, really. The last few weeks had been nothing but a short period of insanity, a reaction against the pressures I was feeling – but it would all be resolved soon.

I had reached the driveway to the Taylor house. As I paused there and looked at the front door, I realised that the man who had been lying on his belly across the back seat of the car had got up and was coming over to me, wiping his hands on a bit of rag. I turned to face him and paused, more out of a habit of politeness than anything else.

I recognised Jonathan immediately from the photograph I had taken from Sophie's flat.

He said, 'You want number thirty-eight?'

'Yes,' I said, before I could stop myself.

'That's my parents' place. There's nobody in.'

'Oh,' I said. The notebook was heavy against my hip, but I didn't know what to do. Sophie wouldn't want me to hand the notebook to him. I couldn't give it to him, not after everything she had told me about him.

'So, what do you want?' he demanded.

I stuttered out the beginning of a sentence – 'I—' but my head was hammering, my heart was racing. I looked at him, at the ugly frown on his face, at the mess of blond hair, at the muscles of his arms. He was the one who had phoned Sophie – it was his fault that she had left, he was the one who was to blame.

He said, 'Are you a friend of Sophie's?'

'No,' I said, too quickly.

He said, 'Who are you?' Then, before I could answer, he said, 'Are you that weirdo who phoned Mum up a few days ago?' I started to deny it, but he was already saying, 'You are, aren't you? The police've been to see you, haven't they?'

I tried to back away, but he was stepping towards me. I said, 'I don't know what you're talking about.'

'So why are you so scared, then?' The frown had grown across his face like a scar. 'What the hell's going on, eh? Where the hell is my sister?'

I wanted to say, 'You should know.' I wanted to say that it was all his doing. I wanted to demand to know what had happened between them. I heard myself saying the words, pictured his silence, imagined how that would change things, how much stronger than him I would be.

He was saying, 'We're all worried sick, and here you are, bothering my family, so you'd better tell me what you're doing here before I call the police.'

If I shouted at him, if I screamed that he knew it was all his fault, if I forced him to tell me what had happened . . .

He had produced a mobile phone from his back pocket, and now started to push buttons.

I said, 'Really, I don't know what you're talking about. I don't know anything about Sophie's disappearance, honestly, I only phoned your mother because I wanted to know if there was any news, that's all.'

He put the phone to his ear. I couldn't tell if he was bluffing or not.

I said, 'You know more than I do. You know why she left.'

He took the phone from his ear. 'What?'

'It's got something to do with you.'

'What has?'

'Why she left.'

He looked at me as if he believed he could read my thoughts. I licked dry lips, looking away, feeling the sweat gathering in my hairline.

'What about me?' he asked.

The notebook was sharp in my pocket, but there was no way I was going to hand it over, not with the mood he was in. I said, 'I don't know, she never told me exactly.'

He had straightened the frown from his face and now I couldn't read his expression. I avoided looking at his eyes.

I said, 'Did something happen?'

'No,' he said.

I pressed on, not sure how to phrase it, not sure how I could stop myself. 'Something happened between you two. I know it. Something happened to make her run away last time. It's the same thing, the same reason.'

He looked confused, but he could have been bluffing.

I said, 'You know why.'

'No,' he said. 'There's no reason.'

But I knew he was lying – I could see it in his face, in the frown that shadowed his eyes. I was close to finding out. I said, 'Is she at Arbor Low? Have you been there?'

He seemed surprised that I knew the name of the place, but he said, 'I checked already. It's all boarded up.'

'You looked inside?'

The surprise, the confusion, was fading from his expression, and I could see that he was growing angry. He hadn't moved at all, as if his feet were nailed to the tarmac. I eased my weight from one foot to the other. He said, 'How do you know about Arbor Low? What are you, some kind of pervert, poking your nose into private business?'

'Of course not,' I said. 'I'm just a friend, that's all.'

'If you were a real friend you'd be helping us find her, not harassing us this way.' Then he looked at me harder and shook his head. 'I really should phone the police.'

I realised suddenly that I was out of time. I said, 'I'm sorry. I'm going now, honestly. There's no need to call them. I didn't mean any harm.' I was backing away as he stood there watching me, and after a moment I turned and walked up the cul-de-sac. I wanted to run, as fast as I could, but he was still holding the phone in his hand.

When I reached the top of the close I stood there trying to catch my breath, and then I started to worry about what would happen next. I wanted to believe that he wouldn't call the police. If he was the one making all the phone calls, if it was him who had forced Sophie to leave, then maybe he wouldn't? But I was beginning to doubt the things Sophie had said; after all, she had been just as sure that it was Jamie who had been calling her – maybe she had got this wrong as well?

But I knew it was crazy to keep thinking about these things. I should never have gone to the house – I had wanted to help, to do what I could to help them while I disentangled myself, but it had only made matters worse. I had to cut myself free from this once and for all, and leave it to them to unravel the mess they had created for themselves.

I walked along the road until I came to a path leading down to the River Leen. I took the path down to a cinder track leading alongside the narrow river, which was little more than a brook with steep banks and muddy water. But it was quiet by the river, and as I walked further along between patches of tall yellow grasses and scrubby bushes the sound of the traffic receded to a gentle hum.

I took the notebook out of my pocket. It was looking more scrappy now, from all the times I had thumbed through it. I realised that I couldn't return it to the family, not now, not after all of this. It wouldn't take the police long to ask me about it, and I didn't think anyone would believe anything I had to say. I tried to breathe normally, sucking in air, blowing it out, trying to decide what to do next.

The cinder path led into a small scrap of wood, by the side of a church that belonged more to a country scene than the heart of the city. There was a bench by the side of the path, and when I sat down I could almost believe that I was in the countryside, that I had left the city behind. But I could still hear the lorries on the main road, and by moving my head only slightly I could see the apex of several warehouse roofs. I looked at the notebook for one last time. Her handwriting was so familiar to me now, as if I had always had that voice to listen to, as if she was a part of me, as if the words on the page were as alive as she was.

I gripped the covers in both hands and wrenched at the notebook, feeling the spine crack and break, seeing the pages start to loosen and spill forward, all her words jumbling together and falling onto the mud. I looked around again, but nobody was watching, and I piled the pages together and weighed it all down with some twigs. Then I took out Sophie's lighter and set the curling corners of the papers alight. They didn't catch right away, and the slight breeze that came through the trees threatened to extinguish the flames, but finally the whole pile began to burn, and the flame grew larger, a yellow flame sucking up the words and twisting and blackening the pages.

I had the photograph that I had taken from her flat in my hands. I looked at the family group standing together in front of the Arbor Low farmhouse, at the expressions that had grown so familiar to me over the last few days. I looked at Sophie, at the smile in her eyes and the way her mouth was still slightly open from speaking. Then I held the photograph out into the flames, and the corner started to curl as the flame caught, and then the flame was running across the surface of the photograph, liquifying the image as the paper burned. I dropped the photograph onto the pile of notebook and watched it crack and shrivel there, the faces slowly blackening and disappearing, until even Sophie was gone.

I crouched there and saw the plastic coating on the notebook catch and warp, the final stage, the end of it all. Once I was sure everything had been blackened, the words obliterated, I stood up and looked around. When I walked away, I could feel the relief starting to sweep through me. I was free of her at last, and my own life was calling me back.

Chapter Twenty

When I got home, Alison was sitting on the sofa watching the news with a mug of coffee in her hands. I had stopped off to buy her some flowers and presented them to her with a flourish. She gave a little laugh, and smiled, and stood up to take them from me. I followed her into the kitchen, watched her unwrap the cellophane and arrange them in a vase.

'They're lovely,' she said. 'Thank you.' Then she turned to the sink and filled the vase with water. 'What are they for?'

'What are they for?' I was a little staggered. 'Can't I buy you flowers, Alison?' I approached her and put my hands on her shoulders. She twisted to look up at me, but she was frowning more than smiling. I said, 'Alison, I love you. I know I've been a bit weird lately, and I'm sorry. I don't know what came over me. Stress, I don't know. But I love you, Alison.' As I said the words I felt a rush of pleasure through me – I saw how she looked, those eyes fixed on mine, that smile. I said, 'Let's go out somewhere for dinner.'

'Dinner?'

'Yes. A restaurant.'

'On a week night?' Then she seemed to hesitate, and laughed a little. 'Listen to me. That would be great, Peter. Where would you like to go?'

I considered that. 'I don't know. How about – how about somewhere in the city centre? Somewhere nice.'

She smiled. 'Okay. I'll go and get changed.'

She went upstairs. I finished putting the flowers in water, arranging them so that each colour, each variety was shown off to its best. I carried the vase through into the front room and rearranged the bits on the mantelpiece to make room for the flowers. Then I sat down and took a packet of Marlboro Lights from my pocket, but when I took a cigarette from the box I didn't light it. I felt its shape, its slight weight, the smoothness of the paper with the rough tobacco just beneath the surface. Then I stuffed it back into the box and followed Alison upstairs.

She was in her underwear, sitting in front of the dressing-table mirror, applying mascara with a long brush. I stood behind her and looked at us in the reflection; she put down the brush and smiled at the reflection, smiled at me. I leaned down and kissed her on the lips, and put my hands against her shoulders, then down towards her breasts.

'No, no, no,' she said, laughing, her hands against my hands.

'I know,' I said, and walked away, but she was still smiling.

I took off my jacket and opened the wardrobe to take out a clean shirt, and she watched me for a moment and then went back to applying her mascara. When I had put my shirt on, I went back downstairs again, phoned for a taxi, then waited for her in front of *EastEnders*.

When she came down, she was wearing her silky lilac dress, the one that hugged her figure loosely, that showed off the shape of her hips and the stride of her legs. She had fixed her hair up in clips to show off the line of her jaw, the slight hollows in her cheeks, her smooth skin. I wanted to take her in my arms, take her right there and then, a vision of beauty, my own vision of perfection.

I said, 'You look stunning. You look like a princess.'

She smiled and accepted the compliment. She seemed to be about to say something else, but then there was a car horn from the road.

'Perfect timing,' I said, taking her arm. 'Taxi's here.'

She raised her eyebrows a little at the extravagance of a taxi, but said nothing. I held onto her arm as we left the house, feeling her warmth so close to me. In the back of the minicab, I sat close to her and sought out her fingers with mine through the polyester fur on the seat covers. Our fingers intertwined and she turned and smiled at me, and I knew she was thinking the same as me, that the spark was back, that it was just like when we first fell in love.

We had a quiet drink in The Peacock and then

found a small table in the corner of a Spanish-Mexican-Italian restaurant on the Mansfield Road. The restaurant was not busy; the sounds of the other diners talking and clinking cutlery against plates was soft in the background. She seemed to be happy, and it was just the way I had dreamed an evening like this one would be.

Half a bottle of red wine later, waiting for the empty plates to be taken away, Alison leaned forward and said, 'So, what's the meal in aid of?'

Her tone was light-hearted. I matched mine to hers. 'I just wanted to take the most beautiful woman in the world out to dinner. What's wrong with that?'

The waiter had appeared and she sat back and sipped her wine while he cleared the plates away. We both ordered a coffee, and then, when he was out of earshot, she leaned forward again. Her tone was serious this time. 'Did I lose you?' she asked.

'Lose me?' I was surprised. I took her hand between mine and said, 'No, no, of course not. I love you. I always have done.'

She was frowning, a dark crease across the smooth skin of her forehead. 'It's felt as if you've been shutting me out,' she said.

'I'm sorry if it seemed that way,' I said. I had to measure each word exactly; I felt as if I was on the edge of a verbal precipice. I said, 'I just – I don't know. I just went a little crazy for a while. Work, life, you know. But I'm fine again now.' I squeezed her hand. 'We're fine again now, aren't we?'

'You're the one who went away,' she said. 'You tell me.'

'It's fine,' I said. 'I promise.'

'I thought I was losing you,' she said, 'but I couldn't see who to.'

'Nobody,' I said, then I lifted her fingers to my lips and kissed them. 'Alison, I love you. That's all I know. That's all I care about.'

She seemed to be finding it difficult to phrase what she wanted to say. 'If you love me, you need to tell me what's going on in that head of yours. Sometimes – sometimes I can't tell what it is you're thinking. As if you're a complete stranger to me. I want to rely on you, I think I can rely on you, but I need to feel that you're telling me things.'

I said, 'I'm sorry, Alison. I was confused, that's all. This promotion, all of that, it got me wondering what I really wanted.'

'And what conclusion did you come to?'

I met her eyes, and saw the reflected candlelight in them. I was slightly drunk, but there was more to it than that; it was a glow, a rush of warmth when I looked at her. I knew with an absolute certainty that this was the right thing to do, this was the way to show her that I wanted to be with her and only her. 'I want you,' I said. 'You're all I want. To spend the rest of my life with you.' She was looking at me, not smiling, not speaking. The anticipation of that moment – I felt as if it would last for ever, suspended in time, trying to read her unreadable expression. I felt the inevitability of it and gripped her hand harder. 'Alison,' I said. 'Will you marry me?'

She looked at me in silence for a long moment, then looked down at the tablecloth. 'You shouldn't say that if you don't mean it.'

'But I do mean it.'

'You're sure?'

'Of course I am,' I said. 'Alison, I love you. What else is there that matters?'

A slow smile crept onto her lips, and she looked at me again. 'I would love to marry you,' she said. 'Yes, I would love to.'

Until she said those words, I had no idea what I would feel, but then I was overwhelmed by the thrill of the moment – it was all I could do not to stand up and shout – I wanted to hug her and kiss her and cry all at once. Until she said those words I wasn't even sure I had meant what I said, but then I just knew it, I just knew that this was right, that she was right, that we would be together for ever.

Chapter Twenty-one

The knock at the door jerked me awake, and I was up and out of bed immediately, emergency reflexes.

Alison stirred and sat up and said sleepily, 'What is it?'

'I don't know,' I said. I pulled on the trousers I'd been wearing the night before. The clock said a little after six. I put my shirt on and went downstairs in bare feet, buttoning the shirt. They were knocking again. I opened the front door.

Joseph and McAllister and three young PCs, one of them a woman. McAllister handed a sheet of paper to me and said, 'Can we come in, please, Mr Williams?'

At the same time, he was pushing past me into the hall. I stayed where I was, holding the door, holding the paper in my other hand.

I said, 'What is this?'

They all followed McAllister in, through into the front room. Alison had come halfway down the stairs, clutching her dressing gown tightly at the neck, looking at me with a question mark for an expression.

I repeated, 'What the hell is this about?'

McAllister had also seen Alison on the stairs and signalled for her to come down into the front room. She came down hesitantly, and I followed her in.

McAllister said, 'We have a warrant to search these premises in connection with the disappearance of Sophie Taylor.'

Confusion was spreading across Alison's face, and her hand went up to her mouth, and she looked at me. I felt a sudden sense of desperation, of things spiralling away. I said, 'But there's nothing here. Sophie's never even been here. I barely even know Sophie.'

McAllister said, 'We'll talk about that later, Mr Williams. For now, we need to conduct a search of this house.'

Alison's breath jerked in suddenly. I opened out my hands, not sure what I could say. I moved over to where Alison was standing, but she shrank further into her dressing gown.

McAllister said, 'Joseph, take Alison upstairs and start in the bedrooms.'

Joseph indicated for Alison to go up the stairs in front of him, and the female PC followed them. I stood where I was in the doorway, watching them disappear up the stairs. McAllister said, 'Right, Mr Williams. Peter. Let's start in here, shall we?'

McAllister pulled out the sideboard drawers and tipped the contents onto the table. All the folder of bills, sorted and labelled, bank statements, receipts, all of them mixed in together. I went to help, to try to keep them in some semblance of order, but McAllister caught my arm and guided me towards a chair.

I stayed standing and said, 'They were all in order.'

McAllister gave a sort of grunt for a reply, running his fingers through a neat stack of bank statements. One of the young PCs looked at McAllister and then at me, but went back to examining the mess on the table.

I leaned against the wall with my arms folded and watched them. McAllister moved on to the cupboard underneath the drawers. Photograph albums, letters, old notepads, out-of-date holiday brochures and Argos catalogues. It felt strange, to see them wade through our possessions, and I thought of Alison, upstairs, watching them empty out the underwear onto the bed.

I said, 'Is this all really necessary? I told you, there's nothing—'

'We need to check,' McAllister said, then flashed me a professional smile. 'If you've nothing to hide, you've nothing to worry about, have you?'

He moved on to the bookcase, and took out the books one by one then shook them to see if anything dropped out. He said, 'So you're a sci-fi fan, then?'

'Yes,' I said. 'I mean, I used to be. When I was younger.'

He got down onto his knees and started checking the bottom shelf. 'Never liked it much myself. Aliens and that, doesn't seem very real, does it?'

I watched him pulling out the books Alison used for her course, opening and shaking them, as if there would be anything among her things. I felt a strange, cold rage building up inside myself. 'That isn't what a lot of sci-fi is about,' I said. Upstairs, I could hear thumps and footsteps as people moved around, and low voices, and I wondered what Joseph was saying to Alison, how Alison was coping with this. 'Sci-fi is about alternative views of this world,' I said, suddenly feeling how frustrating this was, how powerless I was. 'I mean, it all developed out of the Soviet Union, as a way for people to talk about the world they lived in without being arrested.'

'Is that right?' He had his hand down the back of the bottom shelf now, pulling out all the bits of paper and old letters that had fallen down there over the years that neither of us had ever bothered to pick up.

'Yes,' I said, and a new savageness came into my tone. 'A reaction against a police state.'

He stopped and looked at me, then smiled and went back to examining an old Christmas card with a photo of baubles and candles on the front.

I could feel the sweat starting to gather across my forehead, and a sudden, inexplicable fear that he would find something, that he could possibly find something. 'If they wrote a dystopia—'

'A dystopia, huh?'

'Yes, a dystopia about the Soviet system, the censor would have to admit that the nightmare world or planet whatever was actually about the reality of the Soviet system, and that would involve them admitting that there was something wrong with the Soviet system, which would have got them into trouble. So the censors just used to pass the books.'

'Really?' His tone was disinterested now and I doubted he was even listening, but I wasn't sure I could stop talking. He moved on to the box of videos under the TV, and opened each box in turn. I could hear more thumps from upstairs, and I felt a sudden desire to go rushing up there, to check that Alison was okay.

Finally, we moved into the kitchen, and I leaned in the doorway as he went through the drawers one by one. I said, 'There's nothing here to find, I can tell you that, because I haven't done anything wrong.' I was starting to feel more confident, and I said, 'You're barking up the wrong tree, I can tell you. You're going to be very embarrassed to have put me through this, and—' I gulped for breath. 'And my fiancée. She doesn't need to be upset this way. She doesn't need to see this.'

He didn't even glance at me, just kept looking, opening drawers and pulling things out onto the worktop, examining them one by one while I rattled on, hearing nothing but the dull grate of my own voice. Finally he looked up at me, and he wasn't smiling this time. He said, 'Let's go upstairs, shall we?'

He followed me up the stairs. The female PC was standing in the bedroom doorway with her arms folded, and moved out of the room as we entered. Alison was sitting on the bed, holding her hand over her face, a tissue crumpled between her fingers, hugging her stomach with her other arm. I approached her, said, 'Alison? Are you okay?'

She didn't look at me, didn't speak, but I saw the way her shoulders were shaking ever so slightly, and I knew she was crying. I looked around, at the clothes thrown onto the floor, at the books and papers emptied out on top. I went through to the back bedroom, and saw the books from the bookcase emptied out all over the bed, and the spare blankets and sheets in a pile on the floor. In the bathroom, Joseph was looking inside the toilet cistern.

McAllister had followed me around the upstairs, and now he said to Joseph, 'Anything?'

'No, sir,' Joseph said.

McAllister frowned, rubbed his hand across his face. I followed him back to the bedroom, where Alison was rubbing her eyes and blowing her nose. I said, 'I told you. This has been one big mistake, and you're going to be sorry you made it.'

Alison looked up, her eyes red, and managed a smile at me.

McAllister said, 'Oh, I don't know. I still think you can help us with our enquiries, Peter. I'd like you to come down to the station and answer a few questions I have outstanding.'

I said, 'I've already told you that I don't know anything about this.'

Alison said, 'Why do you think he's done anything? What makes you think he's even involved?'

McAllister said, 'We have our reasons. Peter, I would recommend that you come with us and clear your name, then you can go right back to being a happy little family.'

I said, 'But I have nothing to answer to.'

'So come down with us, make a statement and tell us that officially. It's not so difficult. It happens all the time. We're not arresting you.' He smiled, his mouth still slightly open, and part of me read the unvoiced 'yet', and I started to shiver.

Alison said, 'Peter, maybe you should.'

Her voice was sullen. I looked around at the mess, at everything that had been thrown onto the floor. 'But there's a lot to sort out.'

'Pete, just go with them. Get this sorted out and then come home.'

I approached her, tried to put my hands on her shoulders, but she pulled away. I said, 'If you think it's best, of course I will.' I was thinking, at least I won't have to explain to Alison, not just yet, not until I've had time to think . . .

McAllister touched my arm, and I looked at him, and he indicated for me to go down the stairs in front of him. I sat on the sofa to pull on my shoes, and he stopped by the table to pick up a pile of things – photo albums, letters, phone bills, old notebooks – and put them in a large clear plastic bag.

'Why do you need those?' I asked.

'I just want a closer look, that's all. You'll get them back when we've finished with them.'

We went out into the street. It was almost eight o'clock, and people were starting to move about, going off to work and getting the kids ready for school. McAllister opened the back door of the Rover and I got in. Then he got in the front passenger seat, and Joseph got in the driver's seat. Behind us, the police car's engine started up, and it pulled off into the traffic.

It all seemed so unreal, I couldn't really take any of it in. We went to Radford Road Police Station, and they took my belt and shoelaces from me, and emptied my pockets, and then Joseph announced that they wanted to take my fingerprints.

'Why?' I asked.

He looked surprised. 'To help us with our enquiries. Come with me, please.'

I said, 'But I don't have to give them?'

He stopped and turned to face me. 'No,' he said. 'You don't have to, but what are we supposed to think if you refuse us? After all, it's not a problem if you have nothing to hide.'

The sweat was starting to crawl across my skin. There was no way I could say no, so I agreed. They took me through to another office and took my prints, and then they left me in an interview room, my fingers still a little inky where the soap hadn't quite washed it off. It was a small room with bile-green walls. An extraction fan whirred somewhere high up, and the strip light had an irregular flicker. I sat at the table, waiting for something to happen.

Finally, Joseph and McAllister came back into the room, and frowned at me, as if they had the results of some test I had failed. They sat down opposite me, and Joseph opened two tapes and put them into the recorder on the table.

I said, 'I didn't think you'd record this.'

'It's for your own protection as much as our use,' McAllister said. 'But we could use it as evidence later. Now, you haven't been charged with anything, you can go whenever you like. Would you like a cup of tea?'

His question threw me for a moment, but I recovered. 'Yes,' I said. 'Milk no sugar. I didn't have time for any breakfast this morning.'

That didn't make either of them smile.

McAllister said, 'Teas all round, then.'

He was looking at me as he spoke, and Joseph didn't seem to have heard him. McAllister turned to face him and said, 'Well, why are you still sitting there?'

His head jerked up. 'Sir?'

'I said three teas, you dipstick.'

'Sir,' Joseph said, and scrambled out of his seat.

McAllister shook his head, and as the door closed behind Joseph he smiled at me, as if I was somehow colluding with his opinion of Joseph, and said, 'Needs a boot up the backside, that one. Cigarette?'

He was offering me a packet. 'No thanks,' I said.

He shrugged and put the packet back in his jacket pocket.

'Will this take a long time?' I asked. 'Only, I'm supposed to be at work, you know.'

'Would you like us to phone them?'

'No,' I said, trying to imagine Malcolm's reaction if the police phoned up. 'No, they'll cope.'

Joseph came back in, carrying three cups of vending-machine tea, grouped together between his hands. He handed them out, and I sipped my tea while he started up the tape recorder. I didn't want this to begin – I had no idea what I was going to say. I could feel the sweating starting again, cold against my skin, and I concentrated hard on keeping my hands steady.

'Okay,' McAllister said. 'So, you've already told us that you didn't know Sophie very well, and that you were trying to return her security swipecard to her when Jamie Forester met you at her flat. You phoned her parents because you were worried about her and wanted some news. Is that all accurate?'

'Yes,' I said.

'So, why did you go round to her parents' house yesterday?'

'Her parents' house? I didn't.'

McAllister sat back. 'Oh, come on, Mr Williams. We know it was you. Her brother would be able to identify you if it came to it.'

'Okay, so maybe I did.'

'Why?'

My lips were very dry, but the sweat was gathering

on my forehead and under my shirt. I said, 'I wondered if they'd heard anything, that's all.'

'After you decided it was a bad idea to have phoned them?' McAllister sat back. 'Come on, Mr Williams, that doesn't sound like a very good reason.'

I shrugged. 'I know. I was worried, that's all. She seemed like a nice girl. I'd hate anything to have happened to her.'

'So why lie to us about it?'

I moved positions in the chair and heard it creak under me. 'I suppose – well, you have this way of making everything sound suspicious. I haven't done anything wrong. I'm just worried about someone I know slightly who has disappeared. What's wrong with that?'

'Nothing,' McAllister said. 'Very community minded of you.' There was the slightest trace of a sneer in his voice. Then he said, 'Where were you on the eighteenth of May?'

That threw me. 'God, I don't know. Let me think.' Then it came to me. The day after Sophie disappeared. I said, 'Oh yes, I went to a conference in Derby. Community Planning Strategies in the Twenty-first Century.'

He smiled, and I thought, he already knew that. I felt a cold chill settling on the sweat in the small of my back. McAllister said, 'Good conference, was it?'

'As these things go, it was okay.'

'Stay for all of the sessions, did you?'

'Yes.'

'What time did it finish?'

'About four.'

'What time did you get home?'

I said, 'What difference does that make? Why is that even important?' He just looked at me, so I said, 'I don't know, about half six, I suppose. I looked round the shops in Derby before I came back.'

'Did you buy anything?'

'No. What relevance does this have?'

McAllister murmured, 'Stay calm, Mr Williams. We aren't accusing you of anything at all. We're just investigating a number of coincidences that could be construed as grounds for suspicion against you.'

'Suspicions of what?' I could hear the rising tension in my voice and I laid my palms flat on the table to stop my hands shaking, and I thought, Christ, thank God I destroyed the notebook, thank Christ they won't find that.

'Sophie has disappeared. Nobody's heard from her. We can't discount any possibilities, can we?'

'You think something has happened to her?'

McAllister didn't reply. We looked at one another.

I said, 'No, it can't have.' I thought of the notebook again – had that contained clues? Had I destroyed the clues that would find her? I thought about telling them, about recounting everything I could remember from the notebook, everything she had said. They could talk to Jonathan, get him to tell them what had happened, and I'd be in the clear, they would have to leave me alone.

'Why can't it have?'

'I don't know,' I said. 'You're the detective.'

McAllister said, 'Do you know what happened to Sophie after she boarded the Derby train?'

I took a deep breath and tried to keep my voice steady. 'No,' I said. 'I have no idea what happened to her, but I suspect she just ran away. Like you told me before, she did exactly the same thing once before.'

'If you're so sure she ran away, why are you worried about her? It doesn't make much sense to me.'

I said, 'You could turn that around. If I knew what had happened to her, why would I be contacting her family to ask? That doesn't make sense.'

McAllister shrugged. 'A good question,' he said, and for a moment I thought he had an answer, but then he seemed to change his mind. He said, 'So let's go back to how well you knew Sophie.'

'Hardly at all,' I said. 'I never even spoke to her. We just caught the same bus every morning.'

'You never even spoke to her? But you've been telling us how unlikely you think it is that she would kill herself. How do you know that without speaking to her?'

I said, 'I was just guessing, okay?'

Joseph was flicking back through his notepad, a frown on his face. McAllister waited while he flicked, looking at the pages turning, and I began to wonder what they were looking for. Then Joseph said, 'When we spoke to you at your house, you said, and I quote, "She wouldn't let anything get her down that much". How would you know that without speaking to her?'

I said, 'Well, maybe we said a few things to each other.'

'Like what?'

'Like hello, or, the bus is late, or, hard day at work. That sort of stuff.'

'And you could tell she wasn't suicidal from that?'

I shrugged. 'Yes, I think so.'

McAllister narrowed his eyes and looked closely at me. 'I can't tell what's going on with you,' he said. 'I think you're lying, but I can't work out why. I don't like people who lie to me.'

I said, 'I'm not lying.' I could feel the indignation creeping up on me. 'I haven't done anything wrong, and I don't think you should accuse me of being a liar when you haven't yet told me what it is I'm supposed to have done.'

'We don't know if you've done anything yet.'

There was a knock at the door. McAllister sighed and leaned forward to announce to the tape what was happening, while Joseph went to answer it. There was a young policeman in the doorway, and he and Joseph had an urgent conversation, too quiet to hear. Then Joseph shut the door and came back to the table, carrying a piece of paper, which he handed to McAllister. McAllister looked at it, then folded it in half and lay it on the table in front of him.

'This is very interesting,' he said. 'I am wondering how, if you really do barely know Sophie at all, your fingerprints got into her flat.'

'My fingerprints?' I pretended to look confused, but all the adrenaline pumping through my body made me shiver suddenly, and a fresh wave of sweat poured out under my shirt.

'Yes. When were you in her flat, then, Peter? The flat of a woman you claim to have hardly even known. How did that come about, eh?'

I looked up at him, and I realised that there was nothing I could do but tell the whole truth – about the notebook, about how everything had kind of spun out of control for a while. But then, as I began to formulate in my own mind how I would tell it, I realised that he was not going to believe me. I couldn't say the words out loud, all that would happen was I would end up in even more trouble as they decided I really had done something wrong. So I said, 'I would like to go now.'

'I bet you would,' McAllister said. 'Listen, Peter, I don't particularly care whether this is making you feel uncomfortable. I just want to find out what happened to Sophie Taylor.'

'I don't know what happened,' I said.

He leaned across the table. 'Did you bump her off?'

I started to say, 'That's ridiculous.'

'You've done something,' he said, and his voice

was growing louder as he spoke, winding himself up, building up to something. 'Just tell us the truth, Peter. What happened?'

'Nothing,' I said. 'Nothing happened.'

He was leaning closer to me, half standing, his weight against his fists on the table. I found I couldn't look away from his eyes, I had to look right at him, and he was stopping me from moving with the sheer force of his voice.

'All we want is the truth,' he said.

'I – I—'

'Did you do something terrible, Peter?'

'No,' I said. 'No, no.'

'Did you do something that you can't even admit to yourself, eh Peter? Something so unspeakable you're denying it to yourself? Why are you lying to us, Peter? What are you trying to hide?'

'I'm not—'

'And you're just trying to wriggle off the hook, aren't you, Peter? You just want to wriggle away and slink back to your girlfriend, don't you? Sorry, your fiancée. Why did you get engaged to her, eh? Was it because you feel guilty about something? Are you trying to make up for something by walking her down the aisle? Is that what you're doing to her? Because I tell you this, even if you didn't do something to Sophie, even if she strolls into a police station tomorrow to announce that she's alive and well, you're guilty of something. It's written all over your face.'

'That's not true!' I was on my feet now, face close

to his, shouting, trying to drown him out. 'You're wrong, you're wrong.'

'Calm down,' McAllister said, stepping back from the table.

'Sit down,' Joseph said.

I looked from one to the other, and sat down. 'You can't say things like that,' I said. 'They're not true.'

'I can say what I like,' McAllister said. He was walking around over near the door, kicking his shoes against the floor, as if he really was angry.

I addressed Joseph. 'I want to go now.'

'That wouldn't be a good idea,' Joseph said, glancing at McAllister and then leaning in towards me. He was calm, sympathetic even. 'Look, it doesn't look good if you walk out when someone accuses you of something. It makes you look guilty of something.'

I said, 'I haven't done anything wrong.' I was surprised to feel tears rising up through me, tears of frustration, and I swallowed them back. 'I want a solicitor, then.'

Joseph said, 'Why do you need one if you've done nothing wrong? You should just tell us the truth, get it over and done with. You'll feel much better afterwards, I promise you.'

I said, 'He's twisting everything.'

Joseph's voice was low, calm, a soothing voice like running water. 'If you tell us everything then you've got nothing to fear.'

I wiped away the tears that had collected in my eyes with my fingers, hoping Joseph hadn't noticed.

I felt wretched, weak, stupid. I said, 'But I haven't done anything wrong.'

'I know,' Joseph said. 'Tell us about it and you'll be able to go home, forget about all of this. That'll be all right, won't it, eh?'

I knew he was searching out eye contact, so I glanced at him, then wiped my nose on my hand and sniffed back more tears. McAllister was leaning against the door, looking up at the ceiling.

Joseph said, 'Now, tell us. When were you in Sophie's flat?'

'Last week. I found a key in the outhouse.'

'Why?'

'I don't know really,' I said. 'I was curious. I wanted to know what had happened to her.'

McAllister gave a short laugh and came back to the table. 'And you thought you'd find out by breaking into her flat?' He pulled his chair out and sat down. 'What are you, some kind of Hardy Boy?'

'Of course not,' I said, looking at Joseph.

Joseph said, 'Did you find anything in the flat?'

'No,' I said. 'Just her parents' phone number. It looked like someone had searched the place.' I looked up at him, suddenly excited by that thought. 'Yes, someone else had been in before me. That must be who you need to speak to, mustn't it?'

'That was us,' McAllister said, as if I was stupid. 'We went in ourselves. We knew someone had been in after us when we went back the second time. And apart from us, you're the only other person who has shown any interest in what has happened to Sophie.'

'And Jamie Forester,' I said, and felt a sudden surge of hope. 'Maybe he knows more than he's letting on, eh? Maybe he's the one you should be talking to?'

'We are satisfied that he has no case to answer for. You're the one with all the unexplained behaviour, Peter.'

'Or Jonathan,' I said. 'He's suspicious too.'

'What makes you say that?'

They were both looking at me closely. I wondered how I could tell them what I thought had been going on. I didn't think they would even believe me. So I said, 'I think I want a solicitor now.'

'Are you trying to hide something from us, then, Peter?'

'No,' I said. 'I do have the right to a solicitor, don't I?'

'Well, yes,' McAllister said. 'I'm just interested as to why you feel you need one? After all, we're just talking. You're just helping us with our enquiries, nothing more.'

I could hear the petulance in my tone even as I spoke, but I was past the point of caring. I said, 'You tell me not to leave and that I have something to answer for and then you tell me I don't need a solicitor. If I don't need a solicitor, then I think I'll go home now.'

'You're free to do that,' McAllister said. 'But of course, we'd only have to call you back in to answer more questions. This isn't over yet, you know. It'd be much better for you to help us now so that we can find out what happened. You must remember that we're all worried for Sophie Taylor's safety, and if you can help us in any way, I feel that you have a duty to do so, particularly as you claim to be concerned yourself about her safety.'

I sat and looked at him. He had a bit of a smile on his face, as if he thought he was getting somewhere, as if he thought he was so bloody clever. Joseph was looking away. McAllister ran his tongue quickly over his lips, still looking directly at me, as if he was expecting me to say something startling, to break down and confess to something. I had the sudden desire to stand up and swing for him, to punch that self-satisfied smirk off his face, to see the blood running down his chin and dripping onto his nasty polyester tie, mingling in with the shiny blue stripes, seeping onto his suit. I could imagine him coated in shiny red blood. He was never going to understand, he had no way of even conceptualising the situation, and I would never be able to explain it to him.

I said, very slowly in the hope that he would get it, 'I have already told you. I don't really know Sophie at all. I was on the same bus as her the day she went to Derby. I saw her get off at the station. She left her swipecard behind. I went round to her flat to return it and met Jamie Forester there. After that I kept bumping into Jamie and he kept asking me if I had heard from Sophie, and I kept saying no.'

'Why did you tell Jamie that you were a friend of Sophie's if you hardly even knew her?'

'I don't know. Politeness. I was knocking on

her door, for Christ's sake, I couldn't say I was a complete stranger, could I?'

'So you're saying that all of this is some misunderstanding, and you have nothing at all to do with Sophie Taylor's disappearance?'

'Yes,' I said, feeling a sudden relief that we were finally getting somewhere.

McAllister looked at Joseph and then said, 'Okay, let's start from the top again, shall we? And maybe this time you'll tell us the truth.'

Chapter Twenty-two

The police didn't give me a lift home after the interview had ended, but I was actually relieved. The recycled air inside the police station was stifling and it was good to stand out in the open, sucking in traffic fumes by the side of the road while the perspiration cooled in an unpleasant layer under my clothes.

I went into a shop and bought some cigarettes and stood smoking while I waited for the bus. It was early evening. I felt drained, as if the police had sucked everything out of me with their incessant questions. I was just skin and bones, a walking sack, emptied of everything else.

I didn't know what I was going to find when I finally got home. The day was dragging into twilight but there were no lights on in the house, and I imagined Alison curled up on the sofa with the duvet over her, or foetus-like under the covers in bed, or sat in some corner just waiting for me to return. By the time I had been into every room in the house, calling her name, stepping over the mess of books and clothes and papers and objects that had been our life, I realised that I didn't know what I was going to do without her.

I sat down on the sofa among the debris, and then I phoned Steve.

He didn't seem surprised to hear from me. 'Alison phoned,' he said. 'Are you okay?'

'Yes. Did she say where she was going?'

'A friend from work. Don't call her, though . . .'

I felt my heart pound in my chest. 'Andrew?' I asked. 'Was it Andrew?'

He hesitated, just for a moment. 'Yes, but don't call tonight. Give her time.'

'I can't believe she went to Andrew's,' I said. 'Of all the places she could have gone—'

'Listen,' Steve was saying. 'Listen, Pete, leave her, she's upset—'

'And how do you think I feel?'

He hesitated, then said, 'Come for a drink, Pete. Get blasted, get out of your skull. Phone her tomorrow.' I started to protest, but he said, 'Leave it, honestly.'

He had been given a loop message, I could see that – he was just going to repeat the same words. I wanted to demand what he was doing, why he was always siding with her these days, but my mouth was suddenly dry.

'Pete?' Steve said. 'You still there?'

'Yeah.'

'So come for a drink with me. Meet me at the Arms.'

'Okay,' I said. 'I'll do that.' And I cut the connection before he could tell me again not to phone Alison.

Andrew's number was programmed into the phone's speed-dial, and I pressed the button and heard the phone stutter through the tones until it started to ring.

Andrew answered. I said, 'Is Alison there?'

'Peter,' he said. 'Peter, I don't think she wants to—'

'Just put her on the bloody phone,' I said, and he must have put his hand over the receiver, because I heard several seconds of muffled conversation.

Then Alison. 'Hello, Peter,' she said, and I knew she'd been crying.

I said, 'Alison, Alison, how are you?'

'Okay,' she said, monotone. 'They let you go?'

'Yes. I told you, it was a mistake. A misunderstanding.'

'They trashed our house,' she said. I could tell that she was close to crying again. 'All our hard work,' she said. 'Why won't you tell me what's going on?'

'I haven't done anything,' I said. 'You know that. Come home, Alison, please. I need you here.'

She said, 'I phoned work for you. Told them it was a family emergency.'

'Thank you,' I said. 'Please come home.'

'I can't,' she said, and her voice was cracking. Then she said, 'I don't want to.'

'Why not?' But I knew why not, and it cut right into me. 'You think I did something, don't you?'

'No, no—' she started.

I cut her off. 'You do. You really think I've got something to do with that girl disappearing.'

She gave a heavy sigh, magnified by the hiss on the line. 'I don't know what to think,' she said. 'You have been hiding things from me.'

'Nothing like that,' I said. 'Don't start all that again, Alison, I told you.' She had started to cry, and I felt myself hardening, because how did she think I felt, what did she think this was doing to me?

She said, 'You told me you didn't know that girl. You lied to me.'

'No,' I said. 'No, I didn't.'

'You've been lying to me all along,' she said. 'Were you having a relationship – were you having an affair with her?'

'No,' I said. 'Don't be ridiculous, I told you—'

'You're a liar,' she said.

'No,' I started, but I knew she wasn't going to listen to me now. She was convinced, she had been turned against me, it didn't matter what I said. So I said, 'What about Andrew then, eh?' A sense of recklessness, of savageness, surged up through me. 'All these work do's you tell me you're going to. I'm not stupid. Why'd you go running to Andrew, eh? I'm not the one with something to hide.'

'Bastard,' she said. Then, 'For Christ's sake, grow up. I don't want to talk to you any more.'

'Don't go,' I started.

'I'll talk to you when you're more rational,' she said.

I opened my mouth to plead with her again, but she had already hung up. I considered phoning back, but I didn't know what I could say, I didn't even know what I wanted to say. I could imagine her turning to Andrew, and Andrew comforting her, hugging her, telling her that I wasn't worth it, telling her that she deserved better than me. I could picture his smarmy face – I wanted to hit him, feel the strength running through my muscles, feel my bones make contact with his flesh, his bone. I could picture him falling back, clutching his nose, red ribbons of blood streaking down his face, and me standing over him, curled fists, keyed up, alive.

I sat on the sofa in the gathering gloom and smoked two cigarettes, one after the other. I was starting to regret the things I had said to Alison. The house was a mess; I could imagine her sitting waiting for news, waiting for me all day, and all the mess piled up around her, and no escape from looking at it. None of this was her fault. She had to turn to somebody. But Andrew – out of everyone she knew, she had chosen Andrew.

I went upstairs to the bathroom. Alison had piled most of the bottles of shampoo and conditioner and face cream and shaving foam back on the windowsill. The bottom of the bath was scummy with spilt shampoo and conditioner. I rinsed it out with the showerhead and then ran a bath.

I soaked and scrubbed myself in that bath, determined to get rid of the sour smell of stale sweat and tension, to rub off the dirt and sleaze that seemed to ooze from every pore after all that time in the police station. As I ducked my head under the water and rinsed shampoo off my hair, I lay listening to the strangeness of the muffled silence, with nothing but the dull roar of the water tank filling up to consume my thoughts, until my fingers grew wrinkled and the water cooled. Then I got out of the bath and dried myself carefully. I felt cleaner, more alive. And I wanted to get stupidly, recklessly drunk, just me and Steve, like the old days. I couldn't bear to be in the house, not with the mess, not with the air disturbed by the strangeness of the day's events, not without Alison.

It was only when I was walking down towards the Arms that I thought suddenly of Jamie Forester – would he be there? Would he know what had happened today? I nearly turned right around to walk the other way. But where could I go? What could I do to escape everything that was happening? It felt as if the situation was closing in on me, a dark box with a flush lid, blocking out the light and sucking out the air until it was hard to breathe and it was a struggle to stop myself from shaking, collapsing, falling down, my lungs heaving in that desperate gasp for air, stumbling forward.

And then I was inside, and it was just the Arms, with people sitting around drinking, and the two barmaids leaning against the counter, laughing with the regulars, and Steve racking up for a game of pool and sipping his pint and smiling at me.

I staggered over to where he was and sat down

at the nearest table. He said, 'Pete, you look like shit.'

The air was spinning, lilac lights, flashes, and my chest burned as I tried to fight for breath, and I felt a blackness closing in. Then I could hear Steve's voice above me, and the dizziness cleared, and I opened my eyes and I was sitting in the chair. He was saying, 'Are you okay, mate? Pete? What can I do?'

I shook it all away, shook the drowsiness out of my head, forced myself to smile at Steve as my breathing returned to normal. I said, 'Sorry, sorry,' and he waved that away, his face still scored by concern. I said, 'S'okay, honest, I'm okay.'

He said, 'Here, let me get you a drink? What do you want?'

'Whisky,' I said, thinking of oblivion.

He brought a double over to me, then went back to the bar. I took a deep breath and sucked in the whisky fumes, longing for something to shake me up or knock me out. I felt pale, weak. Then I took a sip of the burning liquid, and felt it run down through my throat to my chest, and settle there with a hot glow.

Steve came back with two pints and looked at me with slightly less concern. I said, 'Thanks, mate.'

He said, 'Christ, you had me worried there.'

I nodded, sipping the pint. 'I'm okay.'

He said, 'What the hell's happening? Alison was beside herself. Why'd they take you in?'

I shook my head, not sure what words I could use to explain what had happened. It was all so ludicrous, so ridiculous. How could anybody really think I could do the things they had accused me of? Then I couldn't help smiling. 'I think they think I've bumped someone off,' I said, and then I was giggling into my pint. It was too surreal, too absurd to take seriously any longer. 'I was helping them with their enquiries,' I managed to say, and Steve watched me, and I couldn't explain to him why it was funny.

We drank another couple of pints, and I told him about the police, and what bastards they were, about how they twisted every little thing and made everything seem so important, so different from how it really was. So suspicious. Steve joined me for another double whisky, and I really was laughing by then, until I thought of Alison, with Andrew, not knowing what was going on, being comforted by Andrew. How would she ever look at me again? How could I ever hope to make her believe me again? I felt the long black slide of my life, dizzyingly close.

'She's ruined my life,' I said.

'You can't blame her,' Steve said. 'You need to talk to her. She's upset. Anyone would be.'

'Not Alison,' I said, and I wanted to shake him and tell him to keep up. 'Sophie fucking Taylor, that's who I'm talking about.'

Steve nodded down at his pint and I could tell he wasn't really following what I was saying, he had drunk too much too quickly. I felt a knot of hatred rising through me, sour like the beer. I wanted to explain it to him, because it was suddenly very clear to me. Sophie was jealous, that was what was going on. Sophie knew how much I loved Alison – she knew I wouldn't do anything to jeopardise that, but she never would leave a thing alone. She was teasing me, winding me up, and all the time she was looking for a way to cause trouble between me and Alison. That was her aim all along – getting the police involved was just her way of upping the ante, just her way of pushing her point home. She was framing me, deliberately making me look guilty of something, just to punish me for loving Alison.

'It's all her fault,' I said, but Steve didn't seem to hear me.

So I downed my pint and got up to get another one from the bar. Steve just watched me, in and out of focus as the room swayed. He was only halfway down his pint but I ordered him another anyway. As I waited for the drinks I looked around the pub, and I saw him – Jamie – at his usual table, with his usual mates. Part of me wanted to go across to him, tell him just what I thought of Sophie and all her friends, tell him what they'd all done to my life. I wanted to declare to the world just how much I hated Sophie for the things she was doing to me. But the barman wanted the money for the pints, and the coins refused to add up, and by the time I'd sorted that out and looked back over, Jamie's seat was empty. I wondered if I'd been imagining things.

'You're really going for it, aren't you?' Steve said as I got back to the table with only a little beer slopped out of the glasses.

'I need it,' I said.

'Alcoholism is not the solution,' Steve said in a mock-infomercial voice, but seemed to run out of words then, and fell silent.

I smiled at his weak joke and tried to shake myself out of my stupor, but I couldn't help feeling that none of this was going to get resolved, that these events were going to keep coming round, a feedback loop, a bad dream I couldn't wake up from. I wanted to ask Steve what he thought, but he was talking to himself about Forest's mid-field, and the golden days under Cloughie, and whether Forest would ever regain their rightful place as European champions. I couldn't form any words to interrupt, so I just drank some more of my pint.

Finally, the bell rang for last orders, and Steve said, 'Let's get out of here, Pete. Let's go home. You look all in.'

I shrugged, looking down at the pint I couldn't remember finishing. Then I said, 'Okay,' because I didn't want to be sitting there any more, I didn't want to be occupying a regular kind of space, I didn't want to feel myself being anywhere very much. I stumbled after Steve out into the cool night, and the shock of the air in my lungs seemed to sober me up or at least wake me up, because I managed to respond normally to Steve's conversation. He was going on about the weather, about the bastard thing of going to work the next morning, about how he and Alison and I would have to go out for a meal or something some time soon, celebrate our engagement once everything had blown over because he was sure it all would, me and Alison were made for each other, he'd said so all along. Then we were at the place where our routes home parted company, and he asked me if I would be okay alone, and I convinced him yes without even really trying, without even feeling that anything was going to be okay. I stood there on the corner watching him head towards his house, and then I felt myself swaying as I walked along the road towards my home.

I heard someone coming up behind me, but it wasn't until he said, 'Hey, I'm talking to you,' that the significance hit me, and I stopped and turned. It was Jonathan, swollen with anger, taller than I remembered, leaning towards me as he spoke. I remembered Jamie being in his seat and then disappearing – where was he now? Made a phone call and then legged it – I was almost disappointed that he hadn't stayed around.

I said, 'I didn't hear you. How are you?'

'Don't give me that,' Jonathan said. 'Don't give me any of that crap. I hear the police took you in today. What'd they want, eh?'

'None of your business,' I said, feeling reckless in the face of his aggression.

'It was to do with my sister, and that makes it my business.'

He had bunched his fingers into fists, his arms loose by his sides. I kept a distance between us. 'I don't know what you think's going on,' I said, 'but I haven't got anything to do with your sister running away.'

'The police don't seem to think that. The police were round at my mum and dad's place, telling them how they don't think that—'

'The police are wrong,' I said.

'The police don't make mistakes like that,' Jonathan said.

'They do when people tell them things to mislead them,' I said, and it was suddenly very clear to me. Jonathan didn't want anyone to know the truth – he was as selfish as Sophie – he was quite happy to see me suffer if it kept his hands clean. I said, 'You know exactly what's going on, don't you?'

He seemed surprised. 'What do you mean?'

'You and Sophie,' I said. I felt vicious suddenly. 'Your little secret. The thing you don't want anyone else to know about.'

'What?' He was putting on a good act of ignorance, but I could tell he was worried, I could tell he realised I knew more than he thought. He said, 'What the fuck are you talking about?'

'You know,' I said.

'I don't,' he said. 'What are you saying?'

He wasn't giving anything away, but I knew there was something, I could feel it. I said, 'You can deny it all you like, but I know the truth.'

'What truth?' He seemed more confused than angry for a moment, but then his rage returned in a wave. 'You're a fucking nutter,' he said. 'You're a fucking psycho. You're a fucking pervert, that's it, isn't it?'

'Don't be stupid,' I said. I was getting tired of

his denials. I could barely see him in the darkness; I screwed up my eyes to try to see him more clearly, but I was swaying too much, my eyes were hurting as I moved, my brain was throwing everything out of focus. 'Don't be stupid,' I repeated, louder.

'Why'd the police keep you all day, then?'

I just laughed at that. 'Why'd they let me go without charge?'

Jonathan was stepping closer to me.

I tried to push my advantage home. 'Tell me the truth,' I said. 'It's just me and you. Tell me what your big secret is.'

'There is no secret,' he said. 'If you think you know so much, you tell me.' He was shifting his weight, edging closer to me. 'You don't know nothing,' he said.

I swayed away, tempted to laugh at his double negative, tempted to demand answers, tempted to tell him that he was the pervert.

He said, 'Where's my sister?'

'I don't know,' I said. 'I keep telling you, I don't know.'

In the gloom, I didn't see his fist coming in time. He turned too quickly, caught me off-balance, caught me hard across the corner of my mouth. I was surprised, and fell. The pavement span past my eyes. Then he kicked me, hard, in the gut; I rolled, got halfway up, saw him standing over me.

I said, 'Fuck,' and found blood in my mouth.

He was walking away from me. I struggled to my feet, my hand clutching my side. 'You're the fucking psycho,' I shouted, but he kept walking, not even looking back.

I leaned against the nearest wall and tried to suck air into my lungs. I was shaking. I knew I should go after him, force him to tell me what was going on, but my legs wouldn't respond, I could only move in jerks. I felt a wave of nausea running through me, out through the extremities of my body. I spat blood onto the pavement.

When I felt able to walk, there was no sign of Jonathan. There was nobody at all out on the street. I stumbled slowly towards home.

In the bathroom, I ran a basinful of hot water and washed my face. The heat of the water sucked and burned at my skin. The corner of my mouth was slightly swollen, the lip a little blue, the gums around my teeth bleeding. I crawled into bed and lay there awake for a good long time, feeling the pulse of the swelling bruise, trying not to think, trying to empty my mind. But I couldn't get away from the fact that Sophie had done it again, that even now she was able to control things, able to cause trouble for me. I had the feeling that I would never be free of her, never be completely beyond her grasp, and it was like a knot tightening around my insides, it was like she was trying to hurt me, she was deliberately trying to punish me. I wanted to sleep, but I didn't think she was going to let me. After a while, I turned onto my back and lay there, listening to the sounds from the street outside.

Chapter Twenty-three

I had been too drunk to set the clock radio, but my internal alarm was working and I pulled myself out of bed only a few minutes after my usual time. My head was angry with me, sparking a headache each time I moved too quickly, and my mouth tasted like it had been coated in tar while I slept. After a bath I felt a little more human, and I stood examining my face in the bathroom mirror. I looked tired, my eyes rimmed red, but the bruise on my lip didn't look as bad as I had feared.

The house was quiet without Alison. It seemed to echo more, as if the house itself knew that there was something wrong. The place was still a tip, but I couldn't bring myself to do anything about that.

I made myself a strong black coffee then went through my briefcase. The police had taken my diary and my action book away with them. As I touched my pens and my calculator and the folder of papers I should have been reading, each item seemed strange somehow, the texture of the surfaces suddenly unfamiliar, coldly unresponsive in my hands.

I didn't want to go to work, but I didn't want to stay at home either, so I pulled on my jacket and headed out. Alison's car was still parked in the road and I did consider taking it, but my eyes were not focusing properly in the bright sunlight, so I went for the bus.

Traffic was slow, backed up from the traffic lights a quarter of a mile away, and when the bus finally arrived it was fuller than usual, as if heavy traffic could affect the number of people sitting on the bus. Someone was sitting in my usual seat, a fat girl reading a novel, and I went further towards the rear of the bus and sank down there, feeling the strangeness of the new angle of view, feeling the strangeness of all the people sitting around me buried in their own private worlds.

The work on the tram route was well underway by now, and I watched from above as we crawled past the neon-vested workmen, knee-deep in narrow trenches. Two more years of roadworks, and when it all finished I would still be following this route, going to the same office, the same job, doing the same things every day of my working life.

When we finally pulled up outside the railway station, I watched all the people getting off, all the people hurrying in and coming out of the station building, and I remembered Sophie getting off the bus and disappearing inside. I imagined her at the counter, flush with the excitement of misbehaving, buying a ticket to Derby. What would she have asked for? A single? A return? And what if there was no return?

Then the bus was jolting away again, and heading out towards Trent Bridge. As my stop approached, I considered not getting up, I considered staying on the bus until it looped round through the suburbs and came back into town again, but even as I thought about it, I was getting up and ringing the bell, stepping down the stairs, waiting at the doors. There were other people from my office there, and I nodded hello and forced a smile, and none of them asked where I had been, or what had happened to my lip, or why the sweat was gathering like a descending curtain around my hairline. Soon we were inside the building, in through the cool air of the reception and up the stairs, and I was saying goodbye to the people as I headed for my new office, the Senior Planner's Office. I could see the glances of the women from my section as I headed in there, and when I shut the door behind me and sank down into my chair, I was dripping with sweat and chilled by the air-conditioning pumped out in preparation for a warm day.

I sat looking at the piles of paper on my desk. There was a stack of mail date-stamped the day before and I dutifully flicked through for anything urgent. Then I looked at the folders in my in-tray, and the half-written reports in my action tray, but my eyes didn't seem to focus, I couldn't make any sense of the letters on the pages. It all felt distant, disconnected from my life.

I rubbed my eyes and walked around the room, then sat down and tried again, but there was a noise coming from the air-conditioning vent, and when I got up on my chair and examined the vent, high up in the wall by the ceiling, I saw that it was full of old dirt, grime, dust, blocked by it. I considered trying to clean it, but I had no duster to use. I was trying to dislodge some of the dirt with the end of a ruler when Malcolm knocked and walked straight into my office.

I got down off the chair. 'Vent's making a noise,' I said.

He nodded, not even fazed. Then he said, 'Feeling better after yesterday?'

'Yes, thanks,' I said.

'Flu, was it?'

'No.'

'Oh. Jenny seemed to think it was flu.' I opened my mouth to start some kind of explanation, but then he saw the bruise on my lip. 'God, Peter, what happened?'

'Walked into a door,' I said. I knew I should tell him what was going on, prepare him in case McAllister and Joseph turned up asking questions, but I suddenly felt very wretched, and I couldn't find the words to begin.

He said, 'Listen, about the Park Estate thing. I want you to get together with Jan and work on our response.'

'Sure,' I said, relieved. 'I'll talk to her later.'

He nodded, and left me. He had left my office door open and I could hear the familiar hum of the chat in the main office, and the clatter of fingers on keyboards, and phones ringing. I closed the door and sat down at my desk again, but I couldn't bring myself to open a folder or start actioning the mail. I turned on my computer and checked my email, but there was nothing interesting, only a few circulars about meetings and report deadlines. I beat my own high score on intermediate Minesweeper, twice, and then I surfed the net, but I didn't find anything interesting to read.

When I came back from a particularly unengaging chat with Jan about the Park Estate project, it was twelve o'clock. I was considering taking an early lunch break and went to the window to see what the weather was doing. Bright and clear. A green Rover was pulling into the parking space Anthony usually occupied; I watched, waiting for Anthony to arrive, outraged. He didn't show up, but when the two men got out of the car, it nearly stopped my breath. One was McAllister; it wasn't Joseph with him, but some other CID clone in a nasty suit. I wished I had told Malcolm what had happened when I had the chance earlier – I cursed my own stupidity, that he was going to find out this way. A part of me was ready to rush down and intercept them, or to find Malcolm now and tell him, damage limitation, get him on my side.

But what if they wanted to ask me more questions? I didn't think I could cope with that, not today, not with a hammer striking against the inside of my skull. So I pulled on my jacket and told the main office that I was going into town for lunch, and I headed for the stairs.

They were at the bottom of the stairs; I could see down through the banisters to a corner of the reception desk, and I could hear the security officer telling them that my office was on the first floor. So I went up, to Trading Standards, and stood by their door peering down through the banisters. McAllister was saying something to his sidekick as they came up, but I couldn't tell what over the sound of their feet on the tiled stairs. Then they pulled open the double doors and headed into Planning, and I shot down the stairs and out, quick as I could, head down, not looking back until I was out of view of the windows, behind the next building. There was a bus coming up the road as I reached the stop, and I stuck my hand out and thanked my lucky stars, because I had got away.

The question was what I was going to do next. It didn't seem likely that the police were going to leave me alone. Not content with just wrecking my relationship, they seemed to be determined to cause trouble for me at work as well. But as the bus headed in towards the city centre, I realised that I had no intentions of going back to work, not today at least. So I got off the bus in the Market Square and stood there for a moment, considering what I was going to do.

It seemed to me that if I could only find out what had happened to Sophie, all of this would go away. The police would stop harassing me, Alison would come back home, I would be able to concentrate at work. I couldn't go and talk to Jonathan, I realised that, but I knew Jamie worked in the city, at the Selectadisc record shop just off the square.

The shop was busy, crowded with students and teenagers spending their parents' money. Over the sound system they were playing loud guitar-based commercial retro-punk with someone shouting unintelligible lyrics. The walls were painted black and covered with posters advertising local gigs and local groups. Kids jostled one another as they thumbed through the racks of CDs. I worked my way through the crowd to the cash desk at the back, where a long-haired teenage boy in a Metallica T-shirt was handing change to a younger girl. I asked him where I would find Jamie Forester, struggling to be heard over the music, and he directed me upstairs.

It was much quieter upstairs. The second-hand vinyl section, with a scattering of thirty-somethings looking through the racks. Jamie saw me before I saw him; when I went over to him behind the counter, he already had his scowl prepared.

'What do you want?' he asked.

'I want to talk to you,' I said. He gave his head a dismissive flick and I thought he was going to walk away from me. I said, 'You've got to believe me, I've got nothing to do with Sophie's disappearance.'

'Why should I believe you?'

'Why would I lie about this? Why would I come here otherwise?' But he was turning away from me, and I said quickly, 'It's got something to do with Jonathan.'

'Jonathan?' The scowl had turned to a frown. 'What makes you think that?'

'He's hiding something,' I said.

'Rubbish,' Jamie said, but he didn't seem that certain. 'What would he have to hide?'

'I don't know,' I said. 'That's why I want to talk to you.'

Someone had come to the cash register with a record. Jamie took it from them and rang it into the till. When he had finished serving the customer he came back to me. 'Why should I believe anything you say?'

'I've got no reason to lie,' I said.

'You have if the police think you've done something.'

I said, 'I don't think anything has happened to Sophie. I think she's just run away again.'

'So why are you so bothered, then?'

'Because of the police. They think I'm lying, but I'm not. I want to show them that they're wrong. Maybe then they'll find Sophie and everyone can stop worrying.'

He sighed and shook his head. Another customer had come to the till. He said, 'Look, I can't talk now. I'm on lunch in twenty minutes. I'll meet you in the café on the corner.'

'Okay,' I said, and left him to his customers.

I fought my way out of the shop and walked down the road to the café on the corner. It was one of the trendy new coffee bars that had sprung up like fungus all over the city. I ordered a Mochaccino and sat down at a small table near the back. It did occur to me that Jamie might phone the police, or Jonathan, but I knew I had to risk this.

I had nearly finished the Mochaccino when Jamie appeared. He seemed to be alone. He sat down opposite me, glancing around, as if he was nervous.

'So,' he said. 'You wanted to talk. Go for it.'

He was looking around again. I said, 'Did you tell someone that we were meeting?'

'Why would I do that?'

But he didn't look at me. I said, 'Okay, I think whatever has happened to Sophie had something to do with Jonathan.'

'You said that already,' he said. 'What makes you think that?'

I hesitated. The crunch moment. Should I tell him about the notebook, come clean about everything? I said, 'It's something Sophie said to me one time.'

'What did she say?'

I was struggling to find the words, struggling against all the details I didn't know. 'It was about the reason she ran away last time,' I said. 'There was some sort of trouble. She and Jonathan. Sophie thought all the phone calls she was getting were about that.'

He narrowed his eyes slightly, thinking. 'She would've told me,' he said finally.

'You don't remember anything?'

'No,' he said. Then he gained confidence. 'What would that have to do with it, anyway? What's that got to do with you?'

'Nothing,' I said. 'I keep telling you, I've got nothing to do with any of this.'

'For someone who's got nothing to do with it, you seem to have a hell of a lot of ideas.'

The suspicion had returned to his tone, but he was listening to me. I had the feeling that I could convince him of this, could win him over to my side and use him to challenge Jonathan, to force Jonathan to tell us the truth. I was close to the answer, I could feel it – Jamie could give me the missing pieces, could help me to fit it all together.

But then I was aware of someone striding towards us, through the café, and when I looked up I realised it was Jonathan. As Jamie saw my expression he gave a little cry and turned to look.

Jonathan grabbed at me, grabbed my jacket and shirt in his fists and half pulled me to my feet. I tried to pull myself free, my fingers grappling uselessly against his hands. His face was contorted into an ugly expression; he had his face up close to mine, and I could see the blood vessels in his eyes. He said, 'I thought I told you to leave us alone?'

'We were just talking,' I said.

The chair behind me had toppled backwards; customers at other tables had edged away; the girl behind the counter was poised to come over, caught in a moment of indecision.

Jonathan said, 'You shouldn't be harassing us.'

I was tempted to say that he was the one who could more accurately be described as harassing. Instead, I said, 'I'm just trying to find out what's going on.'

Jonathan seemed suddenly to be aware of everyone looking at us, and released me. I pulled my chair upright and sat down. It was very quiet in the café.

Jamie said, 'He's got some wild idea that you know what's happened to Sophie. He doesn't know what he's talking about.'

I wasn't surprised that Jamie had jumped sides so quickly. He had phoned Jonathan, after all – last night in the pub, and today. I couldn't expect him to see things my way that quickly.

Jonathan said, 'He's a fucking nutter.'

'You're the one with all the secrets,' I said. He turned to face me, standing over me, and I couldn't bring myself to look up at him.

He said quietly, 'I should take you outside and give you a good hiding. I should've done more than split your lip last night.'

I addressed Jamie. 'You see? Now tell me he isn't hiding something. Now tell me I'm wrong.'

Jamie frowned, but said, 'You're wrong. Tell him, Jonathan.'

There was an appeal in Jamie's voice. I looked up at Jonathan. 'Yes, tell me,' I said. 'Tell me all about your little secrets, eh? Tell me all about what happened to make Sophie run away last time.'

'Nothing happened,' he said.

'So what's the big secret, then? Why'd Sophie have to cover things up, to get you off the hook? Why was she frightened of you?'

'Frightened of me?' Jonathan seemed a little nonplussed for a moment, and then he sat down and said, 'You've got a suspicious mind. There wasn't anything, nothing big, not the way you make it sound.'

'Oh, come on,' I said. 'Sophie told me. She said you were lying to everyone. You made her lie to cover it all up. You made her swear to tell nobody, and that's what made her run away before. She couldn't handle it.'

'That's not true,' he said. 'She didn't run away because of that. She'd messed up her college course, they were about to kick her off. She was upset about that. She always messes everything up, and she's such a spoilt little brat she just ran away instead of admitting it.'

Jamie frowned at that, but didn't say anything in Sophie's defence. I said, 'But you made her lie to her parents. She felt terrible about that.'

'Yeah,' Jonathan said. 'So terrible she cleared off and didn't care that they were worried sick about her.'

There was resentment in his tone. I ignored it and pressed on. 'But she was lying to protect you. It had something to do with you. You can't deny it was partly your fault.'

'It wasn't my fault,' he said, and sat back in his seat, looking at Jamie. 'Don't listen to this psycho,' he said. 'It was nothing, really. Kids' stuff. You know how Sophie likes to play the wild child, until it comes to it. We just got it wrapped around our-selves, that's all, but it's all in the past now. It's got nothing to do with why she's run away this time. I haven't even thought about it in a long time.'

'So?' Jamie said. He seemed to be unaware that he had already heard the first lie. 'What happened, then?'

I folded my arms, casually, trying to look disinterested, but I was desperate to hear what story Jonathan would concoct that could explain what had happened.

Jonathan glanced around and leaned in close to Jamie, so that their faces were almost touching, as if he was terrified that someone might overhear. 'Don't you dare repeat this,' he said. 'I'd be in real trouble, I mean, serious.'

'Oh, please,' I said. 'Don't be so melodramatic.'

Jonathan flashed me a scowl, but turned back to Jamie. 'It was only a couple of months after I started working at the garage. I'd been working on a car for some friend of the boss, a BMW, really nice, I mean, a series seven, practically brand new.' He obviously expected more of a response from us. He said impatiently, 'That's thirty-seven-odd grand's worth of car.'

Jamie said, 'Thirty-seven grand for a car? Could buy a house for that round here.'

'Exactly,' Jonathan said. A little smile had crept onto his lips. 'It had everything, I mean, the whole lot.' He laughed. 'I mean, who wouldn't want to drive a car like that?'

Jamie said, 'You didn't?'

'Yeah,' Jonathan said, and flashed an embarrassed

smile at Jamie but didn't look at me. 'Sophie was upset. I wanted to cheer her up. You know she'd love that sort of thing. We were just kids, we were stupid. We wanted an adventure, you know? I'd have backed out, I mean, I wouldn't have gone through with it, but Sophie was really keen, she was always pulling crazy stuff back then.'

'Oh, that's right,' I said. 'Blame Sophie, why don't you?'

He ignored me. 'Nobody would've known. We could've brought it back and nobody would've been any the wiser. It was stupid, I know, but I just couldn't resist. I mean, a car like that – it's a dream, isn't it?'

He didn't wait for either of us to agree.

'We were only going to go round the block,' he said. 'But that would've been daft, I mean, I never even got out of second gear. So we took it on the M1, me and Sophie. It was nearly midnight, there was no traffic, so we opened her up, did ninety-five. Beautiful. So much power I only had to touch the accelerator. Nothing like that feeling. And it was good getting one over on my boss, I mean, he'd have flipped if he knew, sacked me on the spot, and he's such a bastard, it felt great, like putting a giant finger up to him.' He shook his head, but he was still smiling. 'Like I said, we were just stupid kids. I was going too fast, I know, just got carried away. Didn't stop in time, up at Cinderhill island. Got hit by a car coming round the island, not hard, but hard enough. Spun the BMW round so it was facing the other way. Smashed the whole wing in.'

'But nobody was hurt?' Jamie asked, breathless, as if he was buying this ludicrous story.

'No, no, but the other driver was going mental. I dunno what he'd've done if we'd hung around, I mean, it was obvious it wasn't our car. But we didn't stick around to see. We just legged it, left the car there and ran for it.' He gave a slight giggle, as if he was reliving the moment. 'I mean, just left the BMW there, headlights on, doors open, right in the middle of the traffic.'

'Wow!' Jamie said.

I wanted to laugh, but I didn't.

'Well, we were panicking then,' Jonathan said. He seemed to be enjoying telling this story – I wondered if he had told it before, and whether he had embellished the details. 'I was all for walking into a police station and admitting to it, but Sophie said no, said there was no point doing that. She said we should lie about it, fake a break-in at the garage. Well, I wasn't gonna land myself in it if there was a choice, was I? So that's what we did. Kicked the back door in, messed up the office, threw all the car keys around the place, spray-painted the walls.'

'And you got away with it?' Jamie asked, which seemed like a stupid question in the circumstances. 'What about fingerprints, stuff like that?'

'Mine were all over the car,' Jonathan said, 'but I'd been working on it earlier, so that didn't prove anything. They never took Sophie's, thank God. It would've been all over if they had.'

Jamie seemed to be believing him. I tried to rescue the situation. 'What a load of rubbish,' I said. 'What's the big deal? It's hardly the secret of the century, is it?'

Jonathan looked at me angrily and said, 'I'd've lost my job, and probably my licence. I could've gone down for that. And who else would've given me a job after that? Anyway, I told you, we panicked. We weren't exactly thinking straight. What would you have done, turned yourself in and copped for the lot?'

I wasn't going to give in that easily. 'What's that got to do with Sophie running away?' I asked. 'It doesn't make any sense. You're lying, I know you are. There's something else.'

'You just shut up,' Jonathan said. 'I'm not talking to you, anyway.'

I wanted to protest that he was just trying to get himself off the hook, I wanted to shout that Jonathan was the one who had been frightening Sophie so badly, I wanted to shake Jamie for even listening to this nonsense, but Jonathan was rambling on again.

'My boss twigged that it was us right off. I was terrified; I didn't want to lose my job or get arrested, but Sophie said keep quiet, she said it'd all be okay. How was I supposed to know how much aggro there'd be about it? If I'd known I'd've owned up right away, but I didn't, and the longer it went on the harder it was.'

'And that's why Sophie ran away?' Jamie asked.

'No. Maybe. Look, I don't know why she did. She took it all to heart, but I thought she was okay.' He gave me a challenging look, as if daring me to disagree with him. 'Anyway, it was after it all blew over that she went. And she never told me it had anything to do with it.'

'She wouldn't,' I said. 'She was scared of you.'

'That's not true,' he said. He was getting angry again. 'You should just shut your mouth.'

Jamie opened his mouth as if he was about to say something, but then changed his mind and resumed frowning. Jonathan was rambling on again – how he had no idea what made Sophie run away, this time or last time, it had nothing to do with him, he would undo it all if he could, he had hated lying to his parents as much as Sophie had but she had insisted that they keep quiet, keep up the charade until finally it was all dropped.

'Oh, blame Sophie again,' I said. 'It's bound to be all her fault, isn't it?'

He turned suddenly, and grabbed my arm. As I felt the strength in his muscles, I remembered how badly he had frightened Sophie. 'I told you to shut up,' he said. 'I'm sick of you.'

I pulled my arm free. 'That's what you did to Sophie, isn't it? Threatened her? Pushed her up against the wall?'

'No,' he said. 'Of course not.' But I knew he was lying. He said, 'You just shut the fuck up. You need help. Where do you get off, sticking your nose in where it's not wanted?'

I had to laugh at that. 'I just want to know what you've done to Sophie,' I said.

'I haven't done anything,' he said. His voice was getting louder. Jamie looked from me to him, then down at his coffee. 'You're the one who seems to have all the answers,' Jonathan added. 'You tell me where she's gone. You tell me what's going on.'

We were getting nowhere. I could see that Jonathan wasn't going to tell the truth. I said, 'Christ, no wonder she ran away, with you for a brother. Have you even bothered to look for her? Do you even care what's happened to her?'

'Of course I do,' he said. 'I've looked everywhere for her. You just shut up.'

'Even Arbor Low?' I asked. 'Maybe she's hiding from you again?'

'It wasn't like that,' he said. Then, 'Christ, I don't know why I'm even talking to you. She isn't there. I told you that the other day. It's all boarded up. Why don't you just leave us alone? Go and check for yourself if you're so sure that's where she went.'

'Yeah,' I said. 'That's right. Send me away because I know the truth.'

'You don't know anything,' he said, and there was an ugly edge to his voice. 'You've got no idea.'

'She's hiding from you,' I said. 'She's hiding and you can't stand it.'

He leaned across the table, grabbed my wrist in his hand. His grip was tight, squeezing. He said, 'I don't want to listen to you any more. Why don't you crawl off back to wherever you came from? Why don't you just fuck off and leave us alone?'

He was looking right into my eyes. I was suddenly afraid – I didn't know what he was capable of doing. So I pulled free of his grip again and stood up and said, 'I don't have to listen to this.'

'Yeah, yeah,' he said, looking up at me through narrowed eyes. 'That's right, run away.'

'I'm not running away,' I said. 'I'm not the one with something to hide.' I looked at Jamie as I spoke, still hoping for some kind of support, still hoping that I might have convinced him of something, but Jamie didn't respond. I said, 'The police will find out what happened, you'll see. Then we'll know who's right.'

Neither of them said anything, neither looking at me. I felt how flushed I was, how close I was to saying or doing something that I might regret. So I left. I walked unsteadily through the café, feeling everyone's eyes on me, feeling the thickness of the air. When I got to the door, I turned and looked back. Jonathan's head was still bent. I couldn't see Jamie from where I was.

I caught the bus home. I felt almost shaken by the experience, by Jonathan's brazen denials. I had hoped that I could enlist Jamie's help, but it was clear to me now that I would have to find Sophie on my own. It was clear what I had to do – I couldn't trust Jonathan, but Sophie hadn't known that, Sophie had thought she could trust him. She had thought it was Jonathan making those phone calls, and it was obvious to me that there was only one place she would have gone, whatever Jonathan said about having been there to look.

It was a big step, to go all the way to Arbor Low. All I had found out, everything I knew, hinged on whether I was right about her going there. Part of me was hoping that Alison had been home during the morning to fetch the car, but when I reached our street I saw that it was still parked outside our house. There was no going back now that the decision had been made. I went into the house and up the stairs two at a time, and changed into jeans and a sweater. I threw a few things into a rucksack. I felt adventurous, reckless. From the bedroom window I could see the car, the street, all the other houses, and I said a mental goodbye to all the familiar sights. I felt alive at last, back in control as I took the spare car keys from the hook in the kitchen and headed out into the street.

Chapter Twenty-four

I took the car up through the gears and out along the quiet roads towards junction twenty-six of the M1. I gathered speed along the motorway in light traffic, and made junction twenty-five at Stapleford in only a few minutes. Then I was off along the A52, heading towards Derby.

I stopped at a petrol station just outside Derby and filled the car up. I had checked the route on the map before I left Nottingham, but I took the opportunity to run through it again while I ate a plastic cheese and tomato cob on the petrol station forecourt. Then I took the A6 out of Derby, out past the suburban fringes and the sprawl of light industry, out into open countryside, and soon I was heading into the heart of the Peaks. The hills rolled up on either side of the road, the view crowded with trees or dropping away into steep green valleys with grey rocks forming walls. I wound down the window and The Kinks provided the soundtrack as I drove on into a sunny afternoon. There was little traffic on the roads; a blue Mondeo somewhere behind me, a few white vans and family cars heading in towards Derby. The sky was bright and clear and the warm breeze that blew in through the windows filled me with euphoria. I was finally doing something, taking control of the situation, and it felt good.

I had planned to drive straight to Arbor Low Farm, but when I reached the car park at the top of the lane, near the standing stones, I parked the car and got out. The main road ran on past, further into the Peaks. There were a couple of picnic tables by the car park, and a scattering of walkers with fleece jackets and socks rolled over their boots were enjoying lunch in the open air. The blue Mondeo that had been behind me since Derby pulled into the far end of the car park, more city people out for a stroll in the afternoon sun. I locked the car, nodded to the walkers and followed the steep path up to the standing stones.

I wasn't really sure why I had decided to walk up to the stones rather than go straight to the house, but as I got further away from the road I knew it had been the right thing to do. It was a fairly high altitude and there wasn't much cover in the open countryside – the occasional stumpy tree, growing more out than up, or drystone walls topped with barbed wire on which hung scraps of grey wool torn from the coats of the sheep grazing in the fields. The sky was a big blue space above me, almost cloudless, as cold as it was blue.

I reached the top of the slope, and came out to the standing stones. They were in an area marked out by deep hollows within man-made hills, and the stones came through the turf like teeth through gums. They were set out in a rough circle, a mouth open to the sky, with a central stone flattened like a low table. When I stood on the top of the mound I could see the fields opening out flat all around, until they curved at a close horizon down into woods behind me, and to the left curved up into the lip of a hill topped with yet more woods. Directly ahead, I could see the farmhouse, a grotty grey pebble-dashed house, low down in the landscape, as if it was hiding its head from the winter storms.

I sat down on the man-made hill, looking down at the farmhouse. Now that I had arrived, I suddenly wasn't sure what I should do. I think I had expected the answer to present itself to me, but I was stepping into unknown territory now, and I was afraid that Sophie wouldn't understand why I had come.

But I couldn't go back. There were too many difficulties. Nottingham seemed so far away, now that I was here, out on this dark landscape with such a clear, cold sky above me. So I got to my feet again and headed down the grassy slope and onto the lane that led up from the main road and the car park. I walked past sheds that must have once held cows, past the rotting remains of an old tractor. My boots were heavy with mud as I trudged up the gravel track.

I didn't want anyone to see me knocking on the door, so I went straight into the walled yard at the side of the house. The concrete on the ground was cracked and stained with dark brown mud. Under a lean-to against the yard wall, there were rusting bits of farm machinery; what looked like some sort of giant rake to go on the back of a tractor, and a trailer with the tyres flat and cracked open by age. There were bricks and old tyres stacked up against the back wall of the house. A glass pane in the door had broken and been repaired with part of a cardboard box, soggy and stained by rain. The doorbell didn't work, so I knocked and waited, but nobody came.

I pushed the cardboard out of the way and put my hand through the hole in the glass. The key was in the lock so I turned it and went in. When I shut the door behind me I was overwhelmed by the smell of damp and something musty and unpleasant that I couldn't identify. I was in a small room with a tiled floor and some old white units against the wall. There was a frosted glass door opposite me, so I opened that and went through into a kitchen. It was dark; the curtains were pulled, and I couldn't see very clearly in the gloom, but I didn't want to open the curtains in case anyone saw from outside. The kitchen was kitted out in the same units as the previous room, with a nasty swirled patterned carpet of indistinguishable colour on the floor. I pressed on further into the gloom of the house.

The next room was an old sitting room of some sort, and the smell of damp was stronger here, and when I touched the sofa against the far wall my hand felt cold and slimy. The air had a chill to it, and I found myself shivering. There were stairs leading up, old white banisters that didn't look too sturdy, but I ignored them and went on into the next downstairs room. I wanted to call out to see if anyone was here, to see if they were hiding from me somewhere, but I found that I couldn't summon up my voice.

It was getting darker the further into the house I went. I tried the light switch but nothing happened. In the next room, empty of furniture, there were some cardboard boxes in the middle of the floor, and half a dozen candles, unused, on the top. I took a candle and lit it, and the light flared up around me and threw giant shadows of myself on the ceiling. I lifted the flaps on a box and found it was full of cans of food, beans and soup and macaroni cheese, the labels old and peeling off the tins in the damp air.

I went back into the previous room and climbed the stairs. The wood creaked and groaned under me, and I tested each step as I went up. The banister moved as I put my hand against it. At the top there was a landing with more vile swirled carpet lapping up against the skirting boards. It was very dark, and all I could see was within the yellow flickering light of the candle. The first bedroom was completely empty, the windows boarded up with cardboard, the dirty wallpaper coming off the walls, the floorboards bare. I backed out and chose a door that was closed, and when my hand closed around the handle I felt stickiness. I tried to see what it was on my fingers, but all I could make out was darkness.

So I opened the door and went in. The smell nearly forced me out again, a thick metallic smell

that burned the back of my throat and sent my eyes
smarting. There were flies; they reared up at me as I
went further into the room, and I swatted them away
from my face, the candle sputtering as I swung my
arms. The candlelight flared across the room; in the
flicker, I saw more carpet, a blocked-up window, a
mattress with a dark stain like a hole in its centre. I
felt my feet sticking to the floor as I walked. I bent
down and put my palm flat on the clumpy fibres of
the carpet, and it was thick with stickiness, damp,
as if there was too much of something for it to
dry. I raised my hand towards my face, into the
candlelight, and then it hit me what it was, and I
stumbled back, dropped the candle, fell against both
my palms. The candle had gone out. I felt the blood
against my hands, sticking to my clothes, cold under
the seat of my jeans. I scrambled up again, feeling
myself starting to retch, my lungs clogging up in the
thick air, my throat and eyes closing against the air.

I stumbled along the hall, throwing open the doors
I passed, leaving bloody streaks all along the floor
and the walls and on all the door handles, until
finally I found the bathroom. The frosted-glass window was not boarded and bright white light streamed
in, and I saw how much blood was on my hands and
smeared across my clothes. I turned the taps in the
basin, my hands slipping against the metal, and the
pipes gagged and sucked and moaned, but there was
not enough water, it dribbled out cold and I couldn't
wash my hands clean.

And then I had to get out, I couldn't stay in that

house any longer because the smell of the place seemed to be clinging to me, filling my nose and my throat, and my eyes were running, and I couldn't wipe my face, I wouldn't touch my face while there was so much blood on my hands. So I took the stairs as fast as I dared, not wanting to risk the banister, not wanting to touch anything in that place, and I rushed through the rooms to the back door, and out into the concrete yard.

The blue Mondeo from the car park was pulling up along the track as I came out. I fell to my knees, right there on the muddy concrete, and the cold air stuck in my throat, and the bile rose up through my stomach. I closed my eyes, felt my guts tearing at my insides as I retched, felt it all coming out through my mouth and my nose, puking it up over the concrete, retching until there was nothing to retch. I felt a hand against my back; someone was kneeling next to me; I could hear my voice, the words stumbling out of me.

Then I opened my eyes, and saw black lace-up shoes covered in mud, and navy blue trousers with the turn-ups spattered. I looked up, at the person crouching next to me, and I was surprised to see that it was Joseph.

He leaned down and said, 'Peter?'

There was mud and blood smeared on my clothes and my hands. I wanted to wipe my mouth, to get rid of the bitter taste of sick, but my hands were filthy. I used my sleeve, wiped my face, then I managed to say, 'In there, upstairs.'

There was a woman with Joseph, plain-clothes,

blonde hair, but no sign of McAllister. I couldn't look at her. Joseph stood up and said something to her, and then he was gone, towards the house. I wanted to warn him, but my mouth was thick and I couldn't form any words.

I thought I was going to start retching again, but there was nothing to retch, and I felt dizzy instead. The woman helped me to my feet and I stood there swaying, head back, gulping down air, my eyes closed.

The woman said, 'Smoke?'

I opened my eyes and looked at her. She had a pretty face, and that made me want to laugh but I didn't know why. She was offering me a packet of cigarettes. Sophie's brand. I tried to wipe my hands on the front of the sweatshirt, but the stuff wouldn't come off, it had dried in reddish-brown stains across my palms, clotting around my fingernails. I felt myself start to shake. The woman took a cigarette from the packet and placed it between my lips, then held a lighter flame up for me. I sucked in smoke, and then I was shivering, so cold, shivering and shaking.

She said, 'Why don't we sit in the car?'

I nodded. We walked over to the Mondeo, her hand touching the small of my back to guide me. My legs moved in jerky motions, as if I'd never had to walk before. She opened the car's back door and I sat on the edge of the seat, feet still on the muddy track. The car smelled of air freshener and warm plastic, and I wanted the cold air of the hills.

She leaned against the car door. 'So,' she said. 'What are you doing here, Peter?'

I just shrugged. Then I looked at her. 'What are you doing here?'

'We followed you from your house,' she said, no apology, as if I should have realised. 'You gave us quite a shock, running off from work like that.'

There didn't seem to be anything I could say to that. I tried to force my thoughts into some sort of sense, but felt myself start to shake again. I took a deep drag on the cigarette.

'Stay there,' the woman said, and went back towards the house. Joseph had come out and met her halfway. They had some sort of conversation, glancing across at me.

I finished the cigarette and chucked the end out onto the track. A few walkers had come down to the edge of the stone circle and were looking towards me and talking among themselves. I watched them for a moment, and they looked back at me then turned away and headed back up the slope towards the stones.

Joseph and the woman were coming back towards the car. I stood up as they reached me. 'So,' Joseph said. 'I think we'd all better go back to the station and have a little chat.'

I said, 'There's my car to bring back.'

'Don't worry about that,' Joseph said. 'We'll take care of everything from here on.'

His words didn't comfort me.

Chapter Twenty-five

The interview room was hot, airless, a stifling box. I was wearing a disposable suit made from a white plasticky material a little like paper. When I moved, the suit crackled and rubbed against my skin, and the hard edges of the seams scraped at me, and sweat ran down the inside of the suit in streams. My fingers ached where they had scraped out samples from under the nails for analysis, I could still taste the cotton swab they had used in my mouth, and there was a sore spot on my arm where they had taken some of my blood.

The Duty Solicitor sitting next to me was a heavy, sweaty, greasy man who looked like he'd had an uncomfortably large lunch; when he shifted in his seat his body groaned and creaked like the chair, and he was sweating an unpleasant mixture of Italian herbs and red wine through his pin-striped polyester suit. His advice to me had been to tell the truth. I had nothing to hide. I'd done nothing wrong, it was all simply a misunderstanding. I imagined myself helping them with their enquiries, giving them the final piece in the jigsaw of evidence they had already built up that would point irrefutably at the real culprit. The whole mess would unravel neatly around us and, once they were satisfied, they would tell me that I'd been a fool, and we'd have a little joke about it, and then they would send me merrily on my way.

McAllister and Joseph were interviewing. I told them that it was all a mistake, a misunderstanding, and they smiled and nodded and agreed that I was probably right, so we should get on and clear up their questions. Next to me, the solicitor stifled what could have been a yawn or a belch and shifted in his seat again.

So I told them about finding Sophie's notebook, and as I talked the absurdity of the situation kept occurring to me. Accusing me – it was laughable – I'd never done anything wrong in my whole life. Part of me wanted to laugh out loud at being there, but I didn't dare to. They all looked so used to this situation that I didn't think they would understand the joke.

I found myself telling them that I wished I'd never picked the notebook up, or had given it to the bus driver, or had dropped it through the letterbox when I went round to Sophie's flat the first time. It seemed ridiculous to me that I hadn't done that – I realised that I couldn't explain why I hadn't done that. And if I had, none of this would be happening – I would be at home with Alison right now, making lists of who we would invite to the wedding, picking the young cousins to play bridesmaids, asking Steve to be Best Man, looking at holiday brochures to choose our honeymoon. Rome, maybe, or Athens. Venice, Florida, the Dominican Republic. I could imagine that – jetskiing, snorkelling, swimming up to a poolside bar and having cocktails in the water, having glasses of chilled sparkling wine – no, champagne, served in a silver ice bucket – with a view of white sands and palm trees and the most brilliant flame of sunset while the surf cracked on the shore.

McAllister said, 'I'd like you to tell us what you were doing at the house.'

'I've already told you,' I said. 'I feel I've been very clear on this already. I thought Sophie might be there so I went to find out.'

'What made you think she would be there?'

'Her notebook seemed to suggest it. It was where she went last time she ran away. I thought she'd go there to wait for Jonathan.'

McAllister was sitting back in his seat, eyes down, his arms folded across his chest, his fingers tucked into his armpits. I had the feeling that this was just the start, the limbering up exercises for when the questions really got going.

'You went instead of Jonathan?' McAllister asked.

'He said she wasn't there. He said he'd been to check and there was nobody there. I thought maybe she was hiding from him.'

'Why would she hide from Jonathan?'

'Because he was making anonymous phone calls. She was frightened. He threatened her – he pinned her up against the wall, he would have hurt her.'

McAllister said, 'But why?'

I didn't know what to say. I still didn't believe Jonathan about the car theft, but I didn't have anything else to tell him, so I had no choice, I had to repeat the ridiculous story that Jonathan had told me.

McAllister didn't respond for a moment. I suppose I had hoped that this would be enough, that he would see that I was not the prime suspect, but finally he said, 'And this happened over four years ago? Why would Sophie be frightened now?'

'Because of the phone calls,' I said.

'But why would Jonathan make the phone calls?'

'I don't know,' I said. 'You'll have to ask him that.'

McAllister glanced at Joseph, who made a note in his notebook and said, 'We'll look into it.'

He didn't sound convinced. Neither of them seemed to really be listening to my answers. The solicitor cleared his throat and moved in his seat, but didn't say anything. I wanted to shake them all awake, make them realise that I might say something that would piece it all together, if they actually concentrated.

McAllister said, 'And you thought Sophie would talk to you if you turned up at Arbor Low?'

'I'm no threat to her,' I said.

McAllister finally looked up and made eye contact, but I had to look away, I couldn't look into those eyes. 'You're a friend,' McAllister said, a statement.

'Yes,' I said. 'No, I mean, I've never actually spoken to her.'

'But you've been going around telling people that she's a friend of yours.'

'Yes.'

'Why?'

'I don't know,' I said. 'It was a misunderstanding, that's all.'

Joseph had been examining his hands, his fingernails, but now he looked up at me. 'How did you get her diary?' he asked.

'She dropped it on the bus,' I said. 'I've already told you that. Several times. You don't seem to be listening.'

Joseph didn't respond to that. McAllister flashed me a little smile and said, 'We are listening, Peter. We want to hear about what happened.'

'I've already told you,' I said. 'We're going in circles.'

'Okay,' McAllister said. 'So tell us again. We want to be clear.' He had adopted a neutral, almost dead tone. I wondered if he had been trained to do that, or if it was the stale air and the artificial light in the room that had induced a comatose state. 'Why did you burn the notebook?'

I started to explain that I didn't think anyone should read it if Sophie didn't want them to, that she was entitled to her privacy, but even as my words formed into sentences and grew into paragraphs, I knew I sounded ridiculous, and I stopped. Then I said, 'What else could I have done?'

'Given it to us,' McAllister said.

'Well yes, but—' and I managed to stop myself there.

'But what?' McAllister asked.

He wasn't looking at me, and I couldn't tell if he knew what I had been about to say. I looked at my hands, at the fingernails scraped clean. 'But you'd have asked why I didn't give it to you before,' I said. 'It would've seemed odd.'

He glanced up at me now. 'Oh, I think I can understand that. You didn't want us to know that you'd been lying to us all along.'

'No,' I said, but stopped, because he was right, even though he made it sound like something else, like I really did have something to hide. I said, 'It seemed like a sensible idea at the time.'

'But not now?'

'Nothing seems sensible now,' I said, and McAllister laughed. It wasn't a loud laugh, but it was so sudden, as if I'd been wrong about the deadening effect of the room. The solicitor looked up, as if he was as surprised as I was. McAllister suddenly seemed relaxed, in control; I wondered how I could have got that so wrong, how he could stay that cool despite the thick heat. I felt as if I was melting in the heat, as if a little part of me was running down the inside of the suit with every wave of perspiration. When I shifted in my seat, the suit stuck to my legs and pulled against my skin. I could feel the dampness all over my body, a greasy, slimy coating that made me shiver despite the heat.

McAllister said, 'Everything seems suspicious now, that's what you mean, isn't it?'

I said, 'I haven't done anything wrong.'

McAllister brought his hand down onto the table top with a thump. I felt myself jerk with the shock of the sound in the small room. McAllister raised his voice. 'Come on, Peter, you've lied about how well you knew her, you've been questioning her friends and her workmates, harassing her family, you broke into her flat, you burned the one thing that might have helped us find her in time.'

'No,' I said quickly, wanting to stop his words, wanting to shut off his voice. 'I don't know. I didn't think—'

'I put it to you that you are lying to us.'

'No,' I said. 'I'm not.'

'I put it to you that you became obsessed with Sophie Taylor long before she disappeared.'

'No, I didn't.' Turning, appealing to the solicitor, appealing to anyone who might help me out. The solicitor looked back at me, nodded to me, as if he was trying to say I should go ahead and tell them something. I turned back to McAllister. 'It's not true,' I said.

'Come on, Peter,' McAllister said. His tone was friendlier; he was leaning in towards me with a little smile. 'We've all gone a little crazy over a pretty girl at some time or another. There's nothing wrong with that. Maybe things got out of control? I can see how that might have happened.'

'No,' I said, and I realised that I was almost

shouting. I took a deep breath, tried to calm myself. 'No, I didn't do anything,' I said. 'I didn't hurt her. I've never even spoken to her. You need to talk to Jonathan. He's the one who was making all those phone calls. Or Jamie. He was in love with her, he's the one who was obsessed. They're the people you should be talking to, not me.'

McAllister leaned in further across the table so his face was close to mine. I sat back, but I couldn't look away from that face, from those eyes staring right at me. I couldn't avoid what he was thinking – that I had hurt Sophie, that I was the one who had done that. I had tried to keep thoughts about the house out of my mind, but the images were rearing up; the blood on the mattress, the blood on the bathroom taps, my feet sticking to the carpet, the smell.

McAllister said, 'You're just trying to put up a smokescreen by blaming other people. You just want to hide what you've done.'

'No,' I said. 'I haven't done anything.'

He said, 'You're blaming other people because you can't face the truth about what you've done.'

'That's not true,' I said.

He said, 'It must be hard to face up to what you've done. It must be hard even to admit it to yourself. But you'll find once you've told us all about it you'll feel a whole lot better.'

I still couldn't break away from his look, I couldn't move. I managed to stutter out, 'There's nothing to tell.'

McAllister was opening his mouth to say something else when the solicitor finally started to speak. He said, 'Do you actually have any evidence that Peter has done anything wrong?'

McAllister didn't answer for a moment, still staring into my face. Then he sat back and looked at Joseph, then at the solicitor, and said, 'He was at the murder scene. He's been lying to us. There're grounds for suspicion.'

'Yes,' the solicitor said. 'But is there any evidence?'

Joseph said, 'Forensics haven't come back to us yet.'

I looked over at my solicitor, my saviour. He seemed to be getting into some sort of stride. 'Maybe we should continue this when forensics do get back to you,' he said.

I thought McAllister was going to explode, but he swallowed his anger and forced a smile out between his teeth, and finally nodded.

I had my hands flat on the table, and I flopped my head down so I could feel my fingers beneath my forehead. I was exhausted. I heard Joseph announcing to the tape that we were taking a break, and I closed my eyes, and for the first time in a long time I felt myself smile.

Chapter Twenty-six

In the cell, all I could do was wait for them to return. It was a small cell, white-tiled, with a sour smell of bleach masking something more unpleasant. I walked the four paces to the door and back to the bed, waiting for something to happen.

It was all too absurd, too surreal – I had never done anything to hurt Sophie, I never would, not Sophie. I was trying to protect her, that was all I had ever wanted to do. But they turned everything around, they made everything into something it wasn't, and I couldn't see how to convince them that I was telling the truth. Perspiration had formed a cool layer under the plastic suit, and I was tired and thirsty, and even when I squeezed my eyes shut, I could still see McAllister's face and hear his accusations. I felt sick with it all, and a headache was starting to punch behind my eyes, as if the circuits in my brain were burning out.

I tried lying down on my back on the bed, hands over my face to shield my eyes from the light. I should have been trying to sleep – the solicitor's last words to me had been advice to rest, and I knew it was meant kindly, but how could I rest when those accusations kept forcing their way into my mind?

Footsteps in the corridor, and I was on my feet again, looking at that door, waiting for it to open, for something finally to happen. But a key turned in some other lock, and another door opened and banged shut again, all so muffled, as if it was a long way away, as if I was deep underground.

And how could they really think those things? I was Sophie's friend, I was protecting her – why would I hurt her?

But she had been hurt. Someone had hurt her and I hadn't been there to protect her. And then I thought of that room, and running down the hallway and the smears on the walls and her blood staining the grains and lines of my skin.

She knew what she was doing, and I had to hold on to that thought, I had to get them to see that she was in control, that she knew what was going on.

More footsteps along the corridor, and I stood where I was, as metal scraped against metal, and the letterbox flap in the door opened. Two dark eyes looked in at me, two eyes disconnected from a body – I wanted to fling myself at the door, prise the door open, get out, but I couldn't move.

Then the door opened, and Joseph was there, standing there in the doorway looking in at me. I tried to breathe, but the air was too hot in my lungs.

'We've searched your car,' he said.

'Not my car,' I said. 'Alison's car.'

His face was half in shadow, eye sockets dark like I was looking into empty holes. He said, 'We had to look hard, but we knew we'd find what we needed. We knew you did it. We just had to prove it.'

I tried to say that I hadn't done anything, they were wrong, they had the wrong man, but my mouth wouldn't form the words. I hadn't done anything. But what if I had done something? Would that have changed all of this? Would they let me out of the cell if I said I had done something?

'We found fibres in your car,' he was saying. 'Fibres from the carpet in the house. Fibres with her blood on them.'

'Not my car,' I said, but he wasn't listening, so I said it again, louder. 'It's not my car.'

My head hurt. He was still talking, but I couldn't make out his words. The back of my eyes were burning out. I sat down, buried my head in my knees, clasped my arms over my head. The suit tasted papery, plasticky, and stuck to my chin. The door banged shut again and Joseph had gone but I hadn't seen him go. I buried my head again, wishing I could sleep.

Chapter Twenty-seven

Two tiny fibres of carpet caught in the upholstery of Alison's car. Evidence of her blood. I told them, over and over, I told them that they had planted those, that it was a frame, a fit-up, a put-up job. Desperation, they said, I was making wild allegations, trying to wriggle free of the hook, nothing more.

McAllister and Joseph leaned across the table, and I couldn't look at their eyes. The solicitor was slumped in his seat. Where did I dump the body? I didn't, I didn't, but I might as well have screamed that at an empty room.

McAllister said, 'I put it to you that you knew Sophie would be at the house, and you went there and you murdered her. Then you returned to the scene today, and that's when we found you there.'

'It's not true,' I said. 'I swear, I had nothing to do with it.'

I couldn't find the words to destroy what they were saying. I couldn't stop them, they couldn't hear me say that it wasn't me.

'Why did you go back to the house?'

I didn't go back. I'd never been there, it wasn't me. They got it so wrong. I didn't return to the place, they couldn't say that, I didn't know she was dead. And how could they be sure she was dead?

McAllister said, 'There are eight to ten pints of blood in the human body, Peter. How much do you think was sprayed around that room, eh? How much blood?'

Rivers of it. Swimming in it. Talking to them was like trying to swim through it, arms fighting through the thickness, drowning in it. McAllister was walking around the room, playing to an audience, like he was delivering the closing argument. I had to watch him, my eyes had to follow him around the room. He was the star, the pivot on which all the action revolved.

'Rapid blood loss on the scale we're talking about would cause death from shock.' He loomed above me. I thought of blood spraying, splattering, a cut artery, the jugular slashed through. 'This is murder we're talking about now, Peter, not some mix-up. Not some childish crush.'

I wanted to say something, force the words out through my teeth, but I couldn't. I could taste blood, it was everywhere.

He said, 'You must have been covered in blood.'

'No,' I managed.

'And you're lying,' he said. 'I knew the first time I talked to you that you were hiding something.' Then he sat down again and smiled at me, but it didn't make me feel better, it didn't help at all. 'You're a pretty cool customer, aren't you, Peter?'

312

I didn't know what he meant. His words didn't make any sense. I looked at the solicitor, but he just nodded, as if it was a reasonable question, as if I should have an answer already prepared.

So I took a long breath and kept my voice as calm as I could. Fight logic with logic. 'If I had killed her, why would I have gone back to the house?'

'People revisit the scenes of their crimes all the time. Especially this type of crime.' McAllister had a strange, almost twisted smile as he added, 'Crimes with a sexual dimension, I mean.'

'Sexual?' I said. 'There's nothing sexual. You're just reading things in. I haven't done anything wrong.'

'You broke into her flat,' McAllister said. He was watching me closely, as if he could see my thoughts through my face, as if he could see through my skin and right inside my skull. 'We know what you did, Peter. We found the evidence. DNA. Semen on her sheets.'

I had to look away.

'It's not normal behaviour, is it, Peter? We found your semen on her sheets. How can you explain that? What sort of misunderstanding is that, then, Peter?'

I couldn't explain that. I felt my cheeks flush. The disgust, the embarrassment – how could he say those things out loud, in front of other people, with that tape recorder whirring in the background?

'Look at me,' McAllister said.

I glanced up at him, into that face, into a face with no expression at all. I looked away again.

'How can you explain that?'

And how could he expect me to answer? He wouldn't understand – how could he understand the relationship we had, the intimate connection we had built up? That couldn't be put into words, it couldn't be explained, it defied his logic.

'Let me tell you what I think happened,' McAllister said. 'I think you became obsessed with Sophie. I think you were the one who made all those anonymous phone calls. I think when you found out where she was, you went out to the house and when she rejected your advances, you murdered her.'

I managed to force out a laugh, a slight, hollow, unconvincing laugh. 'This is unreal,' I said. Head swimming with it. 'I can't believe you're saying these things. It wasn't me. You've got the wrong man.'

His voice grated, ground away at me, suggestions, insinuations, creeping in, getting under my skin, eating it. I was obsessed with Sophie. I was at the murder scene. I broke into her flat, and when he said that I remembered the smell of her clothes, her scent haunting the clothes, the bedcovers, crawling in and feeling the warmth, closing my eyes and feeling her warmth against me. But I didn't kill her, I wasn't lying to them, I wasn't trying to hide the truth about what I'd done.

Then Joseph was talking, quietly, his voice soft like silk. 'We all lose it sometimes, Peter. We all go a little crazy from time to time. Things take over our lives. This obsession with Sophie, it took over your life, didn't it?'

'No.'

But his voice continued, softly, gently, smoothing a way right inside me. 'We know it strained things between you and your fiancée. Why did you ask Alison to marry you, Peter? Was it because you felt bad about the way you were treating her?'

Alison asking me what was wrong, Alison waiting for me to speak, Alison listening, and all the time I lied to her, I hid things from her, and now she would think the worst, and it was all my fault. I stammered out, 'No, I never treated her badly. Alison has nothing to do with this, leave her out of this.'

'You're not just covering up for this thing with Sophie?'

'No,' I said, voice raised. 'No.' I could feel my feet planted on the floor. I rose from my seat. The solicitor's hand on my arm and I sat down again. 'No. That's ridiculous. Sophie didn't mean anything to me, I was just worried that something might have happened to her. I've told you this already. And I was right to be worried, wasn't I? You should be talking to Jonathan, he's the one you should be talking to. Sophie said he was the one making all the phone calls. She told me that, in her notebook. I've already told you he threatened her. He hit me, look, I've still got the bruise. He hit me.'

'Does he think you've done something to Sophie, then?'

There was no way through the words. Everything was merging, turning against me. They were all against me, longing me to say the words they were waiting for, longing for me to confess, but I did nothing wrong. I was on a smooth slope, a greasy path, and they wanted me to fall, slip and slide down, and I wouldn't be able to climb back up again.

'Everyone else is wrong and you're right, is that it?'

'Yes,' I said.

McAllister's eyes. I couldn't look away now. He said, 'I put it to you that you're lying to us.'

'No,' I said. Broke away from his gaze. 'No, I'm not.'

'You're lying to us because you know it's your fault that Sophie Taylor is dead.'

'It's not my fault,' I said, a rush of words, because I had the notebook, if I had done something, if I had acted . . .

'You knew where she was.'

'But I didn't know she was going to get killed.'

'But you've been telling us how worried you were about her.'

'I was worried,' I said. 'She'd been getting phone calls. I thought something might have happened to her.'

'So worried that you waited a month before you went to the house?'

I wanted to scream the words at them. I didn't know – how could I have known? But I should have realised, I should have acted.

McAllister sat back in his seat. He rubbed his hand over his face. He looked tired.

McAllister said, 'Let's go back. The day of the conference in Derby. The last time you borrowed Alison's car. I put it to you that you left the conference at lunchtime, you drove out to the house and found Sophie there, and when she turned you down, you killed her.'

'No,' I said. Deep breath. 'That's not true.'

'Peter, we've asked. Nobody remembers seeing you at the conference after lunch.'

'They're wrong,' I said. 'I was there. Just because I didn't talk to lots of people doesn't mean I wasn't there.'

'You left early,' McAllister said.

'No, I didn't.'

'You left early and you drove out to see her. But she didn't want to see you, did she?'

'That's not true,' I said. My head was pumping with all the words – I could feel the way they were pushing me, corralling me, willing me to say what they wanted to hear. And they weren't listening, they didn't seem to hear what I was saying. 'This is all her fault,' I said, slowly, trying to make them see. 'She's doing this to spite me. She's setting me up. She just wants to cause trouble for me.' Then I felt more confident, because couldn't they see what she was doing, couldn't they see what she was like? 'She's just a spiteful little tease,' I said. 'She's doing this to punish me because I chose Alison over her. She's doing this because I don't love her, because I don't care for her. It doesn't matter what I do, she won't let go of me.'

I wanted to look up to see what effect my words were having on McAllister, to see whether he was starting to believe me, but I didn't dare. I looked at my hands. 'It's not my fault,' I said. 'It's all her doing. I couldn't have known.'

McAllister said, 'Was she hiding from you? Did you have to search the house?'

I had thought I would find her there, that was true. I had thought she would be waiting for me, maybe even expecting me. That damp, cold house. If I had come earlier, if I had come after the Derby conference, when McAllister said I had, would she have been waiting for me then? Was I just too late? I said, 'I searched the house, and that's when I saw the blood.'

'You searched the house?'

Through those dark rooms. The smell, the smell of the damp earth reclaiming the house. Up the stairs and the metallic taste in the back of the throat. 'Yes,' I said.

'Where was she hiding?'

I could imagine her, hearing footsteps on the stairs, folding herself smaller into a dark corner, hearing her own breath and the thump of her pulse in her ears.

'Was she upstairs?'

'Yes,' I said. 'She must have been.'

'Did you see her?'

I felt as if I was sleepwalking; I could almost feel the stairs under my feet, placing each foot carefully, transferring the weight so the stairs didn't creak, holding a breath in to listen for movement, pausing between each step.

I said, 'It's so dark in that house, he might have missed her. That's what she would have hoped. I can see what must have happened. Jonathan must have found her up there. They must have had a fight. Maybe she had the knife, to protect herself, a big knife, a kitchen knife. They had a fight. Maybe he didn't mean it to happen. Maybe it was an accident.'

'Is that what happened?'

'I don't know,' I said. 'Maybe.'

'Did you see Jonathan there?'

'No,' I said. 'No, I didn't see it.'

I felt as if I was discovering it for the first time. As if I could finally understand what had happened.

'Was Jonathan there at all?'

I realised suddenly that McAllister and Joseph were leaning across the table towards me, as if they had to be closer to me, as if closing the distance between us would make it all clearer. I said, 'I don't know,' but I felt that I did, that I had hit on some kind of truth. 'I don't know,' I repeated.

McAllister's voice was almost breathless. 'Did you kill Sophie?'

If I had acted sooner, could I have stopped it? If I had acted sooner, I could have rescued Sophie, I could have brought her back with me. 'It's my fault that she's dead,' I said, and although I could hear the words, it seemed that I was not saying them, I was not releasing those sounds into the air.

Clare Littleford

McAllister said again, 'Did you kill her?'

'I could have stopped it. If I'd only tried, if I'd only done something about it, I could have stopped it.'

McAllister said, 'Peter.' His tone was sharper, and I looked up from my hands, from my broken fingernails, from the loose skin I had torn away from the edges of the fingernails. He said, 'Peter, did you kill Sophie Taylor?'

I could feel the hard handle of the knife in my hand. I knew how it would feel, its shape and weight. I could see the room with the mattress, the blood collecting, running out across the mattress, onto the carpet. I could have stopped it if I had realised soon enough. Jonathan had lied to me, had lied to everyone, but he didn't understand, he didn't understand Sophie at all. I was the one who had made that connection, I was the one who knew how Sophie had felt when she heard those careful feet on the stairs.

I could barely hear my own voice as I finally answered the question. 'Yes,' I said. 'I did it. I killed her, just the way I said. I didn't mean to, but it was all my fault.'

Chapter Twenty-eight

When I am behind my door, lying on my bed with a book in my hands, sometimes I can even shut out all the noise of this place. There are always voices, arguments or laughter on the landing, keys turning and doors closing further along the wing. All the sounds of men living so close together that we can hear each other growing old.

They don't call them cells here, they're rooms, and we call the screws 'sir', and the governor is only here to help. And it's not con or lag or lifer, it's colleague, thank you very much. I'm locked up here with some of the most dangerous men in the country and they tell me I'm the one who needs counselling.

Alison used to visit every chance she got, but the chances get less as time passes. I know she must be wondering, because it all sounded so certain in court, the case sealed with carpet fibres and my own confession. I have explained it to her; for the first couple of years, I explained it constantly, a record with the needle jammed and jumping. She says she believes me but I don't want to push her for the truth. She says she will stand by me, but time moves at a different speed on the outside and it wouldn't be fair to pin her to her past commitments. Steve still writes when he remembers, but he's never been one for letters.

Sometimes, I can forget about the outside world and concentrate on what I have: the books in the library, playing chess, cultivating vegetables in the garden. Time expands all around me like a bubble of gas in a vacuum.

In Group Therapy, they tell me I have to let go of the past, admit what I did before it eats me away from the inside. I know they all think I'm still in denial, remorseless, cold, shut out from my emotions. They think I wake up in the middle of the night shaking with the fear of what I've done. My neighbours say they have heard me in the night, but it's not my guilt that sneaks into my dreams and turns them sour.

I can tell they hate me a little more each time I plead my innocence. Maybe they hate me because they hate themselves; they hate what they have become, snivelling wretches in an enclosed space, living out their lives in the shadows of the past, caught in a loop of guilt and apology. Or maybe they hate me for being the interloper; they are the elite group, the ones who have seen how easy it is to end someone's life, the ones who know that it takes a long, gradual slide to reach that line but only a second to cross it. The ones who now know there is no going back. Perhaps I skew the group, changing the magnetic poles. They think I am dishonest and feel anger, or they think I am innocent and feel their own guilt.

Sometimes, I can shut all of this out and concentrate on reading. Sometimes, my mind switches channels like a television, and I close my eyes and everything else tunes out, and then, I think about Sophie.

At first, I blamed Jonathan. I was full of revenge fantasies – paint the walls with his blood. I replayed the images in my mind, the story I had told to McAllister and Joseph. I worked through every possible scenario, twisting it, turning it around in my mind, testing it against the things I thought I knew. But whichever way I looked at it, I couldn't find the missing part of the story, the link that told me how, or when, or why. What could have driven him to do such a thing? Why would he have phoned her, have made such a nuisance of himself, when all he had to do was visit her? Logic doesn't give me the breakthrough; I can't complete the equation.

It took me a long time to start to see the truth. If everyone is a suspect it is very hard to see that nobody is guilty. Because who would be capable of doing something like this, of putting her family through so much anguish? I spent so long listening to her words that I failed to notice the voice she was speaking in. She was clever, I will grant her that much. She planted the seeds of her disappearance long before she actually left.

I assumed that she was telling me the truth. I assumed that that notebook was not intended to be left behind. Maybe she hadn't planned to drop it – maybe she was going to leave it somewhere else, in the house with bloodstains on the cover, or post it to someone. Maybe she really did catch that train on the spur of the moment, the crystallisation of a plan that had been forming all along.

Because I know how she did it. I know how she disappeared. I worked it out a long time ago, in the library reading up on anatomy. There are ten pints of blood in the human body, in a body the size of Sophie's. If someone loses two or three pints of blood in one go, if their jugular is cut open or a limb is severed, they die rapidly from shock. Blood pressure drops, and the heart rate increases to compensate, and the body fights to keep blood pumping to the vital organs. Blood stops flowing through the capillaries – oxygen and nutrients cannot pass into the tissue, waste cannot be collected for removal, and the body closes down. Even if she lost that blood more slowly, if it leaked out over several hours, if she had a wound that could not be closed, she would lose consciousness as the blood spilled out around her. The brain, the heart, the lungs, the kidneys, the liver would start to fail. As her organs failed her body would begin to cool, and the blood would clot in her arteries, moved only by the effects of gravity.

And yet, if she lost a little every day, she would live.

I can picture her in that house, decanting her

blood every day into a container, storing it in the fridge to keep it fresh. She had done her nurse's training, she could have done that easily. Rest, eat, wait until the blood supply had built back up and then go for it once more, until she had enough to fake a murder scene. Enough to convince them that she had to be dead.

You see, it's not how much you lose that counts, but how quickly you lose it, and whether you have the strength to carry on.

At first, I pictured Sophie with a knife and a glass, slicing into the flesh on her arm, the friction of the knife burning at her skin as it cut, the blood welling up behind the blade. But it wouldn't have been like that – it couldn't. Other times, I see her sitting on the sofa in one of those damp downstairs rooms, pushing a needle into the veins on her arm, remembering her training, remembering how they took blood when she donated it. I can picture the skin puckering around the needle as she pushes it in, and the deep red liquid running up inside the glass.

Sometimes, I dream that I am in an operating theatre, dressed in a green gown, the bright lights shining down onto green cloth, and a mask covers Sophie's face as she leans in over me with a scalpel in each hand.

Sometimes, I dream that I am back at my trial, and the jury is about to retire to consider their verdict. I dream that I look into the crowd, into those faces twisted with concentration, and sometimes, in among the crowd, I see that Sophie is watching.

Sometimes, she stands up, and the public gallery all turn to stare at her, and as the ripple of recognition spreads through the court, the judge calls for order and snaps me awake with the bang of his gavel against the bench. Sometimes, I try to call to her but nobody can hear my voice, and when I try to point her out the police surround me and hustle me away to the cells beneath the court.

I keep my mouth shut about my theory, even now, because I know everyone thinks I'm in denial, I know they think I'm lying to myself. Every so often, a couple of people from CID will come to visit me and ask me where I buried the body. They tell me that the family need closure, that I'm doing nobody any good by withholding this final piece of information, that I'll be helping myself when I am considered for early release, that it would do me good to get it all off my chest. And I tell them straight that I am innocent, that I was framed, that they have the wrong man. If it is Joseph or McAllister who comes visiting, I remind them about the carpet fibres that they must have planted in my car. They just shake their heads and make a note in their file and go away again. Maybe they think I've lost the plot, maybe they think they can hear the marbles rattling around upstairs. Maybe they're right and they're just being kind by not telling me.

Either that or they think the same things as those people on the outside. They think I'm evil, or sick, or a psycho. The freak who stalked a girl seen at a bus stop and murdered her when she said no.

Beholden

A special feature in the *Evening Post*, coverage on *East Midlands Today*, and all the neighbours saying, 'He seemed like such a nice young chap,' and, 'He always kept himself to himself.' Alison doorstepped by a couple of reporters, some of her friends passing judgement on my character as if they knew me, the City Council giving no comment about their former employee. The media circus, feeding off my flesh, and all because they're secretly afraid that I'm the dark side that rears up through the surface.

Outside the courthouse, Jonathan threw rocks at the van as they drove me away. I heard the thumps of the rocks making contact with the side of the van, and I heard the dull shouts from the crowd that had gathered, and I lurched in my seat as the van slowed and swerved. That ubiquitous crowd, showing a psycho that he has enraged public opinion, that he isn't wanted round here, not in our back yard, not near our kids and our schools and our decent way of life. It's funny, because even as the rocks thumped home and the van pitched, all I could think was that there was no natural place to find rocks around the courthouse so he must have come prepared. He had planned to make a statement – that hanging's too good, that a life for a life is the only kind of justice, that anything less is an insult to the memory of his precious sister.

I found out later that Jonathan was arrested for Breach of the Peace. It made me smile, to think of him cooling his heels in a police cell. There was some small measure of justice in that, even if he did probably have the young coppers hanging around the cell door saying things like, 'Yeah, I understand what you mean, mate, but the law's the law, innit?' or, 'I'd've done the same if it had been me. Bastard deserves all he gets. Cuppa tea?'

Sometimes, on a quiet day, I close my eyes and try to imagine where Sophie is now. I imagine her sailing a yacht around the world, scrambling over the deck in short white shorts, showing off the tan on her slim legs, winding winches and trimming sails, squinting into the sun as she laughs at a joke made by someone I cannot see. Or she's walking along a beach in a flowing white dress, with the white sand sticking to her toes and the surf throwing itself under her feet. She doesn't know what has happened to me, she doesn't know, but some day soon she will find out. Then she will have a choice. She can stay disappeared if she wants to, that's okay by me. She knows how much I love her, even now, even after everything she has done to ruin my life. I can forgive her for that. She knows I understand, she knows I'll always be here for her, she knows I'll do anything for her, anything at all. It might be that she chooses to come back and rescue me, to return the love I've shown for her. I'm the only one who really understands her, who really understands how difficult things have been for her. I'm the only one who was prepared to do whatever it took to set her free, and that is the greatest declaration of love that I am capable of making.